Loving You

By Allie Everhart

Loving You
By Allie Everhart

Copyright ©2014 Allie Everhart
All rights reserved.
Published by Waltham Publishing, LLC
Cover Design by Sarah Hansen of Okay Creations
ISBN-13: 978-0-9887524-6-7

CHAPTER ONE

"I should go back to my room," I whisper to Garret as I push myself up, supporting myself with my hands. He reaches behind my neck and brings me back to him and kisses me.

"It's the middle of the night, Jade. You don't need to go back to your room. Nobody's checking to see if you're there."

"Your family will be awake in a few hours. I can't fall asleep here."

His lips brush mine as he smiles. "Then don't fall asleep."

I hover over him, our breath mingling. "We just did this, like an hour ago."

"Yeah? What's your point?"

He kisses me again, harder this time. Then deeper, as he cradles the back of my head with his hand, his fingers tangled in my hair, pulling me even closer.

I never get around to answering him. I'm too distracted. Garret has a way of doing that. Distracting me from all rational thought as I get lost in how good it feels to be with him.

Hours later I wake up in the guest room to the sound of tiny footsteps sneaking up to my bed. Then I feel a little hand tapping my shoulder and open my eyes to find Garret's sister, Lilly, standing there.

"Jade, will you watch cartoons in my room with me?"

I sit up, wiping the sleep from my eyes. The private Christmas party Garret and I had in his room earlier has left me exhausted. Not that I'm complaining. It was definitely worth losing sleep over.

"Lilly, what time is it?"

She shakes her head and her long blond hair flings back and forth across her face. "I don't know. Will you come to my room?"

How can I possibly say no to those bright blue eyes and that sweet smile? It's impossible.

"Okay. Let's go." I get out of bed and slip on my robe—a white, fluffy robe left for me in the bathroom. In the Kensington household, it's not proper to walk around wearing only your pajamas, not that I would given that I'm braless, wearing a thin t-shirt and pajama shorts.

Lilly holds my hand and leads me to her bedroom. In the short time I've known her, Lilly has decided to make me her big sister. I really don't mind the role. I've never been anyone's sister and it's nice to have someone look up to me that way.

"You sit here." She pats her hand on one side of her twin canopy bed. The bed is all pink. Pink sheets, pink blankets, pink comforter, and pink pillows.

I sit where she tells me to and lean back against the pillows. Cartoon bears are playing on the big, flat-screen TV hanging on the wall. Lilly climbs up next to me, holding two dolls. "This one's yours. Her name is Katy."

She forces the doll into my arms. I feel like an idiot holding it. I never had dolls growing up and I have no idea what you're supposed to do with them.

"Let's fix their hair." She hands me a small, plastic brush. "You do braids on yours."

The door to her room opens. "Lilly, are you—" It's Katherine, Lilly's mom and Garret's stepmother. "Oh. Jade, I didn't know you were in here."

Hearing her tone, I get the feeling that she doesn't *want* me in here. I set the doll down and swing my legs off the bed.

Lilly grabs hold of my robe. "No. Don't go. We're playing."

"Lilly, you need to go eat breakfast. You have ballet class soon."

"Can Jade go to ballet, too?"

"No. Jade's staying here. Now go downstairs. Charles has breakfast waiting."

Lilly gets down off the bed and slowly walks out, dragging her doll behind her.

"I'm sorry she's bothering you like that," Katherine says once Lilly is gone.

"It's no problem. I don't mind playing with her."

"Yes, well, she's used to playing by herself, so don't feel like you have to entertain her."

"Really, it's no problem. I like—"

"Hey, there you are." Garret walks past Katherine into Lilly's room. "Did Lilly wake you up?"

Before I can answer, Katherine does. "Yes, she did. I'll have a talk with her. It won't happen again."

"It's okay," Garret says. "I'm sure Jade didn't mind."

"No. Not at all," I say, going over to stand next to Garret.

"Still, Lilly knows better than to go into someone's room like that," Katherine says as she glares at the two of us. She hates seeing Garret and me together.

In the past, Garret's girlfriends were chosen for him based on how the girl would benefit the family and the family name. Then I came along and changed all that which infuriates Katherine.

Garret's dad seems to have accepted the fact that I'm dating his son. Or at least he acts like he does, especially now, after the scene that happened downstairs almost a week ago. A scene witnessed only by Garret, his dad, and me. A scene that might have changed the future of the United States.

Garret's dad shot and killed Royce Sinclair, the frontrunner nominee for the next presidential election. I'd just learned that Sinclair was my father—the man who raped my mother years ago, resulting in me.

Last week, Sinclair showed up here with a gun, planning to kill me to wipe away the evidence of the horrible crime he committed years ago. He also tried to kill Garret, which I'm sure is the real reason Mr. Kensington shot Sinclair dead.

The incident took place in the study, a room just off the foyer. After it happened, a crew of people came in and cleaned up the scene. The story that came out in the media said that Sinclair committed suicide back at his estate in Virginia.

Mr. Kensington ordered me to never speak of the incident again. After that, he welcomed me to the family. Normally that would sound like a good thing. After all, the guy tried to break Garret and me apart for most of last semester, so I should've been thrilled when he welcomed me to the family. But the tone he used when he said it was eerie. It was like it had some hidden meaning. Like I'd been initiated into some secret club. A club I'm sure I don't want to be part of. And there was a finality to

4

the way he said it. As if I would be forever tied to this family after witnessing the scene in the study.

"So what are you two doing today?" Katherine asks as she nervously smooths her long blond hair with her hand. The woman always seems on edge.

"I don't know yet," Garret says. "Maybe we'll do something with Lilly. Jade and I could take her sledding."

"You know that's not a good idea." Katherine's tone is harsh, almost like she's scolding Garret for even offering up the idea.

"I didn't mean we'd go somewhere. I just meant here on the property."

She considers it. "I suppose that would be okay. I'm taking her to ballet soon, but we'll be back in the afternoon." Katherine turns and walks out.

"What's with her?" I whisper to Garret. "She acts like Lilly can't even leave the house."

Garret checks the door to make sure Katherine is gone, then leads me over to Lilly's bed to sit down. "I told you my dad has a lot of enemies, right?"

"Yeah."

"So because of that, Lilly is a target. If they want to get back at him, they'll go after Lilly."

"Are you serious? Like they'd try to kidnap her or what?"

"Kidnap her. Hurt her. Bad shit. We basically can't let her out of our sight."

"That's horrible. Has anything ever happened?"

"When Lilly was a baby, they had a nanny taking care of her. One day the nanny said she was taking Lilly to the park, but the woman never came back. She took her. My dad had to use his connections and pay a shitload of ransom money to get Lilly back. After that, they never hired another nanny."

5

"What about friends? Can she have friends over to play?"

"After what happened with the nanny, Katherine doesn't trust anyone to be around Lilly. So she doesn't really have any friends. She doesn't even go to regular school. She has a private tutor who comes to the house."

"No wonder Lilly's so desperate for a playmate. That's so sad. I should play with her more."

Garret puts his arm around me. "She's okay. She's used to playing alone. But that's sweet of you to offer. And she would love it if you played with her. I try to play with her but she says boys are no fun to play with."

I lean in and kiss the side of his freshly shaven face. "That depends on what you're playing."

He kisses me back on the lips. "Are you saying you want to play with me, Jade?"

"Definitely. But not right now." I get up off the bed. "Go have breakfast. I'll get ready and be right down."

Garret is already showered and dressed, looking freaking hot as usual in jeans and a super-soft, light blue t-shirt. All of his clothes fit him perfectly. It's like they're specially made for him. He's a swimmer so has broad shoulders, a muscular chest, and a narrow waist. I don't think clothes off the rack would fit him right. He'd have to have them tailored to look that good.

"Before you go, I have a surprise for you." He pulls me down to sit on his lap and I notice a sudden spark of excitement in his gorgeous blue eyes.

"What is it?"

"I'm taking you to New York for New Year's Eve. I thought we'd leave next Tuesday and stay until Friday. That way we won't have to rush to see all the sights. What do you think?"

"It sounds great, but I'm a little freaked out about being there on New Year's with all those people and all that noise."

6

Garret knows about my noise phobia. Growing up, my drunk, pill-addicted mother used to scream and throw things and bang pans together knowing how it scared me. I hated it, and to this day I try to avoid loud noises. I know I need to get over it, but I'm not there yet.

"I already considered the noise issue," he says. "And that's why I got us a hotel right above Times Square. We'll watch the ball drop from our room. You won't have to be anywhere near the crowds."

"But that had to have cost a fortune." I don't like Garret spending money on me. He knows this and sometimes we fight about it. But I hate fighting with him, so I've been trying to let it go. Still, the topic tends to sneak up now and then.

"Jade, don't start with the money thing. It's New Year's Eve and I told you I wanted to make every holiday special for you since you never celebrated any of them. Just let me do this." He smiles, and I have a really hard time saying no to that smile.

"Okay, but I swear I'm keeping track of all this money you're spending and I'm going to pay you back someday."

"As long as we're on this topic, I might as well tell you that I'm getting you a plane ticket to go see Frank and Ryan before school starts again. I know you didn't get enough time with them when we were there and now that it's safe to go home, I want you to go."

Again, I don't want Garret paying for my plane ticket, but I really want to see Frank and Ryan and I don't want to wait until May when school's out.

"Thanks. I really appreciate it."

He stares at me, confused. "You're not going to yell at me about the money?"

I shrug. "I'll just add it to my tab."

"There is no tab. I told you, we'll be married by the time you have the money to pay me back. And then it won't matter because what's mine is yours." He smiles smugly.

"Okay, enough with the marriage talk. And besides, it's entirely possible I'll pay you back long before I'd even consider marrying you. Maybe I'll win the lottery or some long lost relative will leave me an inheritance or I'll get a really good job after college or—"

"Damn. You're not even considering it? I really need to up my game."

"Why are you so anxious to get married?"

"I'm not. I'm just tossing the idea out there. Trying to see if you're even open to it."

"I'm open to it. But not at 19."

"My dad got married when he was 22."

"You said he was forced to by his parents. It's not like he wanted to. And look how that ended. Divorce. He was older when he married your mom."

"Relax. I'm not proposing anytime soon." He kisses my cheek. "And given your attitude, maybe I never will." He says it kiddingly, but for some stupid reason I feel disappointed.

"Hey! I don't have an attitude. Take that back."

"So now you *want* me to propose?" He shakes his head. "I'm so confused."

"Well, yes. I mean, no." I'm completely flustered. "I don't know. Just stop talking about it."

"You should at least consider it, Jade. You're already part of my family. You had Thanksgiving here. You've experienced the Kensington family Christmas. And Lilly's made you her big sister."

Already part of my family. His words send a shiver down me. They remind me of his dad's words, welcoming me to the family. This crazy family that I don't at all understand.

I kiss him quick as I stand up. "I need to shower. I'll see you at breakfast."

He catches my wrist. "Do you need some help in the shower? Because I'm more than happy to help."

Given how hot he looks and how great he smells, it's a tempting offer but not with his family home.

"I can handle it. But thanks."

I go back to my room and get ready, then head downstairs to the dining room where Garret, Katherine, and Lilly are having breakfast. I take a seat next to Garret. Charles, the family cook, has set out a warming tray filled with eggs and sausage. There's also a platter of fruit and pastries. I serve myself some eggs and take a pastry.

Nobody is talking. Katherine is reading the newspaper. Lilly is sitting across from me, bobbing up and down in her chair as she eats.

Mr. Kensington walks in, wearing a suit, which is odd given that it's Saturday and the day after Christmas. Lilly bursts out of her chair and runs over to him.

"Daddy! I'm going sledding! I'm going sledding!"

He picks her up and she plants a kiss on his cheek. "Yes, I heard that. That should be fun for you." He looks at Garret. "Do we even have a sled?"

Garret nods as he sets his juice glass down. "Jade and I bought one over Thanksgiving break. We went sledding at Bryant Park."

"You're not going there today, are you?" Mr. Kensington uses the same disapproving tone that his wife used earlier.

"No, we're staying here," Garret says.

"Good. Have a good time, Lilly." He kisses her, then sets her down. "I have to go to the office, but I'll see everyone at dinner."

"Bye, Daddy." Lilly runs back to her seat.

"See ya, Dad," Garret says.

I smile at Mr. Kensington, not sure what to say. Even though he seems to tolerate me now, I still find him very intimidating.

Mr. Kensington looks at Katherine. She keeps her head buried in her newspaper, not even acknowledging him. They're definitely fighting about something. I hope it's not me. But I get the feeling that it is.

CHAPTER TWO

Once Mr. Kensington is gone, Katherine closes her newspaper and folds it back up, setting it on the table. "Lilly, we need to get going. Finish up." She turns to me. "Does she need anything for this sledding activity?"

I'm not sure what Katherine means. Has the woman never gone sledding? Was she never a child? I basically had no childhood and *I* still went sledding.

"Does she have snow pants?" I ask Katherine.

"No. She doesn't. I'll stop and get her some after dance class."

"Can I have pink ones?" Lilly asks.

"That's the only color you wear," Garret says to her.

She shakes her head back and forth. "Nope. I wear purple, too."

Garret looks at Katherine to confirm. "It's true. She recently expanded her wardrobe to include purple." Katherine gets up from the table. "Let's go, Lilly."

Lilly hops down off her chair and the two of them leave. Garret and I stay behind to finish breakfast.

"Hasn't Lilly ever gone sledding?"

He thinks for a moment. "I guess she hasn't. We didn't own a sled before you came along."

"Thank God I did. I need to loosen you people up. You need some fun around here." I reach for the juice carafe but Garret gets to it first and pours me some.

"So when do you think you want to go to Des Moines? I should probably get the plane ticket today."

"Ticket? Just singular? You aren't coming with me?"

He shrugs. "I didn't think I should. I mean, I totally will if you want me to, but I thought you might want some time alone with Frank and Ryan, without me hanging around."

"Yeah, okay. I guess that would be good. Maybe I'll go next Saturday after we get back from New York."

"How long do you want to stay? For the rest of break?"

"That's two weeks. That's kind of a long time."

"I thought that's what you wanted. You said you had all these plans to do stuff with Ryan."

"Yeah. You're right. Two weeks is good. It just sucks that I won't see you for that long." I stare down at my plate, moving my eggs around with my fork.

Garret takes the fork from me and sets it on the table. "Are you saying you'll miss me? Because if so, I need to mentally record this moment. It may never happen again."

I smile as I roll my eyes. "Yes. I guess that's what I'm saying. You put some kind of spell on me and now I miss you when you're not around."

"I didn't do anything," he says.

I punch his arm. "Yeah you did, and it pisses me off."

He kisses my cheek. "Well, you've done the same thing to me. I'm gonna really miss you, but I know you want to go home."

"Why don't you come to Des Moines for a week? That way I'll have a week alone with Frank and Ryan and a week with you. I don't need to spend every minute with the two of them.

And besides, Frank has to stay home and rest. He'll probably sleep most of the time. And Ryan will be at work or out with Chloe."

Garret pushes his chair back and gets up. "Finally. I was waiting for you to invite me. It took you long enough."

"You're the one who told me to go by myself!"

"I was being polite, Jade. And then you were supposed to be polite back and invite me to go with you." He stands behind me and drops a kiss on the top of my head. "I'll go book the flights."

"Not first class. It's too expensive," I say as he walks out. I'm sure he won't listen.

After lunch we take Lilly outside behind the house. The Kensington property includes several acres of land, mostly woods. We walk through the trees until we find a clearing at the top of a small hill. It's not nearly as big as the hill at Bryant Park but it's good enough for Lilly. The hill at the park would've been too scary for her since she's never been sledding.

Lilly's bundled up head to toe in pink snow pants, a pink jacket, and a pink hat. I can't stand the color pink, but it's cute on her with her rosy cheeks and blond hair.

I get on the sled with her and we slide slowly down the tiny hill.

"Can we do it again?" Lilly's jumping up and down like this is the greatest thing she's ever done.

I spend the next half hour going down the hill with her. Garret can't sled because his chest is still healing from the bullet wound caused by the incident in the study that we're pretending never happened.

"Can I go by myself now?" she asks Garret.

"You're not afraid?"

She shakes her head no, then positions herself on the sled. He gives her a push down the hill. It takes her forever to pull the sled back up to the top, but when she finally reaches it, she's ready to go again.

"I think she likes the sledding," I say to Garret.

"Yeah, it's good for her to get out and do stuff. She spends way too much time in her room." He leans down and kisses me.

I pull back. "Garret. Lilly could be watching."

"She's at the bottom of the hill. It'll take her 10 minutes to get back up here." He kisses me again, slower this time. The cold air circles around us, making me shiver. I reach up and grab his jacket, pulling him closer.

We kiss for several minutes, then Garret breaks from the kiss and looks around. "I thought she'd be back by now."

We both look down the hill. There's no sign of Lilly, but the sled is sitting there.

"Lilly?" Garret sounds panicked.

"She probably went in the woods. Maybe she saw a squirrel or something."

I'm trying to reassure him but Garret's not listening. He starts running down the hill.

"Lilly! Answer me! Where are you?" His voice is frantic now.

I don't know why he's so worried. We're on the Kensington property. There's a tall fence around the entire perimeter. She couldn't get out. But I guess it's possible someone could get in, especially back here where they don't have security guards.

"Lilly!" I yell her name as I follow Garret into the woods. "Any sign of her?"

"No. And why the fuck isn't she answering me?" He takes off again farther into the woods. "Lilly! This isn't funny! Where are you?"

14

I run the other direction, calling her name, but there's no response. It's like she just disappeared. I was trying to stay calm, but now I'm panicking like Garret. What if someone got past the fence? What if they took her?

I run to the right and spot a flash of pink out the side of my eye. I stop and turn to see Lilly sitting down next to a tree.

"Lilly!" I run over to her, kneeling beside her. "What are you doing?"

"Look. She's hurt." She points to a bird on the ground that has a broken wing.

"Why didn't you answer me? Or your brother? Didn't you hear us?" Between the running and the panicking, I'm now completely out of breath.

She looks down at the bird again and reaches her hand out to pet it.

I grab her arm. "Don't touch it. Just leave it alone."

I stand up and call for Garret. He's there moments later.

He picks Lilly off the ground and stands her up in front of him. "Why didn't you answer me?"

Garret's voice is loud and stern and he towers over her. I can tell he's scaring her, even though I know that's not his intention.

"I did, but nobody came," she says.

Lilly's voice is so faint that she probably did answer and we didn't hear her.

"You know the rules, Lilly. No running off. Ever."

"But I saw this bird and she couldn't fly and then—"

"I don't care about the bird! You know—"

I grab Garret's arm, giving him a look to calm down.

Lilly looks like she's about to cry. "I was just trying to help."

"So is this the bird?" I ask, hoping to refocus her attention.

She nods. "She can't fly anymore."

15

Lilly kneels down on the ground again. The bird was twitching a little before, but now it's motionless and I'm pretty sure it's dead. I glance over at Garret. I have zero experience with kids and have no idea how to handle this situation.

Garret kneels down next to her, his voice softer now. "You need to let the bird rest. She'll be okay."

"How do you know?"

"When you're hurt you have to rest to get better. Just like with me. I have to rest to get better, right?"

"Can we take her inside? She can rest in my room."

"This is her home. She lives in the woods. She doesn't want to go inside."

"But nobody will take care of her."

"She has a mom, just like you. Her mom will take of her."

"But what if her mom can't find her?"

"She'll find her. But she shouldn't have left home like that. Just like you shouldn't have run off, Lilly. You can't do that ever again, okay?"

She nods.

Garret takes Lilly's tiny, mitten-covered hand and stands up, pulling her up with him. "Let's go inside. I'm hungry from all that sledding." His tone has lightened, making Lilly smile.

"You didn't even go sledding, Garret."

He smiles back. "I know. But watching you and Jade go sledding made me hungry."

He picks up my hand with his free hand and we all walk back to the house.

When we get inside, Lilly takes off her coat, hat, and snow pants and hangs them neatly on the hooks by the door. Next, she takes off her boots and sets them on a rubber mat. It's funny to watch her. I was never that orderly as a kid. I just tossed all my stuff on the floor. I still do, at least in my dorm room. Here, I follow Lilly's lead and put everything in its place.

Once her snow gear is put away, Lilly runs into the kitchen. I start to follow her but Garret holds me back.

"What happened out there has to stay between you and me," he says. "Don't tell my dad and definitely don't tell Katherine."

"I won't say anything. But won't Lilly say something?"

"No. She knows she'd be punished for running off like that. She won't say anything."

"Sorry, I should've kept an eye on her."

"Don't be sorry. It's not your job to keep an eye on her. It's my job. And I fucked up. If Katherine found out, she'd never leave me alone with Lilly again. She's finally starting to trust me and then this happens."

"What do you mean? Why didn't she trust you with Lilly?"

"Because before I met you I was drunk all the time. And not very responsible. But still, I would never let anything happen to Lilly."

"You know, you were really good with her out there. You knew just what to say."

He shrugs. "I tried. She seemed to believe it. And thanks for calming me down."

"I know what it's like to be small and have someone big yelling at you. It's scary, even if the person doesn't mean to be scary." I stand up on my toes to kiss him. "And you're so big you can be kind of scary to us small people."

Lilly comes running out of the kitchen. "Charles made hot cocoa!" She tugs on both of us. "Come on."

Katherine appears just as we're about to follow Lilly to the kitchen. "Did you have fun sledding, Lilly?"

I'm positive Lilly is going to tell her what happened. Why wouldn't she? Kids her age can't keep secrets.

"I went down the hill with Jade and then I went all by myself," Lilly says. "I wasn't even afraid. And now we're having hot cocoa." She runs back to the kitchen.

Katherine turns to Garret. "Did you have any problems with her?"

"No problems," Garret answers. "Everything was fine."

I hear someone in the foyer and turn to see Mr. Kensington coming toward us in the hallway. He's back from work with his coat still on. He walks up to Katherine. "Hello, sweetheart." Her body stiffens as he kisses her cheek. She gives him a tight-lipped smile and says nothing.

"Hi, Dad. Jade and I are going out tonight, so we'll see you guys tomorrow." Garret grabs my hand and starts walking toward the stairs.

"How was the sledding?" his dad calls after us.

"It was good. Lilly liked it," Garret yells back as he hurries me up the stairs.

We go in his room and he shuts the door. "Let's get out of here. You need to change or anything?"

"I need to shower. I'm all sweaty from running up that hill a hundred times."

"You can use mine if you want. I'll get you a towel." Garret disappears in the bathroom, then comes out again. "It's all set. Go ahead."

"What's wrong with you? What's the big rush?"

"Those two were acting really strange and after the thing with Lilly, I just need to get out of here." He lies down on the bed, staring up at the ceiling. "I'm seriously not going to survive living here until school starts again."

18

"You only have to spend a week here. The rest of the time you'll be with me in New York and then Iowa. And the week you're here, your family will be in the Bahamas."

He sighs. "They're not going."

"Why not?" I sit down next to him on the bed.

"It's not safe to leave right now."

"Not safe? What do you mean?"

He sits up and puts his arm around my shoulder. "Do you want to have an early dinner? Or go to a movie?"

"Garret, stop it. Don't hide stuff from me. You know I hate it when you do that. Tell me what's going on."

He keeps quiet.

"Come on. Just tell me."

He gets up and goes to his closet and takes out a long sleeve, button-up shirt. "There's some fallout from what happened last week."

"Fallout? You mean people wanting revenge or something?"

"Not so much revenge as punishment, although I'm sure there are people who want revenge." He takes his t-shirt off and puts on the other shirt, buttoning it up. "That's why I about had a heart attack when Lilly ran off."

"What do you mean by punishment?"

"My dad broke the rules when he did what he did." Garret still hasn't talked about his dad shooting Sinclair. It's like he's wiped it from his memory. Either that or he doesn't want to admit that his dad killed someone.

"What rules?"

"Just forget it." He goes to his desk and starts swiping through his phone.

I walk over and stand in front of him. "What's the deal with your dad? Is he involved in something illegal?"

Garret keeps his eyes on his phone. "I really don't know what he's involved in."

"He's your dad. How could you not know?"

"I've seen things, but I don't know what they mean. And in the past when I've asked him he wouldn't tell me, so I stopped asking."

"Have you seen him cover up stuff before?"

Garret looks up from his phone. "Why are you so interested in this? It doesn't matter what he does. I'm nothing like him and I'll never do whatever it is that he does. So you don't need to worry about it."

"If he's committing crimes, then I don't want to be around him. I don't want to be staying at his house."

"I never said he was doing anything illegal, Jade."

"He shot someone and didn't tell the police. That seems illegal to me."

"The guy was going to kill us!" Garret raises his voice, then lowers it again. "What did you expect my dad to do?"

"Yeah, he did what he had to do, but then he covered it up. How did he do that?"

"He has friends, okay? Let's just leave it at that." He looks down at his phone again and swipes the screen. "There's a movie starting in a hour. You want to go?"

"What did you mean when you said your dad will be punished?"

"I don't know the whole story. I just overheard my dad talking in his office and it sounded like he's in some serious shit. And then I heard him telling Katherine it was too dangerous to travel. I don't know if that's why she's mad at him or what."

"Are you and I in danger?"

"I don't think so. If we were, he would tell us." He shoves the phone in his pocket. "Let's go. You've got 10 minutes to get ready."

He knows 10 minutes isn't long enough, but he also knows I pride myself on getting ready fast and there's no way in hell I won't meet that deadline. He looks down at his watch, taunting me. I sprint down the hall to my room.

We have dinner at an Italian restaurant in town, then see a movie. Garret seems distant the whole time. I think he's still upset about what happened with Lilly. Not upset with her or me, but with himself for not watching her close enough.

There's definitely more going on with Garret's family that he either doesn't know or isn't telling me. And I'm not surprised his dad's in trouble. You can't just kill a possible presidential candidate and get away with it. Can you?

CHAPTER THREE

The next morning I call Ryan to tell him I'm coming home.

"Ryan, guess what?" I skip the hello when I hear him answer. He knows who it is.

"Is this a trick question or something? If so, I don't know the answer."

"I'm coming home next Saturday. For two whole weeks."

"That's great. How'd you manage that?"

"Garret got me a plane ticket."

"That was nice of him, but I should really pay him back. He already paid to fly you out here once. I've been working overtime and have some money saved. Ask him how much I owe him and I'll write him a check."

"No, you need that money for school and Frank's medical bills. I've already told Garret I'll pay him back someday, so don't worry about it. How's Frank doing?"

"Better. Did I tell you about the new doctor who started working at the hospital last week?"

"No, I don't think so."

"He's from New York. He's supposed to be really good and he knows a lot about MS. I have no idea why he decided to take a job in Des Moines, although I think he's splitting his time between New York and here. Anyway, he's been working with

Dad. It sounds like he's going to get him on some different medications."

"Is Frank getting out of the hospital soon?"

"Probably on Saturday. I wish I'd known you were coming home. I'm not sure if I'll be able to get time off from work while you're here."

"That's fine. Garret's flying out a week later, so I can do stuff with him when you're at work and Frank's sleeping."

"Oh. Okay." Ryan still doesn't fully approve of my relationship with Garret. He doesn't like the fact that I hang out with Garret more than I hang out with Harper or other girls. "Is he staying at a hotel again?"

"I guess he will. There's not really room at the house."

"He could sleep on the couch if he wants."

Garret's so tall he'd never fit on their tiny couch, but it's nice of Ryan to offer.

"I'll let you know. Anyway, I just wanted to tell you I'll be home soon. I'll call you later this week. Tell Frank I said hi."

"I will. See ya, Jade."

After I hang up with Ryan, I go to Lilly's room and play with her for a few hours. I feel bad that she doesn't have anyone to play with. Then again, when I was her age I didn't have anyone to play with either. But I didn't like it. And I'm sure Lilly doesn't like it either.

While Lilly and I play, Garret has physical therapy. When he was shot, the bullet went into his upper chest near his shoulder, affecting the muscles he uses for swimming. The physical therapist is showing him different exercises he can do in the pool so he can hopefully start swimming again soon. He won't be able to compete on the swim team, but he wants to be able to go to practice.

23

At 7, we all sit down for dinner. Garret and I usually go out for dinner so we aren't stuck sitting with his dad and Katherine, but tonight we decided to stay in. A winter storm came rolling in earlier today and I didn't want to go out in the bad weather.

"Any plans for New Year's?" Mr. Kensington asks Garret as the server plates our food.

"Jade and I are going to New York. I thought I told you that."

Mr. Kensington nods. "Yes, you did tell me that. I just didn't remember. So when are you leaving?"

"Tuesday and coming back Friday. And then Jade's flying to Des Moines on Saturday. I'm meeting her there a week later, remember?"

Mr. Kensington doesn't answer. He seems deep in thought. Finally he wakes up from wherever his mind was and looks at me.

"Jade, you must be excited about going home. By the way, how is Frank doing?"

I'm always surprised when he mentions Frank. I never talk about Frank or Ryan around Garret's family.

"Frank is fine. He's still in the hospital."

"I hope he's getting good care. It's hard to find competent medical professionals these days. Does he have a good physician?"

"Actually, I talked to Ryan earlier and he said Frank is seeing a new doctor. Some guy from New York. He's supposed to be really good."

Mr. Kensington smiles. "Excellent. I hope he can offer some assistance to Frank. I know he means a great deal to you."

Garret's eyes dart to his dad, then back at me. He seems just as confused as I am about his dad's interest in Frank.

"Where are you two staying in New York?" Mr. Kensington asks Garret.

"I got a hotel in Times Square for New Year's Eve. I thought we'd stay at the apartment for the other nights. Unless you need to stay there for work."

"No, I won't be in the city next week. I'd actually prefer that you stay at the apartment rather than a hotel. It's in a very secure building."

Secure building? Why do we need a secure building? I almost ask Mr. Kensington what he means by that, but then he starts talking again.

"You're taking the car service, I presume?"

Garret shakes his head as he sets his fork down on his plate. "I thought we'd just take the train."

"You need to take the car service, Garret. You have the number. Just tell them what time to be here."

"But the train is fine, Dad. Really."

"I insist that you take the car service." Mr. Kensington's commanding tone seems to imply we don't have a choice.

"Fine. Whatever. We'll take the car service."

"And if you're going to be in Times Square during the New Year's celebrations, you'll take one of our security guards with you."

Garret's dad is starting to scare me. Is New York City really that bad? He makes it sound like there are people waiting to attack us on every corner. Now I'm wondering if we should even go.

"Dad, we're not going to be on the street when the ball drops. Jade doesn't like being around a lot of noise."

I feel my face heating up. My fear of loud noises is not supposed to be public knowledge.

"It's really more about the crowds," I say. "I don't want to be jammed in with all those people."

"Still, I think you should take Brian with you, Garret. Just in case you run into any trouble."

"We're not taking a security guy with us. Nothing's going to happen. We'll be in tourist areas the whole time."

Mr. Kensington doesn't push the topic any further. He picks up his fork and starts eating his meal. The table is silent until Lilly starts telling everyone about the game she and I played earlier in the day.

After dinner, Garret and I go in the theater room and watch a movie with Lilly. She's so happy getting all this attention from her brother and me.

"Do you have to leave?" she asks Garret when the movie's over.

"It's just for a few days. I'll be back on Friday."

"But Jade's not coming back." She comes over and climbs up on my lap. Even after hanging out with Lilly all this time, I'm still not used to the way she just invades my personal space. She's always grabbing my hand and hugging me and messing with my hair. It's fine because it's Lilly, but I don't think I could take it with some other kid.

"Jade, please don't go. Please." She hugs me as tight as her little arms can.

"We can still play tomorrow," I tell her. "Garret and I don't leave until Tuesday."

"When will I see you again?"

"I'm not sure." I glance at Garret to answer.

"Jade has to go home for a couple weeks. And then school starts. But we'll stop by some weekend and see you, okay?"

She releases her hold on me and turns to Garret, pouting and slumping her shoulders. "That's like forever. And you always say you'll come home and you never do." She crosses her arms like she's mad at him.

"I promise I'll come home more. And I'll bring Jade with me."

"No, you won't. You're just saying that." She repositions herself on my lap and hugs me again, resting her head on my shoulder. "I'll give you all my toys if you stay here, Jade."

I mouth the words "help me" to Garret. He just smiles and shakes his head, leaving me to come up with a response.

"Lilly, I think you should keep your toys. That way they'll already be here when I come over to play with you. And I promise I'll come see you."

She sits up and looks at me like she's not sure she believes me. Then she hops off my lap and runs out of the room.

"Thanks a lot, Garret," I say to him. "Why didn't you help me out? She's *your* sister."

"She didn't offer *me* all her toys. Besides, I wanted to see what you'd say."

"Obviously she didn't like what I said. She just ran off."

"She always runs off like that. Don't take it personally." He reaches over and holds my hand. "You're good with kids, Jade. You'll make a great mom someday."

I shudder. "Ugh. No way I'm having kids. Don't even joke about it."

"Come on. Don't you want a mini you?" He smiles. "Or a mini me?"

A smaller version of him would be pretty damn cute.

"No. Absolutely not. Now stop talking about it. Your marriage comments are bad enough."

Lilly runs back into the room, carrying a doll, a pen, and a piece of paper. She puts the doll in my lap. "You can take Katy home with you so you'll remember me." She gives me the piece of paper and pen. "Sign this."

I read the paper. Garret leans over to read it, too. It says, "I, Jade Taylor, promise to come play with Lilly Kensington." There's a line under it where I'm supposed to sign.

"Did Dad write that for you?" Garret asks her.

She nods, keeping her eye on the paper. "Will you sign it, Jade?"

"Um, okay." I sign the paper and give it back to her. She hugs me quick then runs off again.

"You sure you wanted to sign that?" Garret asks. "Now you're stuck playing with her for the rest of your life."

"I'm not too worried about it." I set the doll down. "Although I'm not sure what I'm supposed to do with Katy."

"Just stick her in your closet at school. Lilly will never know." He pulls me up from my chair. "Let's go plan our trip to New York."

We spend the rest of the night making a list of all the things we want to see and figuring out what we'll have time to do.

Before heading to bed, Garret invites me to come to his room later for a little late night fun but I turn him down. I don't like doing it with his parents home. Plus we'll have plenty of time for that when we're in New York.

I spend most of Monday doing stuff with Lilly while Garret has more physical therapy. Katherine keeps stopping by to check on Lilly, and each time she does, she reminds me that Lilly can play by herself. She almost seems angry that I'm playing with her daughter. I have no idea why. You'd think she'd be happy about it. I don't get Katherine at all.

The next morning I wake up at 5 a.m. and can't get back to sleep. I'm really thirsty, so I decide to sneak down to the kitchen to get a drink. As I'm tiptoeing down the long hallway, I hear

Mr. and Mrs. Kensington talking in their room. It sounds like they're arguing. I know I shouldn't, but I walk quietly to the end of the hall where their room is and listen.

"If you'd never brought her here we wouldn't have this problem." Katherine's speaking, but it doesn't sound like her. Her voice is usually monotone, expressing zero emotion. But now her voice is full of emotion—all anger.

"You know the circumstances. We owed Sinclair a favor." Unlike his wife, Mr. Kensington sounds very calm.

"YOU owed Sinclair. I didn't. And I told you not to allow that trashy girl into our lives. She's caused nothing but problems since she arrived."

"She's not trashy. She came from a bad home, but that wasn't her fault. She's very smart. And very driven. She's excelling at Moorhurst. And she's been an excellent influence on Garret. He was completely out of control before she came into his life. Now look at him. He stopped drinking. He's doing well in school. He's acting responsible for once. You can't deny the positive effect she's had on him."

"Garret is your concern, Pearce. Not mine."

Pearce? I guess I never knew Mr. Kensington's first name.

"How can you act that way after all these years? Like you have no concern at all for Garret? That boy has never done anything to you and yet you continue to reject him. You've never even tried to get to know him."

"And how was I supposed to get to know him? He's been drunk for most our marriage. And don't you dare blame me for that! He got that way because of you."

Mr. Kensington's voice gets louder. "He GOT that way because I gave all my attention to YOU! You demanded it from the second we got married. Making me take you on trips without him. Forcing me to attend your ridiculous society

29

events every night. I was never here for him. You did everything in your power to keep me from having a relationship with my son!"

There's a long silence. I stand there frozen in place, afraid they'll hear me if I move.

Katherine clears her throat. "I don't want that girl near my daughter. If you insist on letting her come to this house, she is not to see Lilly."

"Lilly enjoys spending time with Jade. And Jade is very good with her. There's no need to keep the two of them apart."

"She's MY daughter and what I say goes."

"She is OUR daughter. And I am tired of you acting otherwise. I've had enough of this, Katherine. Lilly will no longer live in this tightly-wound world of yours where she can't interact with other people."

"I'm protecting her! She was taken from us once and I will never let it happen again!"

"We can't shield her from the entire world! She needs friends. Friends her own age. She sits alone in her room all day long. That's not normal. Did you see how happy she was when Jade and Garret took her sledding? Because that's what a 6-year-old should be doing! Sledding. Playing outside."

"I'm not talking to you about this. I know what's best for her. And she hasn't been harmed by her upbringing. She's a perfectly well-adjusted little girl."

"Only because Garret has taken it upon himself to teach Lilly how to be halfway normal. If it weren't for Garret, Lilly would be a smaller version of you!"

"And what is that supposed to mean?" she hisses.

"Don't get me started."

"You think you're a better parent than me? You're never even here for our daughter. You spend almost no time with her."

"You know damn well I have no control over my schedule! They control it and they always will!" He lowers his voice. "The bottom line is that you are not going to dictate how we raise our daughter. I'm her father and I WILL have a say in how she is raised."

"So you're just going to send her outside to play? Let her get taken again? Let her spend time with Jade? Some girl we barely know? The girl who has caused the situation we're dealing with now?"

"None of this is Jade's fault. The situation we're in now is because of me. I'm the one who killed Sinclair."

"Which you never should've done!"

"And what did you expect me to do? The man fired a gun at Garret. And Jade. He would've killed them!"

"Sometimes you have to sacrifice a few for the many." Katherine says it in a low, harsh tone that sends a chill through me.

There's silence and then I hear Mr. Kensington speaking. "I'm going to pretend I didn't hear that."

"There was a plan, Pearce!" Katherine raises her voice again. "A very big plan. And you've destroyed that!"

"Yes, I'm well aware of the plan, dear," Mr. Kensington says, emphasizing the 'dear.' "But I was not going to just stand there and watch that fucking bastard kill my son!"

"You could've just injured Royce. You didn't need to kill him."

"I can't change the outcome. He's gone, and another man can take his place. Obviously Sinclair was a poor choice given

31

how unstable he was, trying to kill his own daughter. He had no reason to go after her like that. She was no threat to him."

"She's trash, Pearce. And trashy people will do anything to get money. It was just a matter of time before she went to Royce and asked for hush money. And after she got it, she would've sold her story to the highest paying tabloid. That's why he went after her. And now you allow that piece of trash to live in this house? Interact with our daughter? Date your son? She wants money, Pearce. That's the only reason she's sticking around."

"Jade isn't like that. The girl you described is the type of girl we've forced Garret to date. Like Ava Hamilton. A spoiled, self-centered girl looking for fame and fortune."

"I want Jade out of this house and she is never allowed back."

"She's one of us now, Katherine, whether you like it or not. She's seen too much. She knows our ways."

"Then pay her off. Pay her to keep quiet. Pay her to go away. I don't care how much it costs."

"I'm not doing that. And even if I made her an offer, she wouldn't accept it. She loves Garret and he loves her. No amount of money will break them apart."

"You know Garret's not allowed to be with someone like her, so why are you letting this continue?"

"That's not an issue anymore. He's not going to be part of it."

"You're delusional, Pearce. He's your son. They'll never—"

"We're done discussing this."

"Fine. If you won't get rid of Jade, I'll throw her out myself." I hear footsteps walking quickly toward the door. My heart stops mid-beat as I prepare for Katherine to catch me standing there.

CHAPTER FOUR

"Katherine!" I hear Mr. Kensington racing after her. "You will not interfere in this! I will handle Jade and Garret as needed. If you even *think* of interfering, there will be consequences. Do you understand me?"

The way he says it scares the crap out of me, but it doesn't seem to have the same effect on Katherine.

"Fine, have it your way," she says in a calm but caustic tone. "Besides, we both know those two won't last."

"I'm going into the office." I hear him walking farther away from the door, probably toward the bathroom.

"Why do you have a such soft spot for that girl?" Katherine asks in a syrupy sweet voice. "Is it because she reminds you of Garret's mother? Another trashy girl from the wrong side of the tracks?"

"Fuck you, Katherine!" A door inside the room slams shut, rattling the door next to me.

I hurry back down the hall. I'm no longer thirsty. Well, I kind of am but there's no way in hell I'm going to the kitchen now. I just want to hide away until I can get out of this place.

I knew Katherine hated me, but not that much. She honestly thinks I'm dating Garret to get a piece of the Kensington fortune? That really pisses me off. I've never once asked Garret for money and I never would. I have no interest in his money or his family's money. If she only knew how much I fight with Garret every time he tries to buy me something.

The woman is mean and hateful and all kinds of crazy. And what was the big plan she was talking about? Apparently she thought it was important enough to sacrifice Garret and me. She probably would've been happy if Sinclair had killed me. But did she really think it would've been okay for him to kill Garret? Who says that about their own stepson? And why the hell is Garret's dad still married to this woman?

I'm back in my room now but it feels different. It feels cold and scary and really dark. I can't be in here. I sneak back out and quietly make my way to Garret's room. He's sound asleep.

I didn't think I could love Garret any more than I already do, but after overhearing that conversation I somehow love him even more. He never told me how Katherine treated him all these years. And he never told me how his dad basically ignored him when he married Katherine. It sounds like Garret's life went to hell after his mom died. And although most people would say my life has been a million times worse than Garret's, I feel worse for him than I do for myself. I guess it's harder to accept someone you love being hurt than it is yourself.

I go over to Garret's bed and slip under the covers, trying not to wake him.

"Jade?" He yawns. "What time is it?"

"A little after 5."

"Come here." He puts his arm out and I snuggle up beside him, resting my head on his chest. "Is something wrong or did you just stop by to say hi?"

"Nothing's wrong. I just wanted to be next to you." I pull the blankets up all the way to my chin. This house seems so much colder now.

"Are you sure you're okay?" Garret kisses my forehead. "I feel like you're not telling me something."

"I'm okay. What time are we leaving for New York?"

"I have the car scheduled for 9. Why?"

"Is there any way we could leave earlier? Like maybe 7 or 8?"

"We'd have to get up right now if we did that."

"Yeah. I guess. Goodnight."

He falls back asleep. But I can't. I keep replaying that conversation in my head. Parts of it made no sense. Like when Mr. Kensington said that I know their ways? What ways? What does that mean?

He said I was one of them now. I don't want to be one of them. If Garret and I ever got married, I'd want to run as far away as possible from them, or at least Katherine. I still don't know what to think of Garret's dad. Part of me thinks he's okay, but another part of me knows he can't be trusted. He's definitely involved in something I probably don't want to know about.

I can't decide if I should tell Garret everything I heard. I'm thinking I should only tell him some of it, like the part about Katherine trying to get rid of me. But then again, maybe he'd be mad at me for listening in. Maybe he doesn't want me knowing about the things I heard. I decide to keep quiet for now.

At 6:30, I go back to my room to shower and dress. Then I pack everything in my suitcase. On a chair by the bed I spot the Katy doll that Lilly gave me. It's ironic she gave me a doll that has the same name as her mother. I consider poking pins in it and making it a voodoo doll. But that would be stooping to Katherine's level and I'm better than that.

I pick up Katy and take her over to my suitcase. But before I can pack her I hear faint knocks on the door. I open it to find

35

Lilly standing there. She has on her pink pajamas, pink robe, and pink bunny slippers.

"Mom said I'm not supposed to come in your room without asking first. So can I come in your room?"

"Yes, you can come in."

She notices Katy in my arms and her eyes get big. "Did Katy sleep in your bed? I let my dolls sleep with me, too, but they take turns because they don't all fit in the bed."

"Yep, she slept right beside me."

"Are you leaving now?" She sounds so sad.

"I think we're having breakfast first. You want to come with me?"

She nods repeatedly and grabs my hand.

Katherine's already in the dining room having coffee. Lilly runs up and hugs her. "Hi, Mom."

I remember Garret saying that Katherine doesn't allow Lilly to call her 'mommy' because it sounds too babyish and she wants Lilly to act mature for her age. But Lilly still calls Mr. Kensington 'daddy,' so he must've won that battle.

"Good morning, Lilly. Jade." Katherine smiles at me. Her smile always looks forced. Now I know why.

"Good morning, Katherine." I sit down across from her, smiling back. "So I guess you'll be glad to finally get rid of Garret and me."

My comment makes her spill some of her coffee. She sets her cup on the saucer. "Not at all. Mr. Kensington and I love having you both here. We're sad to see you go."

"Please don't go, Jade," Lilly says. "Please!"

"Lilly, it's rude to beg," Katherine scolds. "And we've talked about this. Jade is very busy with school. She doesn't have time to play with you anymore."

"But she signed a paper. Now she has to play with me."

36

"What paper?" Katherine asks.

"I signed a document saying I would play with Lilly," I answer. "It's very official. Your husband made it himself." I smile again just to piss her off.

"I see." Katherine's normally expressionless face springs to life. She's definitely pissed. To the point that she can't sit at the table a second longer. She gets up from her chair. "I need to attend to some things. Have a good trip, Jade. And good luck with school next semester." She hurries out of the room.

Garret walks in moments later. "Hey, breakfast with my two favorite girls. How did I get so lucky?" He's in a really good mood. Probably because we're finally getting the hell out of here.

Lilly hops down from her chair and gives him a hug. She's big into hugs, just like Garret. He obviously taught her that. I've never seen Katherine hug anyone.

"Are you ready to go?" I ask as he sits down across from me.

He grabs a pastry from the tray. "Yeah, I just need an okay from the doctor before we leave."

"Why? Is something wrong?"

"He just wants to check that everything's healing like it should. Then he's giving me a shot to curb the pain. The pills just aren't doing the job."

"Garret, why didn't you tell me you were in pain? Let's just forget the trip. We'll do it later when you feel better."

"We're not doing it later. New Year's Eve only comes once a year. I'll be fine." He pours himself some juice. "Have you seen my dad? He told me to check in with him before we left but I can't find him."

"I think he's already at the office," I say, knowing he left hours ago.

"Then I guess whatever he had to tell me wasn't that important."

"Garret, are you ready?" An older man in a suit walks into the dining room. It's the same man I saw the night that Garret was shot. He was one of the four men who came in and took Garret away in a van. Mr. Kensington said the men were doctors and that the van was a mobile medical unit. I never did find out where they took Garret that day.

Rule number one. Don't ask questions. Mr. Kensington told me that several times after the incident with Sinclair. So I never asked. And Garret never told me.

"Yeah, I'm ready." Garret finishes his orange juice and follows the man out.

The car service arrives promptly at 9. We get in the back seat of a black luxury sedan with dark tinted windows. Why do all car services use the same type of car? It's just like in the movies. Do rich people only ride in black luxury sedans with tinted windows?

"What did the doctor say?" I ask Garret as we drive away.

"He said it's healing really fast. After he gave me a shot for the pain he gave me another shot to help speed new tissue growth. He said it should feel a lot better in a week or so." He wraps his hand around mine. "Just in time for me to come see you in Des Moines."

"Where is your doctor from? Does he have an office in town?"

"No, he's more of a consultant-type of doctor. He works with private clients." Garret gazes out the side window.

"I've never heard of a doctor like that. Is he your family doctor?"

Garret shifts in his seat. "I don't want to talk about doctors right now. Let's talk about where you want to go for lunch."

He starts telling me about some of the restaurants we could try in New York, but my mind is still on his doctor. He's not a normal doctor, and neither are the other three men who took Garret away after he was shot. Well, they're probably real doctors but they know about the cover-up of Sinclair's death, which means they're somehow part of whatever it was that happened that day. They saw everything.

I really want to know what's going on with these doctors, but whenever the topic comes up Garret changes the subject, like he did just now.

We get to Mr. Kensington's apartment midmorning. It's on the Upper East Side of Manhattan, which Garret says is the rich, fancy part of town. A doorman greets us in the lobby. Well, he greets Garret. He doesn't seem that interested in me. They spend a few minutes talking before we head upstairs.

The apartment has an open floor plan with the kitchen and living room all together in one space. It has a very masculine feel, decorated with dark wood furniture, a black leather couch, and leather chairs. The kitchen cabinets are a dark brown, almost black color, and are surrounded by stainless steel appliances.

Garret takes me down the hall and shows me two bedrooms, one big and one small.

"Do you and Lilly share a room when you come here?" I ask him.

"This isn't really a family apartment. It's just for my dad when he's here for work. Sometimes Katherine stays here, but she prefers to stay in a hotel where she has people waiting on her. The second bedroom was for me. My dad thought the two of us would have father-son weekends in the city. Go to a ball game or a museum. But that never happened. As you can tell, we're not exactly close."

Knowing that Katherine was the reason for that only makes me hate her more. Garret and his dad would actually get along if it weren't for her. And Garret probably wouldn't have drank away his teen years.

"This place is smaller than I thought it would be," I say as we walk back to the living room.

"My dad doesn't need much space. He's not here that much. Besides, Manhattan real estate costs a fortune. This place was $5 million and that was 7 years ago."

I almost choke when he says it. "Dollars? Five million dollars?"

"That's normal for this neighborhood." He picks up a remote control on the living room table and clicks a button that opens the blinds on the windows.

"That's a lot of money. That's gotta be more than your house cost."

"Uh. No. The house cost a lot more than that." He sets the remote down and goes into the kitchen.

I'm not sure how much "a lot more" is and I don't ask. I can't even comprehend numbers that big. And to think that they have five more houses and two more apartments. Where do they get all this money?

CHAPTER FIVE

"Do you want some water or a soda?" Garret opens the large stainless steel refrigerator which is stocked with food and drinks.

"Why do you have all that stuff in there? Did your dad stay here recently?"

"I had it stocked for us. We have a service where you just order what you want and they stock the apartment for you. Not just food, but anything. Do you need anything? Because I can call them right now."

"No, I don't need anything." I take a soda from the fridge. "Why did you hire people to buy this stuff? Couldn't we just go buy it ourselves?"

"We could, but why waste time doing that when we could just use the service?"

"Garret, I think you've been around your family too much. You're starting to act like them."

"What do you mean?"

"Making people get you stuff. Having your fridge stocked instead of buying your own groceries. I thought you didn't like that."

"Don't worry about it." He takes the soda from my hand and sets it on the granite-topped counter behind me. He steps closer until I'm backed up against the counter, then puts his lips to mine.

I pull back. "Garret, I'm serious. Is this the type of life you want? Having people wait on you all the time?" I turn my head so he can't kiss me again.

"It's just a stocked fridge. It's not that big a deal. And there aren't any grocery stores nearby. Just little corner stores. And if we find one of those we have to carry bags of groceries and cases of soda down the street. It's not as easy to get stuff here as it is back home."

"I guess I didn't think about that." I face him again. "Okay, but I better not catch you hiring someone to fill your dorm fridge."

"My dorm fridge. That's a good idea." He kisses me again before I can even get a good eye roll in. His tongue teases my mouth as his body presses against me. A wave of heat courses through me and I get all tingly inside.

I break from the kiss. "Let's go to the bedroom." I didn't mean to say it like that, all forceful and demanding, but I really want to be with him and we're finally alone. I don't have to worry about his dad walking in. Or Lilly. Or Katherine. Or any of the hired help.

"Already? We just got here. Shit, that must have been some kiss." He flashes that cocky grin that for some stupid reason always turns me on.

I reach under his shirt, feeling his rock-hard stomach. "Are you saying you don't want to?"

"Hell, no." He grabs my hand and takes me down the hall to the master bedroom.

I yank him back. "That's your Dad's bed. Gross! There's no way I'm doing it in there."

"It's a king-size bed. The other room has a queen." He tugs on me again but I won't budge. "Jade, the cleaning lady was just here. The sheets are all fresh and clean."

"Forget it. We just won't do it." I wait, knowing there's no way in hell he's forgetting it.

"Oh, we're doing it." He leads me to the other bedroom. "Is this better?"

"Much better." The room is very modern with a sleek platform bed and dark wood furniture. It looks like an expensive hotel room.

As I toss the decorative pillows off the bed, I notice Garret struggling to take his t-shirt off.

"This is so embarrassing but I need some help here." He laughs as he tries again. "That shot the doctor gave me made my shoulder stiff and now I can't get my shirt off. Can you help?"

"Can I help you get naked?" I smile. "Yeah, I can do that." I maneuver the shirt over his head and arms and toss it on the floor. "You need some help with your pants, too?"

He tilts his head and smiles. "Yes, please."

"I was kidding. You don't need help."

"No. But I *want* help."

I take the rest of his clothes off and he gets into bed. I start to quickly take off mine, but then slow down, giving him a show.

"What's this? A striptease?" I can hear the excitement in his voice. Guys are so freaking easy to please.

"Yeah, so sit back and enjoy." I slowly slide my jeans off.

"Damn, I'm taking you to New York more often."

It makes me laugh. "It's not about New York. I'm just spicing things up a little." I leave my black bra and panties on and climb on top of him.

"What about the rest of it?" He whispers as he kisses my neck.

I sit up on my knees showing myself off. "You're supposed to look at it first. The bra matches the panties. I swear. You guys tell us you like this stuff, so we wear it for you and then all you want to do is take it off."

He takes a moment to look at it, then focuses on my face again. "Okay, I've seen it. It looks great. Now take it off."

"Stupid boys." I give him a kiss before I strip the rest of the way. I stay on top of him because he can't put any pressure on his injury. And despite the fact that we've had sex this way several times, I still don't feel confident. And it's never as good as when he's on top. I must be doing something wrong.

When we're done I lie back on the bed, exhausted. "That's a lot of work."

He laughs. "Now you see what I go through. It gets tiring being on top."

"Oh, please. I don't want to hear you complain."

"I'm just saying. It's a workout." He puts his arm out above my head. "Come over here and rest."

Now he's just making fun of me, but I asked for it by even bringing up the topic. I grab a pillow and bury my head in it.

He's still laughing. "Maybe we could try some other positions. Ones that aren't so taxing on you."

"Okay. Enough. I never should've said anything."

"I mean it." He nudges me. "Next time, we'll do it a different way."

I lift my head up slightly. "What way?"

"I don't know. We'll experiment and see what works."

I toss the pillow aside and lay my head on him. "I'm not ready for something new. I'm still trying to figure out the whole being-on-top thing. I'm not very good at it."

44

He kisses the top of my head. "You're good at it."

"I don't believe you. I know you wouldn't tell me if I wasn't."

"Trust me. It's all good, so stop worrying about it. Now do you want to go get some lunch? I'm sure you worked up an appetite exerting yourself like that."

I sit up. "Are you never gonna let this go?" I try to be serious but I'm laughing.

"Come on. Let's have lunch." He gets out of bed and picks his clothes up from the floor. "Remember that deli I told you about? We could go there."

"That sounds good."

As I'm getting dressed I hear Garret behind me.

"Jade, I can't dress myself." He's barely able to say it he's laughing so hard. I look over to see his boxer briefs only halfway up his legs. He's sitting on the edge of the bed, trying to pull them up with one hand. His other arm is stuck down by his side like he can't move it.

"What the hell did that doctor do to you?" I go over and help him with his boxers.

"I'm going to call him and find out. He said that shot might make my arm and shoulder numb but this is ridiculous. I can't even use this arm."

I help him into his jeans and shirt, then put on my own clothes while he makes the call in the other room.

"What did he say?" I ask when he's done.

"He said it should wear off in an hour or so. The numbness means the medicine is working."

"Are you okay to go out?"

"Yeah, but you might have to feed me." He's laughing again. At least he's not upset by it. I wouldn't be too happy if I couldn't move my arm and shoulder.

We have lunch, then go to the Museum of Natural History. I've seen it in movies but I wanted to see it in person. It's huge and you could spend all day there reading all the historical facts and listening to the guides. But we're done in a few hours. I just wanted to walk through and see stuff. Garret's been there several times, so he acted as my tour guide.

Afterward, the car service guy drives us back to the apartment. He's like our own personal chauffeur. We just call him whenever we need a ride and he's there.

"I've got dinner reservations at 7," Garret says as he hands me a bottle of water from the fridge.

"Where are we going?"

"I'm taking you to that place I told you about at the top of a hotel. We have a table right by the window. You can see the whole city lit up."

"When do we get to see the tree?"

My excitement always brings a smile to his face. "We'll go see the tree after dinner. We can go every night if you want."

I always tell Garret I don't care about Christmas, or any other holiday, but he knows it's a lie. That's why he brought me here this week. He says we're here for New Year's, but I know he wanted me to see all the holiday lights before they take them down. And I'm dying to see the Rockefeller tree.

"Could we have a snack before dinner? I'm starving."

"Sure. What do you want?" He starts opening cabinets. A bag of potato chips falls out and lands on the floor. "Well, look at that. Your favorite food. What are the odds?"

As I pick up the bag, I notice something stuck between the stove and the cabinet. I reach in and pull it out.

"What's that?" Garret asks.

"It looks like one of those security badges people use to get in a building."

46

Garret sighs and holds his hand out. "Let me see that."

I hand it to him. He holds it up, staring at the photo. "I knew it was her."

"What are you talking about?"

"This woman was at the company conference in Houston. The one my dad made me go to."

"Yeah. So?"

"Remember how I said my dad was having an affair? I didn't know who the woman was but I was guessing it was her." He tosses the ID on the counter. "And obviously it is or she wouldn't have been here."

"Maybe she was meeting your dad here to go over business stuff."

"He has an office just down the street. He wouldn't have business meetings here."

"Do you know anything about her?"

"She works for an investment firm in DC. That's all I know." Garret places the ID badge in one of the kitchen drawers. "When we leave here on Thursday, remind me to set this out on the table so he can see it. I want my dad to know that I know who his mistress is."

"Why? Are you going to blackmail your dad again?"

"If he starts interfering with us again, then yeah."

"Maybe your dad should just divorce Katherine. It doesn't seem like they get along very well." I consider telling Garret about the fight I overheard but then change my mind.

"He won't divorce her, because if he does he knows Katherine will try to take Lilly away from him. And he doesn't want Lilly caught up in a custody battle." Garret takes the bag of potato chips from me. "Aren't you gonna eat these?"

"I changed my mind. It's already 6. I might as well wait for dinner."

An hour later the driver picks us up. Garret has on a suit and tie and I'm wearing my one and only black dress. Katherine gave me a red dress for Christmas which I actually like, but I didn't want to wear it because it would remind me of her. And the dress Garret bought me for the fundraiser last fall is too formal for dinner. So the black dress is my only option, but seeing it next to Garret's designer suit, my dress looks really plain and cheap. And I only have one winter coat and it's sporty not dressy. It doesn't match the dress at all.

The driver stops on the street in front of the hotel where we're having dinner. "I'm sorry, sir, but I can't drop you off at the entrance with all this traffic, unless you want to wait 10 or 15 minutes for it to move."

"No, this is fine," Garret says. We get out of the car and join the crowds of people on the sidewalk.

The hotel entrance is about a half a block away. As we're heading down there, Garret stops suddenly.

"What do you think of this one?" He's pointing to an engagement ring that has a diamond solitaire that's at least 2 carats. I recognize the signature blue in the store and look up to confirm that we're standing in front of Tiffany's.

"Yeah, you're funny, Garret." I tug on his coat. "Come on, let's go."

"Do you like it or not?" He puts his arm around my waist and moves me closer to the window.

"Well, yeah. What's not to like? Look how much it sparkles. And the diamond is huge. That ring must cost $10,000."

"More like $100,000," he says.

"Are you serious?" I look at it again. "How do you know that? There's no price on it."

"I just know." He leads me to the next window. "How about this one?"

48

"I don't like the diamond. It's too big," I say, playing along. "I like the other one better."

He laughs. "I've never heard a girl say a diamond was too big."

"I just think when they get too big they look fake."

He leans down. "I say the same thing about breasts."

I shake my head and smile as we walk to the last window.

"Okay, here's another one."

"Garret, come on. Let's just go to dinner."

"Not until you tell me if you like this one."

I get up closer to the window. "Nope. I don't like it."

"Why not?"

"I don't like the round shape of the diamond. I liked the square shape better. And I don't like gold. I prefer silver or whatever that first one was."

"It was platinum."

"Whatever. Can we go now?"

I wait for him to move but he stands there with his eyes shut. "Two carats. Princess cut. Platinum. Got it." He opens his eyes, takes my hand, and starts walking again. "You're going to love this restaurant, Jade."

Garret begins telling me about the restaurant but I'm not even listening. I'm still trying to figure out what the hell just happened. Did I just pick out an engagement ring?

CHAPTER SIX

I feel Garret's hand on my lower back as he leads me through the hotel lobby.

"So what do you think?" he asks as we wait for the elevator.

"About what? The hotel? It's nice." I look up at the giant chandelier hanging above us.

"I wasn't talking about the hotel. Did you hear anything I just said?"

"I think you said something about the restaurant."

He rolls his eyes, smiling. "I was telling you how the restaurant rotates. But I guess you didn't find it that interesting."

We're on the elevator now with people all around us, so I don't want to ask about the rotating restaurant even though I'm dying to know more. How does a restaurant rotate?

My ears pop as the elevator takes us to the top floor. It opens to the restaurant which has windows on all sides showing off views of the city.

Garret leads me to the coat check room where a tall, dark-haired woman in a red dress is waiting. She's very pretty and looks like she's only a couple years older than me. We take off our coats and hand them to her. Her face puckers up as she holds mine between her thumb and index finger, like it's dirty or something. There's not a speck of dirt on it, but compared to the long expensive coats hanging behind her, mine looks pretty shabby.

Garret doesn't even notice the rude but beautiful coat check girl. He slips his arm around my waist and goes up to the hostess. "Kensington for two."

When he says it I feel like we're a married couple and a stir of happiness goes through me. Damn Garret and those damn rings! What is he doing to me? I'm not even the marrying type. Or at least I didn't think I was.

The hostess seats us at a small table next to the window.

"It's great, right?" Garret says, checking out the view.

"Yeah. I love seeing the city up high like this." I glance around. "So what did you mean when you said this place rotates?"

"It slowly rotates while you're eating, so by the time our dinner arrives we'll probably be over there." He points to the other side of the room."

"How do they do that?"

"Well, if you'd listened to me earlier you would know." He pretends to act annoyed.

"I'm sorry. Now tell me."

He smiles. "I was kidding. I have no idea how it works. I just wanted you to admit you weren't listening."

We open our menus. Everything is a la carte. The main dish is just a piece of meat and you order the sides separate. I notice the person next to me eating a pork chop topped with some type of sauce.

"What do you think you want to order?" Garret asks.

"Probably the pork."

"And what else?"

"I'm not sure yet." I glance at the menu again. "Why aren't there any prices on here? How are you supposed to know what things cost?"

He leans in and lowers his voice. "Because if you have to ask you shouldn't be here. A lot of fancy restaurants don't list the prices."

"Oh. Well, that's just weird."

Garret reaches across the table and pushes my menu down. "I don't want you to talk about, or even think about, how much this costs, okay? I've been wanting to take you here for a really long time and I just want you to enjoy it. I don't want a lecture about how I'm spending too much."

"I'm not lecturing you. I just—"

"Jade. Please."

"All right. I won't say anything."

"Hey, look." He points out the window. "We're at a different spot now. That building that was in front of us is behind me now."

He's right. The restaurant moved and I hadn't even noticed. "Okay, whatever this costs, it's worth it. This is really cool."

The waiter comes by to take our order. Just as he's leaving our table, we hear a girl squealing across the room. We look over and see a guy on his knee, putting a diamond ring on her finger.

"Looks like she said yes," Garret says.

"Then why is she crying?" I glance over to see the girl wiping her tears with her napkin.

"Because she's happy. They're tears of joy."

"I don't get that. I've never understood the crying-because-you're-happy thing."

"Yeah, I don't get it either but a lot of people seem to do it."

The newly engaged couple is now eating dessert, holding hands across the table.

"Garret, did you really never want to get married?"

"What are you talking about? I tell you I want to get married all the time."

"In that notebook you gave me at Christmas you said you never wanted to get married."

"Yeah, that's true. I told myself I never would."

"Why? Because of your dad?"

"He's not the best role model for marriage. My grandfather's not either. They've both had affairs. Several. But I don't think my dad ever cheated on my mom. At least that's what he told me and I actually believe him. I think she was the only woman he ever really loved. Katherine's just a trophy wife. She fit the mold. She's the type of woman he's supposed to marry, even if he doesn't like her."

"And you didn't want to end up the same way. That's why you never wanted to get married?"

"I used to think marriage was stupid. I decided I'd rather be a lifelong bachelor."

"So what changed your mind?"

"You already know the answer to that." He picks up his water glass and takes a drink.

"Are you saying *I* did?"

"I told you that in the notebook."

"And it didn't make sense."

"It makes perfect sense. When you meet the right person, you see things differently. You do stuff you didn't think you'd do." He glances over at the newly engaged couple. "A year ago, I would've made fun of that guy, saying what a huge mistake he was making. Guessing how long the marriage would last. But then I met you and now I understand why he just got down on one knee in front of a room full of people and asked a girl to marry him."

"So what's the reason? I mean, I get the whole thing about being in love, but why get married? Why not just live together or date forever?"

He considers it. "I don't know. I guess I'm old fashioned. I like the idea of the woman I love being called my wife and me being her husband. When you're married, it seems like you're more of team and not just two people sharing a house. And I like that it's not so easy to break apart. If you have a fight, the person can't just leave and never come back."

"That's the reason I'm scared to death to get married. I like the idea of being able to walk away. If things aren't going well, I just want out."

"So you've got commitment issues." He nudges my foot under the table. "I guess I've got some work to do on you then."

"You've already got me changing my mind, which is really annoying by the way. I can't figure out how you do it. I swear you have some kind of mind-control abilities."

He leans back. "Damn, my secret's out."

"Even if I'm open to marriage, it's not going to happen for a long time. I have stuff to get done before I even think about that."

"Like what?"

"Finish school. Get a good job. Pay you back all the money I owe you."

"Hey. No talking about money."

"Yes, I know."

The waiter brings our food. As a side dish to the pork, I ordered mashed potatoes. They aren't served with gravy like I'm used to, but I'm guessing they're so good you don't need gravy. I take a small bite. Yep, you definitely don't need gravy.

"Jade, look how much we've moved. That building that was next to us when we got here is way over there now."

I look across the room and see the building on the other side. "I should've been watching this whole time. It goes so slow you don't even feel it. We'll have to get dessert so we can spend more time here. Maybe we'll go around again."

"We're definitely getting dessert. They have this awesome chocolate cake. You have to try it."

The great dinner. The rotating restaurant. The amazing views. It was all way more than I was expecting. As we're waiting outside for the car, I get up on my tiptoes and give Garret a kiss. "Thank you. I loved the meal. And the restaurant." I kiss him again. "And my dinner companion."

"You're welcome. I'm glad you liked it. We'll have to go again sometime." He takes my hand and starts walking down the sidewalk. "I see the car. Let's just head down there so we don't have to wait."

Garret waves at the driver. He sees us but has to get over a few lanes. We wait for him in front of the jewelry store. I glance back at the ring I liked in the first window. I can't imagine wearing a ring that sparkly and beautiful. And that expensive.

Garret sees me looking at it and squeezes my hand. "You really like it, don't you?"

"I was just checking out how much it sparkles. That's all."

He leans down and kisses my cheek. "I won't talk about the marriage stuff anymore. I know it bugs you and you're probably sick of it. I'll just have to find a new topic that drives you crazy."

Where did that come from? I was just kidding when I told him not to talk about marriage. I actually like it when he teases me about it. It's kind of become our thing. It doesn't bug me. I just said it did because that's what I do. I say the opposite of what I want. I've been doing it forever and although I'm trying not to anymore, I'm not doing a very good job.

I glance back at the ring one more time, then feel Garret tugging me forward to the car.

Crowds line the entrance to Rockefeller Center. We weave through the people until we're right in front of the magnificent tree.

"Wow." It's the only word that comes out as I stare up at the sea of lights.

"Pretty impressive, huh?" Garret stands behind me, his arms holding me close to him to shield me from the frigid wind.

Never in a million years did I ever think I would be standing in New York City in front of the Rockefeller Christmas tree wrapped in the arms of a super hot guy who I love more than anything. I swear I'm going to wake up from this one day and realize it's all been a dream.

"Do you want to walk around?" Garret asks after a good 10 minutes of standing there.

"Yeah. Sorry. I guess I have a thing for Christmas lights. I didn't know that until you put those blue lights in my room. So it's all your fault that we've been standing here so long."

"I don't mind. We can stay as long as you want."

"No, I'm ready to go. We've been out a long time and your chest is probably hurting."

He doesn't deny it.

I turn to face him. "Garret! You have to tell me if you're in pain. We could have skipped this tonight and gone tomorrow."

"I wanted you to see the tree. And I wanted you to be next to it when I do this." He leans down and holds my face in his

56

hands and kisses me. A gentle, sweet kiss. The kind that makes me feel calm and safe and warm inside. It's just what I need right now in the chaos of the crowds with the cold wind blowing by.

He keeps me close as people swarm past us. "This has been a perfect night, Garret. I'm pretty sure you can't top this one."

"I'm up for the challenge. We still have New Year's Eve."

"Why don't you call the driver? I need to get you back to the apartment now that I know you're in all this pain."

"I'm fine, but we can go." He gets his phone out. "I can't hear with all the noise. I'm gonna go over to the side where it's not as loud. Wait here. I'll be right back."

Garret disappears into the crowd while I get another look at the tree.

As I'm gazing up at it, someone bumps into me so hard it moves me forward and I almost trip.

"Excuse me, miss." I hear a voice next to me and glance over to see an older man, nicely dressed in a dark wool coat, wearing one of those stiff hats you always see men wearing in black and white movies. "I'm terribly sorry. Some kids were running up behind me and they pushed me into you."

"Yeah, don't worry about it." I focus back on the tree.

I feel his hand grip my arm. "Are you sure you're okay? I feel terrible for bumping into you like that."

"I'm fine." I pull my arm away, keeping my eyes on the tree.

"Do you happen to have the time?" He moves right in front of me, blocking my view.

As I see his face, he seems very familiar. I check my watch. "It's 9:50."

"Thank you." He smiles and then stands there for a moment, staring at me, almost like he wants me to get a good look at him. Like I should recognize him.

When he finally turns and walks away, it hits me. I *do* recognize him. I'm almost sure I saw him at the fundraiser for Royce Sinclair last November. And I saw him somewhere else. But where? I try to remember his face. I think I saw him on TV. Yes, I know I did. When Garret and I were in Des Moines watching the news about the caucus, that guy was standing behind Sinclair as he talked to reporters. The old man is somehow connected to Sinclair!

My pulses races as I search for the old man. But he's gone. I don't see him anywhere.

What is he doing here? Does he know I'm Sinclair's daughter? The only evidence of Sinclair's crime years ago? He had to know! He had to have purposely bumped into me. He wanted me to see him.

I scan the crowd trying to find Garret. He was just over to my right, but now he's not there. Where the hell did he go?

People are streaming past me. Laughing. Talking. Coughing. Clearing their throats. Kids are screaming. Babies are crying. It's too much noise. Where did all this noise come from? I didn't hear it before.

I make my way through the crowd to the place I saw Garret last. But he's not there. He's not anywhere. What if someone took him? That old man, or people connected to him, could've taken Garret to get revenge for his dad shooting Sinclair.

"Shit! Shit! Shit!" I say it repeatedly to myself as the noise around me gets even louder.

"Garret!" I scream it into the crowd. The people next to me give me an annoyed look and quickly walk ahead. "Garret!" I scream it again, but there's no way he'd ever hear me in these crowds.

I don't know what to do. I'm too panicked to think straight. I start walking around, searching for him, but I just keep bumping into strangers. Maybe Garret had to use the restroom. But he'd tell me if he was doing that. He wouldn't just leave.

CHAPTER SEVEN

I notice an old lady getting up from a nearby bench. I hurry over and take her seat.

Everything around me seems to be spinning at a rapid pace. It's like being on one of those carnival rides that spin you so fast you only see blurred versions of people as they go by.

I close my eyes for a moment, trying to calm down so I can think. I brought a small purse with me and I'm clutching it so tightly it's making my hand cramp up. I open my eyes as my brain finally wakes up and realizes that I have a purse. And inside it is a phone! Damn! Why didn't I think of that before? I'm not used to having a cell phone. Garret got me one a few weeks ago and I always forget I have it.

I get the phone out and turn it on. The battery's almost dead. Note to Jade: Always charge your phone! I call Garret's phone. It goes straight to voicemail. What does that mean? It's turned off? He's on the phone?

The battery symbol on my phone is flashing at me like it's taunting me, reminding me what an idiot I am for not charging it. Sometimes I really hate technology.

I try Garret's phone again before my battery dies completely. His phone rings repeatedly and then finally—finally!—he picks up.

"Jade, where are you?"

"I'm on a bench just down from the tree. Where are you?"

"I'm in front of the tree where I left you. Why did you—"

My phone dies before he can finish. I'm so mad at the phone I'm tempted to slam it against the pavement, but instead I shove it back in my purse. I get up and hurry back to Garret's location, hoping he isn't going to where I just left.

I spot him in the crowd and push past the people in front of me. When I reach him, I collapse into his arms, holding onto him and not letting go.

"Jade, why did you leave? I told you to stay there."

"I *did* stay there, but this man came over and—"

Garret peels me off him and grabs my shoulders. "What man? What happened?"

"A man bumped into me and he uh—" I glance around and notice the security cameras all around us. Maybe I'm paranoid now, but the cameras are making me nervous. Who knows who's watching us. "We need to get out of here. Did you call the driver?"

"Yeah, he's down there waiting." He points behind me at the street.

"Let's go." I grab Garret's hand and pull him through the crowd until we're at the car.

On the ride back to the apartment, my fear turns to anger. "Garret, where were you? I thought you were gone. It's like you disappeared."

"I just had to move down a little because the people next to me were so loud. I wasn't that far from where I said I'd be."

"What took you so long? How long does it take to call the driver?"

"As soon as I got off the phone with him my dad called so I picked up. He's been texting me all day."

"Why? Is something wrong?" I start to panic again.

"He was just checking in. He wanted to make sure we made here it okay."

"Did your dad sound like he was worried about us? Or did he sound weird at all?"

"I don't know. I couldn't hear him that well. What's with all the questions?"

"I'll tell you when we get back."

The driver drops us off at the apartment. As soon as we're inside I tell Garret about the strange old man.

"I'm almost positive he was at the fundraiser," I say as I take a water from the fridge. "And I know I saw him on TV at least once standing next to Sinclair."

"Are you sure it was the same guy? It's dark out and it's hard to get a good luck at someone in the dark."

"There were lights all around us. And he stood right in front of me, practically forcing me to look at him. Like he wanted me to see that it was him."

"But then he just walked off?" Garret gets a bottle of soda, then takes a seat on one of the barstools next to the kitchen island. He's being much calmer about this than I thought he would be.

"Yes. It was almost like a warning of some kind." I pick Garret's cell phone off the counter and hand it to him. "Call your dad. That man was at your house. Your dad might know him."

Garret holds onto the phone but doesn't call. "What did the guy look like?"

"Old. Probably in his seventies. White hair. Maybe 5'10 or 5'11."

"Jade, almost every guy at the fundraiser looked like that. My dad won't know who that is." He sets the phone down and drinks his soda.

"Why aren't you more worried about this? If this guy knows Sinclair, he could be dangerous."

"But he didn't do anything, so maybe it's just a coincidence he bumped into you. Why would Sinclair's guys come after you? He's dead. There's no reason to. If anything, they'd come after *me* to get back at my dad for what he did."

"Yes! Exactly!" I reach for Garret's hand and hold it tightly in mine. "That's why I was so freaked out when I couldn't find you. I thought they'd taken you. I was sure of it. I thought you were gone." Before I can stop it, a tear runs down my cheek.

"Are you crying?" Garret asks.

"No," I say, stubbornly.

"You're crying because you thought someone took me?"

"I don't know. Maybe." I try to turn away, but he won't let me. He gets off the barstool and pulls me into his arms.

"I guess you really do love me."

"You know I do. I tell you that all the time."

"Yeah, but you also push me away all the time so I'm not always sure."

"I love you, okay? And you scared the crap out of me by hiding from me like that. Don't ever do it again."

"Jade, I wasn't hiding from you." He lets me go and wipes the tear from my cheek with his thumb. "If you're really worried about this guy, we'll leave and go back to my house. Or I'll get Brian, my dad's security guy, to come down here."

"No. Forget it. You're right. If the guy really wanted to do something to me he would've done it, not just walked off." I picture the old man's face in my head again. "Maybe it wasn't the same man who was at the fundraiser. A lot of old guys look the same."

"Still, if you'd feel better being back at my house, we'll leave. We'll just try this again next New Year's Eve."

The thought of being back at his house with Katherine confirms my decision. "I want to stay here. I don't want to go back to your house."

"I need to get a pain pill. I'll be right back."

While he's gone, I bring our drinks to the living room and take a seat on the leather couch. He comes back in the room and I hand him his soda as he sits down.

"Garret, I need to tell you something."

"That doesn't sound good." He takes a drink and swallows his pill.

"I overhead a conversation between your dad and Katherine."

He leans back on the couch, still holding his soda, and waits for me to continue.

"I got up early this morning to get a glass of water downstairs and I heard the two of them arguing in their room. So I kind of listened in."

"Why would you listen in?" Garret sounds mad. I probably should've kept this to myself.

"Because it sounded like they were talking about me. And they were. Katherine told your dad she wanted me out of the house and that I was never allowed back."

"Did she give a reason?"

"She uh . . . she said she didn't want trash like me in the house."

"That bitch actually called you that?" Garret bolts up from the couch and goes to the kitchen.

"Yes. And she banned me from seeing Lilly again."

He returns with his cell phone.

"What are you doing? You can't call her!" I try to grab his phone but he holds it away from me.

"She needs to know she can't talk to you that way. And she can't ban you from seeing Lilly or staying at the house. I can't believe she fucking said that." He starts calling, but I snatch the phone away before he can finish.

"She didn't say it to my face. She said it to your dad. I told you I overheard them. And your dad totally stuck up for me, which made Katherine even more angry. That's why I don't want to go back there right now."

Garret looks like he might punch in a wall. "I fucking hate that woman. She's ruined my life. And my dad's life. And Lilly's life."

"She said something else. She said I was the reason for the problem they're dealing with now. What problem? Do you know what she's talking about?"

"She's probably blaming you for whatever's going on with my dad. I told you he's in trouble for what he did to Sinclair."

"I know, but what does that mean? Is someone trying to kill him?"

"No. These people like you to suffer. Killing you is too easy. Instead they attack your company. Or your reputation." He pauses. "Or they kidnap your little girl. That's why my dad is so on edge right now."

"And it's all my fault. I guess Katherine has reason to hate me and want me gone."

"None of it was your fault, Jade. And my dad will take care of it, like he always does."

"Who are these people? Does your dad even know who wants revenge?"

"I don't know. I don't even know if it's about revenge. That day I overheard him on the phone he said something about how he knew he would be punished for what he'd done, but he didn't say what that meant."

"So how do you know you're safe? Or how does your dad know? Maybe these people are planning to do something to *you* and not Lilly."

Garret leans over and kisses me. "They're not going to do anything to me."

I'm not convinced. I don't know what Garret's dad is involved in, but I don't like the fact that he has enemies or people looking to punish him for what he did to Sinclair. They could easily target Garret. Lilly's locked away in her house all the time. She's safe. It would be way easier for them to do something to Garret.

"You want to watch TV before bed?" Garret asks.

"Yeah, okay." I snuggle beside him as he turns on the TV.

He finds a movie to watch and I try to focus on it, but instead my mind keeps imagining bad people trying to hurt Garret. After an hour of that, I force myself to stop thinking about it. I can't keep assuming bad things will happen. It's what I used to do and I'm trying to change that about myself. Everything will be okay. Garret will be okay. When we get in bed later, I keep telling myself that until I fall asleep.

The next day we sightsee but cut our itinerary down to just a few tourist spots. I'm worried that Garret's overdoing it. I don't want to make his injury worse or make him run around New York City when he's in pain. That night, he offers to take me to Rockefeller Center again to see the tree, but I insist we stay home. As much as I'd love to see the tree, I'd rather have Garret rest and get better.

Thursday morning I wake up to the feel of kisses on the back of my neck and Garret's strong arm around my waist. "Happy New Year's Eve," he says softly.

"What time is it?"

"Nine. You can go back to sleep if you want."

"Then why did you wake me up?"

He laughs. "Purely selfish reasons." He slips his hand under the hem of my pajama shorts. The feel of his warm hand moving along my lower abs instantly wakes me up.

"I don't know what you mean," I say, innocently.

"I'm a guy. And it's morning." He tugs me closer against him and I feel what he's referring to. "And you're freaking hot and right here next to me." His warm breath tickles my neck. "You smell good. You feel amazing. What can I say? I had to at least try."

I yawn and adjust my pillow. "I think I'll just go back to sleep."

"Damn. Seriously?" He sighs. "Okay."

He sounds so disappointed it makes me laugh. I flip around to face him. "I'm kidding. You know I won't turn you down, especially since I have to go without you all next week."

He eases me down on my back and starts kissing me, then stops suddenly.

"Hey. Why'd you stop?" I sound annoyed but it's only because I was really liking his kisses.

He has this huge smile on his face, which I find extremely sexy, especially combined with his tousled morning hair. "I love you. So freaking much. You know that, right?"

I nod, smiling. "Yeah. I know. I love you, too. Now are we going to do this or what?" I sit up a little and rip my shirt off, tossing it on the floor.

He laughs. "And I thought *I* was the impatient one." He tosses the covers back, then leaves kisses along my stomach as he slips my shorts off. I close my eyes, arching back to stretch a little.

Even if I wasn't leaving on Saturday, I still wouldn't turn him down. I love this way too much. In fact, I wish he'd wake me up like this every day.

Later that morning, we go out for an early lunch, then pack up our things and head to the hotel in Times Square. The streets are already packed with people waiting to see the ball drop. It's a cold, windy day and a light sleet is falling. Everyone on the street is bundled up in coats, hats, and gloves. Standing out there all day and night does not look like a fun way to spend New Year's Eve.

"Are you ready?" Garret asks as he slides the key card into the door of our hotel room.

"Ready for what? I've seen a hotel room before."

But it's not just a hotel room. He opens the door to a massive suite. We walk into an open space that includes a kitchen, a small dining area, and a living room with a long couch and two chairs. Across from the couch is a wall of windows that face Times Square, giving us a perfect view of the ball drop tonight. Off to the side is a master bedroom with a separate sitting area near the window. Next to it is the biggest bathroom I've ever seen. The bathtub is almost as large as a hot tub. The shower could fit at least five people in it.

"Garret, this place is huge."

"Check this out." He flips a switch on the wall and a TV appears in the bathroom mirror. He takes a remote control from the counter and tosses it to me. "Try it."

I point the remote at the mirror and start flipping channels. "This is crazy! But come on. Do people really need a TV in the bathroom?"

"It's a want, not a need." He comes over and takes the remote back, shutting the TV off. He takes my hand and leads me back to the living room. "I had them make you a concession stand for tonight." He points to a basket of snack foods in the kitchen. "Obviously, I would've done a much better job but I didn't have time."

"It's great. Thank you."

"And . . ." He picks up a bottle from a silver ice bucket. "Fake champagne for our toast at midnight."

"I think that's real champagne."

He reads the bottle. "I told them no alcohol. What the hell? I'll call the front desk and have them replace this."

"It's okay. I actually want to try some. It's New Year's Eve. You gotta have champagne."

"But, Jade, you don't drink."

"I've been thinking about that a lot and I'm not as worried about it anymore. I mean, my mom was only an alcoholic because of those pills that doctor gave her. The pills made her an addict. It wasn't genetic. Her parents didn't have problems with alcohol."

"I know, but still. You've only had alcohol one time. And it didn't end well."

"That was totally different. This time I'll be with you and we'll just have one glass." I take the bottle from him and set it back in the bucket. Then I drag him to the couch to sit down with me. "I'd rather have my first real drinking experience be here with you than at some college party. And it's not like I plan to get drunk. It's just a glass of champagne."

69

"I'm still going to call down and get the nonalcoholic version just in case you change your mind." He gets his phone out and calls the front desk.

When he's done, I take his phone and set it on the table, then lean over and kiss him. "You're a really nice boyfriend, you know that?"

"I just want you to have a great New Year's Eve."

"This is more than great. This is an awesome New Year's Eve. What do you have planned for Valentine's Day? On second thought, let's skip that one. I've never liked Valentine's Day."

He nudges me. "We're not skipping Valentine's Day. It's a holiday and I'm making you celebrate all of them. Even President's Day. And Arbor Day."

I run my hand along his soft, black t-shirt that fits snugly over his muscular chest. "So how's your gunshot wound?"

He smiles. "It's fine. And from now on, you should ask me *that*, instead of 'How's your chest?' It sounds better. More masculine."

I shake my head. "Whatever. Is it really better or are you just saying that?"

"It's really better. In fact this morning I didn't even take a pain pill."

"Good. Because you were starting to worry me with the numb arm and then the constant pain." I climb onto his lap, straddling him and giving him a hug. My actions cause movement in his pants.

"I'm just hugging you, Garret. That's it."

"I can't help what he does. He's got a mind of his own."

I sit back, my gaze drifting from Garret's bright blue eyes to his sexy smile. "I guess if your chest, or gunshot wound, is better, we could maybe try out the bed."

70

He grins. "Or we could just stay here. Try out the bed later."

"On the couch? That's gross. People sit here."

His eyebrows raise. "Like it hasn't been done before?"

"Eww." I start to scoot off his lap. He reaches around my lower back, keeping me on his lap and pulling me closer until I'm pressed up against him. He kisses me, then moves his hand to the back of my neck and takes the kiss deeper. My concerns about the couch quickly disappear.

After a few minutes, he stops. "Get up for a minute."

I scoot off his lap. He stands up and takes his shirt off and lays it over the couch to keep it clean. At this point I really don't care, but his attempt to keep it clean is very sweet. He slips my sweater off and unhooks my bra as I get to work on his pants.

I hear some sirens out on the street and glance behind me. "Garret, we're right by the window."

"Yeah. And we're thirty stories up. Nobody can see."

"They could if they had binoculars and were in a really tall building. Or a helicopter."

He laughs. "You worry way too freaking much about that shit. You always think people are going to see us or walk in on us." He tugs my jeans down and I step out of them.

"Because I don't want people watching or—" I stop when I feel his hand doing something seriously amazing between my legs.

"I obviously need to do a better job of distracting you." He looks right at me and smiles. "Now what were you saying?"

"I don't remember," I say, bringing his face to mine and kissing him.

After a few minutes, he slowly sits down and I straddle him again and try out this new position.

When we're done, he smiles at me. "So what do you think? Better that time?"

"It wasn't as tiring if that's what you're asking." I get off him and we both get dressed.

He pulls me back on his lap. "Good. Because I don't plan on going anywhere today, so if you're up for it I figure we could do that a few more times before midnight."

"A few more times? I didn't think you could do it a few more times." I'm totally kidding but he takes it seriously.

He huffs out a breath. "What's that supposed to mean?"

I shrug and adjust my sweater, trying not to laugh. "I thought guys could only do it once or twice a day. And we've already done it twice today."

"I'm 19, not 40. I can do it a lot more than that."

"Oh. Sorry. I don't know how all that works."

He rolls his eyes at me but smiles. "What I was going to say before you insulted my manhood is that I'm really going to miss you when you're gone next week."

"It's just a week."

"Yeah, but I have no distractions to keep my mind off you. No school. No swimming. Nothing."

"You have physical therapy." I half smile.

"I'm done with that now. I just have to do the exercises he taught me for range of motion and then check in with him in a couple weeks."

"How were you able to heal so fast? What was in that shot the doctor gave you? Because whatever it was, it really worked."

Garret reaches over and adjusts the pillow on the couch, which doesn't need adjusting. "I don't know. I didn't ask."

I take the pillow from him. "What's going on with you? You always act weird whenever I ask you about this doctor. And now you're acting weird when I ask about the shot."

"I'm not acting weird." His eyes remain on the couch.

"Garret, I know you're hiding something from me and you know I won't let you get away with it. So tell me. What is it?" I get off his lap and sit next to him, waiting for an answer.

He sighs, then looks at me like he wants me to just forget about it. But I won't let him keep secrets from me.

CHAPTER EIGHT

"What is it, Garret? What's the deal with your doctor?"

"He's just part of a . . . I don't know what to call it. It's a medical group that very few people know about. Honestly, Jade, I don't even know that much about it."

"What are you talking about?"

He hesitates. "You can't say a word about this to anyone, okay? I'm serious."

"Yeah. I got it."

"Like I said, I don't know all the details about this group. Nobody has ever come out and told me anything about it. I don't even know if I'm right. I'm just making assumptions after seeing what they can do. I have a regular doctor. I've only gone to these people when I've been really sick."

"Why? Do they have magical healing abilities?" I joke.

"No, but close. They have advanced treatments that most of the public doesn't have access to. I think they might even have cures for certain illnesses, like serious disease shit."

"Yeah, right. I think you've been watching too many movies. That doesn't sound like real life."

"I know, and I can't prove it, but the more I think about it the more I believe it. My grandfather had lung cancer a few years ago and it just went away. He didn't have chemo or radiation. Nothing."

"Maybe he just got better. Do you seriously think doctors would hide a cure for cancer?"

"I don't want to believe that but my grandfather's cancer was pretty advanced. How did he get better like that?"

"If what you're saying is true, that would be pure evil. To only let some people have access to these treatments but not others? I suppose only the rich have access?"

"Rich. Or important. This group is headquartered in DC. They take care of some of the important people there."

"Like the president?"

He shrugs. "President, senators, judges. This doctor who's been taking care of me was down in DC last summer when I was an intern. He came into the office of the senator I was working for."

"So you think that shot they gave you isn't available to regular people? What's so special about it?"

"The doctor said it speeds tissue growth so you heal way faster than normal. I've never heard of anything like that. Have you?"

"No, but maybe it's just new and you're one of the first to get it."

"Think about it, Jade. It should take months for this to heal." He points to the area on his chest where he was shot. "But the doctor said it should be back to normal in a week. I can't compete in swim meets, but he said I'll be able to swim during practice without any pain. Don't you think that's strange?"

"Okay, now I wish I never asked. This is really messed up. But it's just your theory, right? You don't know this for sure."

"I don't have actual proof, but there's no other way to explain this stuff."

"Did you ask your dad about it?"

"No. He'd never tell me. Plus, I think you've figured out by now that you don't ask questions in my family. It's another one of those unspoken rules. Things just happen and you go with it. Things are explained on a need to know basis. And for most of the shit that goes on with my family, I really don't want to know the truth."

There's a knock on the door and Garret gets up to answer it.

"Mr. Kensington," I hear a man say. "I'm so sorry for the mixup. The champagne is on us, of course. And here's the bottle you requested. No charge."

"Thank you." Garret takes the bottle, tips the guy, and closes the door. "There. Now you can pick what you want." His serious tone is gone and he's back in his cheery, holiday mood.

I consider asking him more about this secret medical group, but don't. I'm not sure I want to know any more.

"What should we do now?" I take the bottle from him and place it next to the other one in the ice bucket.

He goes and looks out the window at the revelers down below. "Those people look like they're freezing to death and they have 7 more hours to go."

"I know what we could do." I join him at the window. "Let's take a bath and watch TV in the mirror."

He turns to me and tucks my hair behind my ear. "I don't take baths. That's more of a girl thing. How about a shower instead?"

"But it's not like a regular bath. That thing is huge. And it's one of those bubbly tubs. It's more like a hot tub. Come on." I smile. "I'll be naked."

He laughs. "Yeah, I would hope so."

"You get the bath going and I'll grab some snacks and drinks." I head back to the kitchen.

"We're eating in the bathtub? That's disgusting, Jade."

"Just some chocolate." I grab a fancy chocolate bar from the basket and a couple bottles of soda from the fridge.

Being together in the bubbly bath somehow lands us in bed. I'm pretty sure Garret is just trying to prove to me that he can do it several times a day.

"I guess that bath thing wasn't so bad after all." Garret gives me a quick kiss, then gets out of bed and goes over to his suitcase.

"What are you doing?" I take a swig of my soda. "You're not supposed to get up right after sex. You could at least lie here a couple minutes."

"We need to get ready for dinner."

"I didn't know we were going out. I thought you wanted to stay here." I get out of bed and pick his t-shirt off the floor and slip it on. It's soft and comfy and smells like him.

"We *are* staying here. We're eating in the hotel restaurant. It has a great view. Not as good as the view from the other night but it's still good."

"Why didn't you tell me this earlier?"

"I got the reservation but I wasn't sure if we'd go or not. But I think we should go."

"Aren't you even going to ask me first? Maybe I don't want to go."

He walks over to me and holds both my hands. "Jade, would you like to have New Year's Eve dinner with the guy who loves you with all his heart and would do absolutely anything for you?"

"Well, damn, if you're going to put it that way, I don't have a choice. But I'll have to wear the same dress as the other night.

I hope it's not all wrinkled." I go over and pull it out of my suitcase.

"Check the closet," he says as he puts on his suit pants.

"Why? I didn't put anything in the closet."

"Just check it."

I open the closet door. There's a black dress hanging inside. "Whose is this?"

"It's yours. I got it for you and had them leave it here for when we arrived."

I take the dress out and hold it up. It's a simple but elegant, black sleeveless dress, like one of those little black cocktail dresses everyone says you have to own. "Garret, why did you do this?"

"I wanted you to have it in case we went to dinner tonight. The shoes you brought should go with it, right?" He buttons up his white shirt, a tie hanging around his neck.

"Yeah, but I don't need this. I could've just worn the dress I wore the other night." It's true, but this new dress looks a thousand times better than my old one.

"Like you said, it's probably wrinkled. This way you have one that's not wrinkled."

I don't know what to say to him. I love the dress, but I'm upset with him for buying it for me. It's a designer dress and I'm sure it cost a lot and he's already spent enough money on me this week. But I don't want to ruin our evening with a fight. And maybe he knew that. Maybe that's why he did this on New Year's Eve.

I'm still holding the dress as I watch Garret knot his tie over his shirt. As much as I love him, I do worry he won't be able to break away from the lifestyle he's used to. The one in which people are always doing things for you and money is spent without even a thought. It's a lifestyle I don't want. Because as nice as it sounds, that lifestyle isn't free. It comes weighted down with rules, and punishments for not following those rules.

Garret notices me standing there with the dress folded over my arm. He comes over and gently takes it from me. "I'm sorry, Jade. I shouldn't have bought you the dress. I know how you feel about me buying you stuff. You've been really great this whole trip, not mentioning the money thing. And if it makes you feel any better, the dress really wasn't that expensive. But I'll just take it back." He hangs the dress back in the closet.

It's like he could read my mind. Now I feel bad, because I know he likes buying me things. That's how his family shows love. Buying stuff for each other. That's all he knows. And that concerns me, but I know deep down he understands that material stuff isn't love. He's proved that just now.

"Garret, I like the dress. It's the type of dress I can wear a lot. Plus it's black, which you know is my color. I'll just keep it."

"You don't have to wear it to save my feelings. I don't have a problem taking it back. Really, it's not a big deal."

"Did you pick it out or did someone else do it?"

"I kind of picked it out. I worked with the same woman who helped me with the dress I got you for the fundraiser. I described what I thought you'd like and she sent photos of some different options. Then I picked the one that looked most like you."

The dress does look like something I would pick out. How does he know that about me? It's not like we ever talk about clothing. He sees me in the same old boring clothes every day.

I get the dress back out of the closet. "I'll keep the dress, but I need you to tell me next time. Ask me before you buy me any more dresses. Or any other clothing, okay? No more surprise purchases."

I put the dress on. "Could you help me with the zipper?"

Garret's dressed now, looking so freaking gorgeous with his dark suit, crisp white shirt, and silvery blue tie. He moves behind me, his hand on the zipper, pausing to kiss the back of my shoulder. "What about lingerie? Can I buy you that?"

"Yes. You can buy me that. I'm too embarrassed to buy it myself."

He zips up my dress, then walks over to the dresser. He opens the top drawer, takes out a box, and hands it to me.

"Garret, seriously? When did you buy this?'

"Before we left. Open it."

Inside the box is a cream-colored silk nightgown. Nightgown is not the right term but I don't know lingerie terminology. It has thin straps and hits about mid-thigh. A pair of matching panties is also in the box, along with a matching robe. The whole set is very classy and elegant.

"Do you like it?"

"Yeah, I do." I hold it up. "And I really like the color."

"I almost got black, but then I changed my mind. I'll get you black some other time."

"You must've had someone else buy this. There's no way you went in a store and shopped for lingerie."

"Actually, I did. I went in this small shop a few towns over thinking nobody would be there and guess who walks in?"

"I don't know. Ava?"

"Close. Sierra. She stands there wanting to talk, knowing I was trying to leave. But she didn't see what I bought."

"When did all this happen? We've been together since classes ended."

"I went shopping the week of finals. I was going to give that to you when you got back from break. I was planning this whole welcome back night. But then you ended up staying here so I decided to save it for tonight."

80

"I'm interested in what this welcome back night would've been like."

"It was gonna be great." He smiles. "But I guess you'll never know. Now hurry up or we'll be late and they'll give our table away."

As I put my makeup on, Garret goes in the other room and turns on the TV. I try my hair a bunch of different ways, but can't decide what to do with it. "Garret, should I wear my hair up or down?"

"Up," he calls back. "Down is for later."

I smile, pulling my long, dark, wavy hair up into a loose and low knot at the nape of my neck, just like Harper showed me.

"I'm ready." I slip my shoes on and meet him at the door.

"You're more than ready. You're beautiful." He lifts my hand to his lips and kisses it, then opens the door for me.

We go to the hotel restaurant and have another really great dinner with more amazing views of the city. Again, there are no prices on the menu, so I'm sure it cost a fortune.

Later, we go back to the room and I try on my new lingerie, which leads to where lingerie always leads.

"Okay, Garret. I believe you," I say out of breath. "You can do it several times a day. Although technically I did all the work."

"Hey, I still had to perform." He shoves another pillow behind his head, propping himself up more. "We have another hour until midnight. What do you want to do?"

"Let's check out the New Year's Eve stuff on TV." I toss him the remote and slip my lingerie back on.

His eyes drift over me. "Um, you probably shouldn't wear that."

"Oh, please. We're not doing it again."

His brows raise like I've challenged him.

"Fine." I take it off and put on one of his t-shirts. "I'll be right back. I'm going to grab some drinks."

At 11:50, we go into the living room and look out the wall of windows at the crystal-covered ball. Garret grabs the bottles of real and fake champagne.

"Which one?" He holds them up.

"The real one."

He pops the cork like he's done this a million times before. He pours the champagne in the glasses, then sets them next to us on the table.

He holds me close in front of him as the countdown begins. The ball drops much faster in real life than on TV. It's cool to see, but not worth standing outside in the freezing cold all day.

At midnight, Garret turns me toward him and gives me a kiss. Sweet, loving, hot, sexy. It's all those things. My first New Year's Eve kiss. And it just happened to be with the person I love most in the world.

"Happy New Year, Jade." He lets me go, then hands me a glass of champagne and holds up his own to toast. We clink glasses and I take a tiny sip.

The last and only time I drank was at a party a couple months ago. I was angry, panicked, confused—basically an emotional mess—and I swallowed the vodka without even feeling it in my mouth. I let the fiery liquid go straight down my throat as deafening music blasted all around me and that asshole, Blake, stood beside me. It was awful. The whole scene was awful.

But this time is different. So much different. I take another sip of champagne. It doesn't burn. Instead it tickles my mouth and throat. It has a slightly sweet taste that's a little fruity.

"It's good. A lot better than vodka."

"Yeah. It is." Garret slips his hand in mine and we sit down. His eyes linger on my face and it makes me glance away.

"Why are you looking at me like that?"

He sets his glass down. "I was just thinking that last year at this very moment I was somewhere else. Somewhere completely different from where I am now. I don't even know how I ended up in that place, but I never want to go back there."

I set my glass down. "You won't go back there, Garret."

"I won't, because of you."

"*You're* the one who decided to stop drinking so much. I just asked you to."

"But I wanted to because of you. And now I can have a glass of champagne without needing to finish the whole bottle. I don't have to drink until I pass out. It's just hard to believe I used to be that way. I don't even feel like the same person."

"I don't either. Last New Year's Eve I was asleep in my room at Frank's house. I didn't care about New Year's, or anything, really. Thinking back, I was pretty miserable a year ago. I just wanted to go to college and get as far away as possible from my old life."

"This will be a better year for both of us." He leans over to kiss me. "I love you, Jade."

"I love you, too." I take one last sip of the champagne. "Let's grab some snacks and watch a movie in bed."

We get into bed, but there isn't much to watch on TV at this hour, so we end up doing it again. What can I say? That kiss got me going. And sex with Garret is a great way to ring in the New Year.

CHAPTER NINE

In the morning as I'm getting ready, I hear Garret in the other room.

"Jade, get in here."

"What?" I stagger into the room with only one shoe on, holding the other one in my hand.

Garret points to the TV. "They're talking about Sinclair. This is old footage at his house. Check out the people around him. Do you see that old man anywhere?"

I get up closer to the screen. "Yes. Right there." As I point him out, the camera moves. "You can't see him now but I swear that was him."

"So he's definitely connected to Sinclair. And he's too old to be a campaign worker. Maybe he's just a donor."

"Are donors really that involved? Going to Sinclair's house? Traveling to his speeches? I thought they just wrote a check and that's it."

"My dad travels to political speeches all the time. And if he donates a lot of money, he gets invited to events at the politician's house. So it's not that unusual that the old guy was at Sinclair's house. It just seems odd that a guy who was that involved with the campaign just happened to bump into you like that. Maybe it wasn't a coincidence."

"I'm done worrying about it. He had his chance to do something to me and he didn't. Besides, what's he really going to do? The guy's in his seventies."

Garret turns off the TV and gets up from the couch. "Be careful when you're in Des Moines. Don't go anywhere alone. Take Ryan with you."

"Ryan'll be at work. But I'll be home with Frank the whole time so you don't need to worry."

"I'll still worry because I won't be there myself to protect you."

"I'm not helpless, Garret. I don't need you to protect me."

"Just promise me you'll check in with me a couple times a day so I know you're okay."

"Yes, I promise." I kiss him quick. "I'm ready to go if you want to head out. Although I'm really dreading having to go back to your house. Even if it's just for one night."

"We're not going there." Garret takes my suitcase and wheels it to the door next to his. "I booked us a hotel in Hartford. I knew you didn't want to go back to the house. I'm not ready to, either. I'll just end up yelling at Katherine."

"When you see her later, please don't say anything. She can't know I was listening in."

"I won't. But I'm not letting her keep you away from the house. I want you to be able to come over and not feel like you shouldn't be there. Plus you signed that agreement with Lilly. You have to go see her."

"At least one person in your family likes me."

He holds the door open for me and drops a kiss on my cheek. "My dad likes you, too. And I love you. So that's two likes and a love. You should feel pretty good about that."

The driver takes us back to Garret's house, but we only stop there to get his car and then we drive to Hartford.

We spend the night in the hotel, and the next morning he takes me to the airport. Saying goodbye to him sucks, as saying goodbye always does, but it's just a week. And I really do need that week without him so I can give all my attention to Frank and Ryan.

"You'll call me every day, right?" Garret asks. "And you'll keep your phone on?"

"Yes, and I won't hang out in any dark alleys."

"This is serious, Jade. I need to make sure you're safe."

"Nothing's going to happen to me. If anything, *you* should be the one being careful."

"I'll just be hanging out at home all week. And tomorrow I'm going over to Sean's place."

"Harper's boyfriend?"

"Yeah. He has friends over every Sunday to watch the game."

I glance back at the long line forming at the check-in counter. "I should probably go. Hey, you didn't get me another first class ticket, did you?"

He kisses me. "Guess you'll have to check in to find out."

"Garret!"

"You're scared to death to fly. And first class is a much calmer environment. I had no choice."

"It's too much money. But thank you." I kiss him. "I love you."

"I love you, too. Call me as soon as you get there."

When I land in Des Moines, Ryan's waiting for me right outside security. He looks better than when I saw him last. The dark circles under his eyes are gone and he has some color back in his face.

I run up and hug him as soon as I see him.

"Hi, Jade. How was the flight?"

"It was fine. I'm getting better at flying. As long as I can sleep, I'm good."

"Let's get your bag. Then we need to pick up Dad at the hospital."

He hangs his arm around my shoulder as we walk to baggage. His dad must be doing well because Ryan seems happy and not so serious. It's good to see him that way again.

Frank is ready to go when we arrive at the hospital. He's dressed in a flannel shirt and jeans, sitting in a wheelchair. His suitcase is packed and next to the door. I race over and give him a light hug, not sure if he's hurting anywhere.

"Jade, it's so good to have you back. And for two whole weeks. We'll have to find something to do."

"We'll have plenty to do," I tell him. "I know how to play poker now."

"Poker?" Ryan gets that concerned older brother look on his face. "What kind of poker?"

"Regular poker, Ryan. No stripping involved." I turn back to Frank. "You look a lot better, Frank."

It's true. The last time I saw him he looked like he was on death's door. He was weak and pale and so skinny. He's still thin but his face has life to it again.

"I feel better than I have in a long time. But let's talk later. I need to get out of this place."

We take Frank back to the house and as soon as we get there I feel like we're a family again. It's nice to have just the three of us there together and nobody else. I'm glad Garret suggested I spend this week with just the two of them.

Garret! Crap! I forgot to turn my phone on after I got off the plane. I turn it on and find two voicemails and three text messages from him. I don't bother checking them. I just call him.

"Hey, Garret. I made it to Des Moines," I say when he answers.

"Jade, I told you to call me when you got there. That was hours ago."

"Sorry. I kind of forgot."

He laughs. "You forgot about me already?"

"No. I was just busy. We had to pick up Frank at the hospital and then stop at the drugstore and now we're finally home."

"You sound okay, so the flight must've gone well."

"Yeah. First class was a good idea. It was really quiet, so I slept the whole time."

"How's Frank feeling?"

"He's doing so much better. He looks really good. I'll send you a photo so you can see."

"Well, tell him I said hi. And Ryan, too. I'll let you go, but keep your phone on, okay? And call me once in a while."

"I will. Bye."

That night for dinner Ryan orders a pizza and then the three of us play poker, which I've decided is my new favorite game. Frank is really good. Ryan's not too bad either. I'm surprised they never taught me how to play all those years I lived with them.

"Tomorrow we're having Christmas," Frank announces as Ryan deals the cards. "Ryan and I kind of skipped it since you weren't here and I was in the hospital, so we decided to celebrate it tomorrow."

"So what are we doing?" I ask.

"We're going for our usual Christmas dinner at the casino, but Ryan and I aren't having our eating contest this year. I'd never be able to keep up with him. My stomach shrunk while I was in the hospital living on gelatin and broth."

Frank and his dad have this contest every year at Thanksgiving and Christmas to see who can eat the most food at the buffet. Ryan almost always wins.

"I could beat you, Ryan," I say, challenging him. "It's about time you let me compete in that contest."

"You weigh like 100 pounds. I can easily eat more than you."

"More like 115. And weight doesn't matter. I know I can beat you."

The next day, we go to the buffet and Ryan ends up eating more. I didn't even come close to beating him.

Back at the house, Ryan pulls out a small stack of presents from the coat closet. I have gifts for them, too, but I didn't expect anything in return. With all the stuff going on with his dad the past couple weeks, I was sure Ryan wouldn't have time to shop.

"You first, Frank." I hand him my gift, which is a photo album I put together. It's nothing fancy. Just some photos I took over the semester that I printed out and put in an album.

"I love it. This is perfect." Frank is almost crying as he flips through the pages. The meds he's on must be making him emotional because he isn't a very emotional guy and the album isn't that great.

"It's not much," I say. "But since you can't get to Connecticut to see where I live I thought I'd show you in pictures."

"That was really nice, Jade." Now Ryan seems emotional. What's the deal with these two?

"Open yours." I hand Ryan a small package. Inside is a collection of cassette tapes I found at a used record store in New York. They were super cheap so I got a bunch. "Now you won't be stuck listening to the radio when you drive out to get me. I figure there's enough there to fill 22 hours of driving."

"Thanks, Jade. This is awesome." Ryan likes my gift more than I thought he would. I guess I didn't do too bad this year on present selection. I'm usually not very good at it.

"I know you'll probably have that car for a few more years, so you might as well make use of the cassette player. I picked your favorite bands."

"I see that. Thanks." He gets up and hands me a small box. "Now your turn."

I rip off the paper and find a wooden box containing a set of five black and silver pens. I kind of collect pens. I'm not sure when it started or why, but over the years I've accumulated quite a few. Most of them are freebie pens from hotels or banks, so it's not that great of a collection.

"Thanks. These are really fancy. And they have their own little case."

"We figured since you're in college now, it was time to get you some higher quality pens."

Ryan hands me an envelope next. Inside is a gift card for my favorite sporting goods store so I can replenish my running gear as needed.

Frank and Ryan exchange gifts next and then Frank goes to take a nap while Ryan and I watch TV. It turns out to be a really great Christmas, even though it's not actually Christmas day.

The rest of the week is filled with movies, bowling, and playing cards. Ryan convinced his boss to give him some time off from work so he could do stuff with me while Frank rests. Chloe, Ryan's girlfriend, has to work all week, which I'm secretly happy about. I like her, but I'm still not that comfortable around her and it would've been awkward to have her hang out with us.

On Friday, Ryan and I take Frank back to the hospital. He has an appointment with the new doctor Ryan told me about.

After an hour of sitting in the waiting room, a nurse finally comes up to Ryan. "The doctor will be out shortly to take you back to his office. He'll be going over your father's test results."

"Okay, thanks." Ryan turns to me. "You can wait out here. It shouldn't take long."

There's a stack of magazines on the table next to me and I've already gone through all of them. They're celebrity gossip magazines that are mostly pictures with really short articles.

The person next to me gets up to leave and I snatch her magazine before someone else gets it. My eyes stop at a photo on the top right corner of the cover. I instantly recognize the smiling brunette with the fake boobs and overly white teeth. Next to the photo it says, *Ava Hamilton returns for a Prep School Girls' reunion! Details inside!*

Ava was Garret's fake girlfriend last semester before I ended the fake girlfriend tradition. Ava was on Prep School Girls, some reality show on cable. It was a year ago, but apparently she's doing a reunion show. Like the girl needs more attention. Who would want to watch her on TV anyway?

I flip to the article about her. It's just one page, mostly photos. My stomach drops when I spot a photo at the very bottom next to a caption that says, *Will they get back together?* The photo shows Ava and Garret at a charity function last fall.

Garret has his arm around Ava, and even though I know it's all for show I still cringe seeing them together.

I quickly scan the article. *It's rumored that Ava is getting back together with Garret Kensington, a prep school classmate of hers. Some say they're already a couple again.*

Already a couple again? What the hell? Who's saying this? They were never a couple. She was just his fake girlfriend. I keep reading. *Garret is the son of billionaire Pearce Kensington, owner of Kensington Chemical.*

Billionaire? I thought he was just a millionaire. Everything I'd read about Garret's dad said he was worth millions, not billions. But I suppose several millions make a billion.

The article continues. *Garret and Ava are currently attending Moorhurst College in Connecticut, an exclusive private college attended by several of their prep school classmates. Fans of Prep School Girls are hoping Garret will make an appearance on the reunion episodes. Ever since photos of this hottie were released last year, Garret has developed a large fan following with girls begging to get another glimpse of those famous swimmer abs. Check our website for more photos of Ava and Garret along with updates about the Prep School Girls' Reunion episodes.*

Photos? What photos? And since when does Garret have fans?

"Jade." Ryan is nudging my arm. I'm in a complete daze. The magazine falls out of my hand onto the floor. Ryan picks it up and sets it on the table. "I'm going to meet with the doctor."

My mind comes back into focus as I see Ryan standing there waiting for my response. "Yeah. Okay. I'll wait here."

Ryan walks off and I hear him talking to the doctor. The man's voice sounds familiar. I glance up and realize that I know the doctor. The gray-haired man with black-rimmed glasses standing next to Ryan is one of the doctors who took Garret the day he was shot by Royce Sinclair. I'm 100% sure of it. I remember Garret's dad talking to him while Garret was being carried out on a stretcher.

What is he doing in Des Moines? And what is he doing to Frank?

CHAPTER TEN

I race up next to Ryan. "Do you care if I sit in?"

"Um, no, I guess not," he says, giving me an odd look.

The doctor glances at me. Does he remember me? I'm sure he does. The incident with Sinclair was just a few weeks ago. He extends his hand. "I'm Dr. Cunningham. And you are?"

"This is Jade," Ryan answers for me. "She's my younger sister."

"I didn't realize Frank had other children," the doctor says.

"He doesn't. She's more like an adopted sister."

"I see. Well, she's welcome to come back with us if it's okay with you."

Ryan agrees and we all go to the doctor's office where Frank is waiting. My heart is beating really fast and I'm tapping my foot on the floor. I need to calm down and act like everything is normal.

The doctor goes over Frank's lab results which are all improving. Then he tells Ryan that he's reducing Frank's medications, saying that Frank will continue to improve when he doesn't have the side effects of all those meds he was taking.

By the time the doctor is done talking, it sounds like Frank is doing really well. So is this doctor helping him? Or is he lying about Frank's test results? I think back to what Frank said about the doctor who took care of my mother for all those years. He said Sinclair paid the doctor to give my mom pills that made her hallucinate so people would think she was crazy. What if this doctor is doing something bad to Frank? But Frank seems to be getting better. He definitely looks better.

Ryan and Frank ask the doctor some questions before we leave. Then the doctor escorts us back to the waiting room.

"It was nice meeting you, Jade." The doctor smiles at me. He seems like a nice guy. So maybe he's actually helping Frank. But he's part of that secret medical group that only works with rich, important people, so what is he doing here?

As we're walking out, I go over and take the magazine that had Ava on the cover. I know it's stealing, but I have to show this to Garret.

During lunch, I keep quiet while Frank and Ryan talk. I don't even hear what they're saying. My mind is too busy thinking about that doctor as well as that magazine article. I really need to talk to Garret about all of this. But not over the phone. I need to wait until he gets here.

Garret arrives at Frank's house around noon on Saturday. I greet him at the door, beyond excited to see him. A week apart seems more like a month. That's completely pathetic and I'm ashamed of myself for even feeling that way, but it doesn't change the fact that I miss that boy like crazy when he's not around.

"It's good to see you again," Frank says as Garret walks in.

Ryan says hello as well. We all sit and talk for a few minutes, then I take Garret back to my room. We kiss the second the door shuts.

"Damn, I've missed you," he says against my lips, his forehead resting on mine.

"Did you check into your hotel, yet?"

"Not yet." He steps back and smiles. "Do you want to come with me to check in?"

"Definitely. Let's go." I drag him back to the living room where Frank and Ryan are watching TV. "I'm going with Garret to check into his hotel. I'll be back soon."

There's awkward silence. I feel my cheeks heating up as Frank and Ryan look at me like they know exactly what I'll be doing there. I race outside before either one of them can say anything.

At the hotel Garret and I can't get to the room fast enough. He opens the door and we kiss as it closes behind us.

He takes my shirt off as we walk to the bed. I undo his pants, not breaking the kiss. In less than a minute our clothes litter the floor. I lie down on the bed and he gets on top of me.

"What about your chest?" I ask between kisses.

"Don't worry about it." His lips trail across my cheek and down the side of my neck.

"But I thought you couldn't—"

"It's okay." His hand skims over my hip making me shiver. Going without him the past week has made my body extra sensitive to his touch. His mouth moves to my breast and I arch back as sensations ignite through my core. He rotates off me onto his side and his hand moves farther down. He runs it along the inside of my thighs, just barely brushing the area between and driving me crazy.

His lips return to mine and his tongue thrusts into my mouth as his hand finally hits the spot that is now aching for him.

I reach down and touch him.

"Jade." His voice is deep, his eyelids heavy. His kisses grow slower and deeper.

My body's on fire, desperate to be with him again. I pull on him to get on top of me, but he resists.

"What are you waiting for?" I whisper.

"What's the rush?" He runs his tongue along my bottom lip, then slips it back inside my mouth. I've really missed this. His kisses. His touch. Him.

He's right. There's no rush. I want this to last.

We keep it going as long as possible, which isn't that long since it's been a whole week since we've been together.

After what might be the best sex we've ever had, we lie back on the bed, sweaty and out of breath.

"I don't know what you did just now, Garret, but that was amazing."

"Thanks." His famous cocky smile appears. "I thought so, too."

"It must be the week off. I told you we do it too much. We need to take longer breaks."

"I don't think that's it. And I have no intention of taking a week off from this again anytime soon. Or a week off from seeing you."

I turn on my side and place my hand over the bandage that still covers his wound. "So this must really be healing if you were able to put weight on it like that."

"Yeah, it's a lot better. Last week I was even doing some laps in the pool. The doctor said I was healing faster than he expected."

His comment reminds of Frank's doctor. "Garret, I have to tell you something. I met Frank's new doctor yesterday and he's the same doctor who was there the day you were shot."

"I just saw my doctor yesterday, so it couldn't have been him. It must've been someone who looked like him."

"It wasn't the doctor you're seeing now. It was one of the other doctors who showed up at your house that day. I'm 100% sure. I memorized their faces as they took you out of that room on a stretcher."

"Why would the guy be in Des Moines? His team works out of the East Coast. Mostly New York and DC."

"I know, but I swear it was him. And he *does* work in New York. He's only working here part time."

"Unless..." Garret pauses. "I'm just guessing here, but maybe my dad had something to do with it."

"Your dad? What do you mean?"

"My dad might be trying to help Frank. He knows Frank is like a father to you and because of that, he might've sent that doctor out here to see if he could help Frank."

"Why would your dad do that?"

"Because you're like part of the family now."

"No, I'm not. Katherine hates me."

"It doesn't matter. My dad knows how much I love you and he knows that you and I are getting more serious."

"That's not enough of a reason for him to send that doctor out here to help Frank. I think it's something else."

"Like what?"

"I think your dad is trying to keep me quiet. If he helps Frank, I'll owe him. I'll owe him my silence. It's a way to make sure I never say anything about Sinclair."

Garret sits back, distancing himself from me. "Can't you just accept that maybe my dad did something nice for once?"

"Why are you getting mad about this? You're the one who told me your family is all about bribes and favors. So it makes sense that your dad would bribe me into keeping quiet."

"He didn't even tell you about it. If he was bribing you, he would tell you. And you said you'd never tell anyone about Sinclair so he doesn't have a reason to bribe you."

"I don't want to fight about this. Just forget it. Frank's getting better and that's the only thing that matters."

Garret doesn't respond. I figure since he's already annoyed with me I might as well bring up the other topic that's bugging me.

"So I saw this magazine when I was at the doctor's office. It was one of those celebrity magazines. And it had a story about Ava. And um, you."

He glances up. "What about me?"

"There was a photo of you and Ava at a charity event last fall. The article made it sound like you two really dated and that you might get back together. Actually it hinted that you already *were* back together."

"And?" His eyebrows creep up. "You're not telling me you believed some stupid article in a gossip magazine, are you?"

"No, but I'd like to know where they're getting this information. Is Ava telling them this?"

"I haven't talked to Ava for over a month. I have no idea what she's telling people."

"The article said the show has all these photos of you. Where did they get those?"

"I don't know. Probably from the show last year."

"You were on Prep School Girls?"

"No, but they made it look like I was."

"I don't understand."

"On the last few episodes of the season, Ava made it sound like she and I were dating. She started talking about me, making up all these stories about us going out. Then the producers got footage of me at school and at parties and the way they edited it, it looked like Ava and I were dating. It's just fucked-up Hollywood shit. Those reality shows are anything but reality."

"They did that without your consent? Why didn't you do something about it?"

"I was only in a couple episodes so my dad didn't want to make a big deal about it. If we sued Ava's family or the production company, it'd be bad publicity for the Kensington name and my dad didn't want that. Plus Katherine actually liked my brief celebrity status. It got her invited to more social events."

"Why didn't you tell me about this?"

"There's nothing to tell. It's just Ava making up lies. I was never even on the show."

"Well, apparently the fans are hoping you and Ava get back together during the reunion episodes that come out in March."

"Yeah. So the fans will be disappointed."

"Doesn't it bother you that a national magazine is making it sound like you two are a couple? Because it bothers me."

"Just ignore it. Why are you getting all upset about this? It's a gossip magazine. They make up shit like that all the time to get people to buy the magazine."

"I know, but I don't like them saying that stuff about you."

"Then stop reading it."

"Did you know they were doing this reunion show?"

I'd heard rumors about it, but I didn't think they'd involve me again. I thought Ava would find a new guy. But if she's already making up stories about her and me, then this is just the beginning. She'll do whatever she has to do to make sure people watch the show. If that means making up more shit up about me, she'll do it."

"Then do something. Call her and tell her to find some other fake boyfriend."

100

"That would only make it worse. You know that. She loves pissing me off. It's better to just ignore whatever she's doing."

"It's not just Ava. You have all these people talking about you on the Internet. Teen girls downloading photos of you."

"Nobody's doing that, Jade."

"They are, too. Girls are talking about you online. Saying how hot you are."

"Whatever. Just stop reading that stuff, okay?" He gets up, dragging me off the bed. "Let's go back to the house. We don't want Frank and Ryan to think we're doing anything here at the hotel."

"Did you see their faces when we left?" I pick up my clothes and start dressing. "They totally knew what we were doing. I'm so embarrassed. I don't know if I can go back there."

"If you act normal, they won't even think about it."

"Hey, Ryan has to work tonight, but I was going to make dinner for the three of us. Can we stop at the grocery store on the way over there?"

"Sure. What are you making?" Garret is shirtless and just now putting his jeans on. I'm already fully dressed. I don't know what takes him so long.

"I was thinking of making chili and cornbread. It's one of Frank's favorite meals."

Garret finally puts his shirt on and I go over and button it up to speed things along.

He leans down and kisses me. "Can I help?"

"Of course you can help." I grab his coat from the chair as he puts his shoes on. "You forgot to get your suitcase from the car. You want to go get it before we leave?"

"I didn't forget it." He takes his coat from me and kisses my cheek. "You just distracted me. I'll get it later."

When we get back to Frank's house, Ryan's already gone and Frank is sleeping. Garret and I start on dinner. He insists on making the chili, so I work on the cornbread.

"Is this some secret recipe?" I ask as I watch him add spices to the pot.

"Yeah, and I'm not telling you what's in it, so stop looking over my shoulder."

"Why won't you tell me?"

He sets the spices down and turns to me. "Because once you taste this chili you'll want it again and again. And the only way you'll have it again is if I make it. It's another way for me to make sure you keep me around."

I loop my arms around his neck, pulling him down for a kiss. "You don't need chili for that. What you did before we got here makes me want to keep you around."

"So you're just using me for sex?"

"Pretty much." I let go of him and turn toward the fridge.

He grabs me around the waist, hauling my backside against him and talking softly by my ear. "How is it possible that just being in here cooking with you is totally turning me on?"

"You, too? I thought it was just me."

His hands move where they shouldn't, making my legs so weak that I practically melt into him as he holds me.

"We're not doing it in this house, Garret," I say, breathless.

"I know. So stay with me tonight." He moves my hair aside and kisses the side of my neck.

I force my legs to work again and turn to face him. "I want to, but I really need to be here with Frank."

"It's just overnight. Frank will be asleep. He won't care if you're gone while he's asleep. I'll make sure you're back here first thing in the morning."

"It's tempting, but I still think I should stay here."

He sighs and returns to the stove. "Okay. But you need to keep away from me because you're driving me crazy. And stop rubbing up against me every time you walk by."

"It's a small kitchen. I can't help it." I go over to the stove and reach in front of him for the salt shaker, causing my butt to brush against his jeans.

He backs away. "Jade?"

"What? I need the salt."

"You're evil." He watches me as I go to the fridge and grab a couple eggs and the carton of milk and bring them to the kitchen table where I'm making the cornbread.

Garret turns away from the stove and leans back against the counter across from me. "We should do this more often."

"Do what more often?" I pull on each side of the plastic bag that contains the cornbread mix but it refuses to open. I tighten my grip on it and pull even harder.

"Cook together." Garret comes over and takes the bag from me, opening it without any effort at all.

I look at the bag, annoyed. "We don't have a kitchen."

"So let's get one."

"I don't know what that means." I dump the mix in a bowl and add the milk and eggs.

"Let's get an apartment."

"So we can cook together?" I stir the cornbread, not really paying attention to what he's saying.

"No. Let's get an apartment so we can live together."

"But we're in college. We live in the dorms."

"We don't have to live in the dorms. We can live off campus. There are plenty of apartments close to campus." He waits for me to pour the batter in the pan. "So what do you think?"

I set the bowl down, finally getting the fact that he just asked me to move in with him. "Are you serious?"

"I'm totally serious. Living in the dorms sucks. And you always say that you hate sharing a bathroom with 20 girls. This way you'd only have to share with me."

I was not at all expecting this and now I'm not sure how to react. Move in together? At 19?

"Garret, my room and board is paid for. I don't have money for rent. You know that."

"I'll have my dad put your room and board money into a rental fund."

"I don't have a car. How am I supposed to get to class?"

"Hmm. That's a problem. What if I bought you a car?" he asks cautiously.

"No. Absolutely not. You are not buying me a car."

"Then I'll drive you to campus. Or we'll get a place on the bus line."

I watch him as he continues to think, trying to find a way to make this work. It's so sweet. He really wants this, and I think I do, too, but it seems too soon.

"Let's just put a hold on the moving-in-together idea, okay?"

He goes back to the stove and stirs his chili. I can tell he's disappointed and I hate disappointing him.

I put the cornbread in the oven and go stand beside him. "It's not that I don't want us to live together. I just think we should wait. At least one more semester. And besides, I practically live with you already. I'm always in your dorm room."

"That's not the same as having our own place. We need an apartment, not a dorm room." He adds another secret spice to the pot. "Once you taste this chili, you're going to want a kitchen so I can make this, and all my other secret recipes, all the time."

I take a whiff of the chili. "You have other secret recipes?"

"Tons. This is just one of many. And you could have them every night if we lived together."

I turn him away from the stove and give him a hug. "Garret, I love you and I really do want to move in with you. Just not this semester, okay?"

"You haven't even tried the chili yet." He pulls away and takes a spoon from the drawer, then dips it in the chili, holding it out for me to taste. I take a bite.

"It's good. Really good. Way better than the chili I normally make."

"Yeah, so?"

"I still can't move in with you. Not yet."

"All right." He kisses my forehead. "At least you like the chili."

"What smells so good in here?" Frank appears, rolling his wheelchair into the kitchen.

"Garret made chili," I answer. "And I'm making cornbread."

"One of my favorite meals," Frank says. "Thanks for making dinner. I thought you two would go out for dinner tonight."

I take a seat at the table next to Frank. "We wouldn't leave you all alone. I'm here to spend time with you."

Garret sits next to me. "Is there anything you want to do tonight?" he asks Frank. "I could go get some movies."

"Thank you for offering, but Jade and I have already watched plenty of movies this week. Maybe we could play some cards."

"Sounds good to me," Garret says. "The chili's ready, so whenever Jade's cornbread is done we can eat."

I get up from the table. "It just needs a few more minutes in the oven. I'll get the drinks ready."

Frank starts wheeling himself back down the hall. "When you're done, Jade, could you help me get a sweater from the closet?"

Garret jumps up. "I can help you. Just tell me what you need."

I watch him follow Frank to his room. He's so eager to help. How did I end up with this guy? He's too good to be true. Seeing him act all nice like that to Frank makes me want to take him up on his offer to get an apartment. I should just do it. I love Garret more than anything. I want to be with him all the time. So I don't know what's stopping me.

CHAPTER ELEVEN

The week goes by quickly and in that short time Garret manages to totally win over Frank and Ryan. He'd already won over Frank the last time he was here, but I never thought Ryan would come around. He's way too protective of his little sister. But after watching Garret help take care of Frank, Ryan got to see the kind, generous, selfless side of Garret that I love so much. And that was all that was needed for Ryan to finally accept that Garret was worthy of dating me.

On Saturday morning, Garret checks out of his hotel and comes to the house. We still have a few hours before the flight leaves, so Ryan makes everyone breakfast.

"Are you two ready to go back to class?" Frank asks.

Before either of us can answer, the doorbell rings. Ryan gets up to answer it.

"Dad, Dr. Cunningham is here with your new medication," Ryan says as he walks to the table with the doctor.

"Garret, what a surprise." Dr. Cunningham doesn't act at all surprised to see Garret, despite what he said. "What are you doing all the way out here in Iowa?"

"I'm here to see Jade, my girlfriend," he says, playing along. "She goes to Moorhurst with me." Even though I told Garret

107

about the doctor, he seems a little shocked actually seeing him here.

Frank looks at Garret, then back at the doctor. "You two know each other?"

"Yes, I know Garret's father." Cunningham turns to Garret. "I heard you suffered an injury recently. Would you like me to take a look at it?"

"No, that's okay," he says. "It's fine."

"Well, be sure to tell your father hello for me. Frank, let's go to the other room and I'll tell you about this new medication. I have to catch a flight back to New York in a couple hours."

Cunningham leaves about ten minutes later. It's time for Garret and me to leave, too.

I give Frank and Ryan each a long hug. Since Garret entered my life, I've become a real pro at this hugging thing. A year ago I never would've given them a hug. I couldn't stand to be that close to someone.

"We'll see you in May, honey," Frank says.

Garret looks at me. "Maybe she can make it back for spring break."

Frank shakes his head. "Jade, don't feel like you have to. You should do something with Garret or some of your other friends. May will come soon enough and then we'll have you for the whole summer."

I don't say anything, but I'm kind of thinking of not coming back here for the summer. I'd rather get a job in Connecticut and spend the summer with Garret. Then again, I don't even know what Garret's doing this summer. Maybe he won't even be in Connecticut.

We say a final goodbye before heading out.

"I told you it was the same doctor," I say to Garret on the ride to the airport.

"Yeah. My dad must've paid him to come out here. But I'm not going to ask him about it. And don't you ask him either. He has his reasons for not telling us."

Never ask questions. I understand why that rule applies to me, but why Garret? Why does his dad need to keep secrets from his own son? And why does Garret just accept it instead of demanding answers? It's strange, but I guess it's just how their family works.

As we're walking in the airport Garret's phone rings. "Hey, Dad." He listens. "Yeah, I'm fine. We're at the airport now. I'll call you when we get there." He puts the phone in his pocket.

"What was that about?" I ask him as we stand in line with our luggage.

"It's nothing."

"It's *not* nothing. Your dad's been calling you all week. It's like he's worried about you." We inch forward as the line moves. "Is there a reason your dad is worried about you? And don't lie to me."

"We'll talk about it later."

"Did someone make threats against you? Is it the same person who threatened to do something to your dad? And Lilly?"

He leans down and lowers his voice. "Not here. This is not the place to talk about this."

I glance around and notice people staring at us. I keep quiet until we're on the plane, in first class of course.

"You should've told me someone's making threats against you," I say as I fasten my seatbelt.

"Nobody's made any threats, so you don't need to worry."

"I *do* worry, because I love you and I don't want anything bad to happen to you." I reach over and hold his hand.

109

He kisses my forehead. "Nothing bad will happen to me. I don't know why my dad's acting so overprotective like this. He's probably just being overly cautious."

"Yeah, because he thinks you're in danger."

The plane starts taking off. I move closer to Garret and rest my head on his shoulder.

"Get some sleep," he says. "I'll wake you up when we get there."

We arrive in Hartford a few minutes early and our luggage is the first to appear on the belt.

"I guess it's our lucky day," I say, grabbing my bag. Garret grabs his, then wheels both of our bags to the car.

Garret's car had to be delivered to us from a private storage facility because last time we left it at the airport someone disabled the brakes. Sinclair admitted he hired someone to do it, but even with him dead, Garret didn't trust that the car would be safe sitting at the airport parking lot for that long.

As we drive away from the airport, Garret checks to make sure the brakes work. Then he tests them again as we get on the main road. "Okay, they work this time."

"I should call Frank quick and tell him we made it." I take my phone out of my purse and turn it on but nothing happens. "The battery's dead. And the charger is in my suitcase which is in the trunk."

Garret reaches into his pocket and hands me his phone.

I start to call Frank, then stop. "I should've said this earlier, but thanks for coming out to see me. It was nice that you spent time getting to know Frank and Ryan like that. I think they might actually like you now."

He laughs. "I wasn't aware that they didn't like me before. But I'm glad they do now."

I call Frank, but Ryan answers. "Hi, Ryan. We made it to Connecticut. We even got in early."

"So are you guys headed to campus now?" Ryan asks.

"Yeah. The fun is over." I glance at Garret. "It's back to homework, tests, and cafeteria food."

"Well, thanks for letting us know you got there. I've gotta run to work. Dad is sleeping, so we'll call you later this week."

"Okay, bye." I hang up just as another call is coming in. A photo appears on the screen and I stare at it as the phone continues to ring. Garret reaches for the phone, but I hold it away from him.

"Jade, who is it?" He reaches for it again, making the car swerve. "Give me the phone."

But I won't do it. I'm too angry. Too hurt. Too confused.

The phone finally stops ringing and the photo goes away.

"Why is she calling you?" There's a tightness forming in my chest that's making it hard to breathe.

Garret shifts in his seat, keeping his eyes on the road. He knows who it was without me even saying her name.

"Garret, why is she—"

A text pops up on the screen. It's from her.

My heart beats faster as a lump forms in my throat. "How long has this been going on?"

"It's not like that. There's nothing going on. She just needed a friend. That's all."

"She doesn't have any other friends? You expect me to believe that?" I turn my back to him and read the text. I swore I'd never be the girlfriend who spies on her boyfriend's phone, but tough shit. I'm her today.

The text reads: *Are you back yet? Can we meet?*

I toss the phone on the floor of the car.

111

"Jade, stop it." Garret reaches over to hold my hand, but I won't let him. "She's just a friend. I swear to you, that's it."

"Have you been seeing her? Did you see her while I was gone?"

"No! She doesn't even live around here."

"That doesn't mean she couldn't drive here. Or take a plane. It sounds like she's here right now."

"Why? What did she say?"

"That she wants to meet. Why does she want to meet with you, Garret?"

"Because her fucking father died, Jade! That's why. Do you seriously think I'm cheating on you?"

"Oh, yeah. I'm being so unreasonable. Your ex-girlfriend, a girl you actually *chose* to date and weren't forced to date by your family, has been calling and texting you for God knows how long and you don't even mention it once to me? No, I shouldn't be mad. Why would I be mad?"

"I'm with *you*. Not her. She's just a friend. I have no interest in dating her now or ever again. She has a boyfriend, Jade. You met him."

"It doesn't matter. You should've told me. The only reason you'd hide this from me is if you felt guilty. Like you were doing something you shouldn't."

"I didn't tell you because this doesn't concern you. So I talk on the phone to her. Big fucking deal. Why do you care?"

"Don't you dare act like I'm overreacting! If I had an ex-boyfriend calling and texting me all the time, you would beat the shit out of him and then monitor my calls from that point forward."

"What the hell? I would never do that. You can talk to whoever you want. I trust you."

112

"I don't think we should talk right now." I lean against the door, getting as far away as possible from him.

It starts to rain and I focus on the drops as they hit my window and slide down the glass. It's a steady rain and the rhythmic sound of it helps calm me down.

We drive in silence all the way to campus. Garret parks the car in front of our dorm. It looks like only about half of the students are back. It's still raining and dark clouds hint that there's more to come.

As I start to get out of the car, Garret grabs hold of my coat sleeve. "Wait."

"I want to unpack. Let's just go."

He lets go of my coat and takes my hand. "I'm sorry, Jade. I should've told you. I was just being selfish. I didn't say anything because I didn't want to have this fight with you."

I sigh as I sit back in the car and shut the door. "So are you going to tell me what's been going on with you two?"

"Yes." He turns to me, keeping hold of my hand. "Sadie called me right after you left for Des Moines. She was crying and saying how nobody would talk to her about what happened. Her boyfriend wasn't supportive at all, which doesn't surprise me. I thought he was a real ass that night we met him. Anyway, he didn't even go to the funeral with her. He said that a guy who kills himself and leaves his family behind like that shouldn't have anyone at their funeral, so he refused to go. Sadie was really close to her dad. She always has been. She took his death really hard. She's still a mess."

"Did you see her while I was gone?"

"No. We only talked on the phone. And I had no idea she was coming to Connecticut, so I was surprised when you said she wanted to meet." He pauses. "Jade, I don't want this thing with Sadie to come between us. I thought I was doing the right

113

thing helping her out like this. The first time she called she sounded so upset and I felt guilty because of, well, you know."

Thinking about it, I guess it makes sense that Garret felt he had to help her. His dad killed Sadie's father, Royce Sinclair. The man who is also *my* father. It's still hard to believe that Sadie is my half sister and she doesn't even know it.

Garret continues. "We only talked a few times that week you were gone. The first time was for about an hour and then the other times were short, maybe 10 or 15 minutes. And we haven't texted that much. You can check my phone if you want. You can read the texts and see when she called and how long we talked. And I swear, Jade, I never went to see her. You can ask my dad. He'll tell you I was home that whole week you were gone."

I'm not sure if I should believe him. I could check his phone, like he said, but I don't want to. I don't want to be the jealous girlfriend. And I really do want to believe him.

"You can't keep hiding stuff from me, Garret. You know I have problems trusting people. Even you. And then you hide this from me and I feel like I'll never be able to trust you."

"If you don't want me to talk to her anymore, I won't."

"She wants to get back together with you. She's not going to stop calling you. She won't give up that easily."

"She has a boyfriend. She doesn't want to get back together with me. She just wanted to talk."

"Why can't she talk to someone else? I thought you only dated her for two months. You can't be that great of friends."

"No, but I understand what she's going through."

"Because your mom died?"

"It's more than that. Whenever I asked anything about my mom's plane crash, people brushed me off. I never got answers. Sadie's describing the same thing. She can't understand why her

114

dad would kill himself, so she keeps asking questions but doesn't get answers. You and I know what really happened to her dad, but she doesn't."

The raindrops pelt harder against the window of the car. They almost sound angry. As I listen to them, I think about Sadie and what she's going through. To her, Sinclair was probably a loving father. It's hard for me to imagine that, given what he did to my mother and me. But he lived a double life. Sadie only knew the good Sinclair, so of course she's upset. Still, I don't like her confiding in Garret. There's a history between them and no matter what Garret says, I don't believe that Sadie only sees him as a friend.

"What do you want me to do?" Garret squeezes my hand to get my attention. "I won't fight with you about this. It's not worth it."

"I feel bad for her, but I don't think it's a good idea for you two to keep talking like this. What if you accidentally let something slip out about what really happened to her dad? Plus, she's my half sister. And your ex. That makes this whole thing really weird."

"All good points. I should've just told her I couldn't talk to her. She should be talking to Evan about this. Or one of her friends."

My eyes focus on the water droplets streaming down the window, racing each other to the bottom of the glass. "I'm sorry I accused you like that, but when I saw her face pop up on your phone it was an automatic response."

"I know, and I totally get that. And what you said earlier was true. If the situation was reversed, I'd react way worse than you just did when you saw Sadie calling me."

The rain is now coming down even harder and the cold air is starting to turn it into an icy sleet. I zip up my coat and pull my hood over my head. "We should go. We're gonna get soaked carrying everything inside."

He shrugs. "So we'll stay here until it stops."

"And do what?"

He slides my hood off and reaches behind my head, bringing my face to his. "Steam up the windows?"

A minute ago I was flaming mad at him and now I'm kissing him. I've got to learn to get more control around this guy. But not now. His kisses feel way too good.

The sound of the icy rain hitting the windows is so loud that I almost don't hear Garret's phone ringing. When it continues to ring on the floor of the car I pull away from him and pick it up. I don't even want to see who it's from.

I hand him the phone. He sighs and shakes his head as he answers. "Hi, Sadie."

He puts the phone on speaker and Sadie's voice fills the car. "Hey, Garret. I've been trying to get a hold of you. Are you back yet?"

"Yeah, I'm back, but—"

"I need to see you. Can we meet somewhere? I'm in New Haven visiting Evan."

Garret looks at me. "And Evan doesn't care if you meet up with your ex?"

"Forget about him. Will you meet me somewhere? I don't care how far a drive it is. Just pick the place and I'll be there."

"What's going on? Why do you want to meet? Did something happen while I was gone?"

"No." She's quiet for what seems like a really long couple of seconds. "I just miss you. I want us to try again, Garret. I want us to get back together."

CHAPTER TWELVE

I throw my hands in the air, mouthing *I told you* to Garret.

"Sadie, you know I'm with Jade now."

"Yes, but you're not serious with her, are you? She's not even one of us. I thought you were just dating her to piss your dad off."

The one and only time I met Sadie I thought she was nice. But apparently she was just putting on an act. If she only knew that we shared the same father. That I actually am "one of them" or least half of me is. I open my mouth to say something, but Garret puts his hand up, shaking his head side to side. I cross my arms over my chest and gaze out the side window.

"I'm not dating Jade to piss off my dad." He pokes my arm to get my attention. "I love her."

Sadie doesn't respond.

I turn back toward Garret, my arms still crossed.

He keeps his eyes on me as he continues. "And it's not fair to Jade for you and me to keep talking like this. I'm sorry, Sadie. I really am. But you can't keep calling me."

We hear her quietly crying now. I'm not sure if it's an act to get Garret to change his mind or if she's really crying. But now that I know she's trying to steal my boyfriend, I don't care if she really *is* crying. She can go cry on Evan's shoulder. The guy she's supposed to be dating.

"Last summer, we had something, Garret. It was real. I never should've broke things off like that. It was a mistake. Can't we just meet and talk this out?"

"Sadie, did you not just hear what I said? I love Jade. Nothing's going to change that. You and I are over. You have a new boyfriend now."

"But he's not like you. He doesn't listen to me. He doesn't even care that my dad died."

"Then dump him. Find someone else."

"*You're* the someone else. I want us to be together again."

I roll my eyes. Garret reaches over for my hand which is still tucked under my crossed arm. He manages to free it and hold it in his.

"It's not going to happen. I told you. I'm with Jade now."

"Yeah, and I liked Jade. She seemed nice. But she's not for you. She doesn't fit in our world. I mean, come on, it's not like you're going to marry the girl."

Garret locks his eyes on mine as he gently squeezes my hand. "I *am* going to marry her. If she says yes."

My jaw practically drops to the floor. I can't believe he just said that! Out loud! To his ex-girlfriend! And me!

There's silence on the other end of the phone. Then Sadie finally speaks. "So when is this happening? Did you already propose to her?"

He smiles at me. "Jade would kill me if I proposed now. She thinks we're too young. So I'll wait. I'll wait until she's ready."

"She's not racing to marry into the Kensington fortune? That's a shock."

"She's not like that. Jade doesn't care about money."

118

"Everyone cares about money, Garret. She just won't admit it to you."

"I need to get going and you should get back to Evan. I really am sorry about your dad and I hope things start getting better for you."

"Whatever, Garret." She hangs up without saying goodbye.

Garret turns his phone off. "Jade, I seriously didn't think she wanted to get back together. I thought she just wanted to talk. And I can't believe she said that stuff about you. She's never acted like that before. I didn't think she believed in all that dating-within-your-social-class shit. Or at least she didn't act like it when we were dating. She's always been—"

I lean over and kiss him before he can finish. I don't want to talk about Sadie anymore. Garret made it clear that she's his past and I'm his future. That's all I needed to hear. Whenever I think things won't last between us, he does something like this and I have faith in him again. I wish I could stop doubting him and just accept that he wants to be with me.

I sit back, keeping hold of his hand.

"Does that mean you're not mad at me anymore?" he asks.

"I don't know. Do you have any other ex-girlfriends trying to get back together with you? Any other secret phone calls to tell me about out?" I say it kiddingly but Garret looks serious.

"No. And I never should've hid that from you."

I smile, trying to lighten the mood. "Let's go inside. We'll get our stuff later."

We run through the frigid wind and sleet to the dorm. The inside of the building is almost as cold as the outside and Garret's room feels even colder than the hallway.

"Did they forget to turn the heat on?" I grab an extra blanket from his closet and curl up on his bed, wrapping the blanket around me.

"They turn it way down during breaks." He takes his coat off and drops his keys on his desk.

"Get over here. I need your warmth."

"You're so demanding," he kids. "You could at least ask, especially when you're just using me for my body."

"I'm not using. I'm just borrowing."

"You're borrowing my body heat?" He laughs as he joins me under the blanket. "So you plan on giving it back someday?"

"Yes. Now let me in." I sit up a little, waiting for him to move his arm.

"Let you in where?" He smiles and remains on his back, keeping his arms at his sides.

I make a circle in the air below his shoulder where his arm meets his chest. "That little nook area that's all warm and cozy."

He's laughing at me again. "Little nook area? I'm sorry. I don't have one of those."

"Yes, you do. Now come on. I'm freezing here."

He puts his arm out and I slide up next to him, wrapping my arm around his chest and resting my head in that spot just below his shoulder.

He closes his arm around me. "Better now?"

"Much better." I pull the blanket over us. "So about that proposal thing. I probably wouldn't *kill* you if you proposed. Kill is kind of a strong word."

"Well, you'd definitely freak out. Look how freaked out you got when I asked you to get an apartment with me."

"I didn't freak out. I just thought this semester was too soon. Plus I'm not ready to take the bus to class every day. It's easier living here." I move even closer to him, trying to steal some of his warmth. "So what are your plans for the summer?"

"I don't know yet. Why?"

"It's not that far away and we'll have almost four months off. I'm just trying to figure out when we'll see each other. Are you staying in Connecticut? Or going somewhere for an internship like last summer?"

"I might stay in Connecticut, but I really don't know yet."

I was sure Garret would tell me he wanted us to spend the summer together, but he didn't and now I'm confused. Does he really want to be apart for four months? We could barely stand being apart for one week.

My finger starts making small circular movements on the blanket. It's what I do when I'm not sure what to say.

"What are you thinking, Jade?"

"I just don't want us to be apart all summer. That's a long time."

He picks my hand up to stop the circling. "So what are you suggesting?"

I hesitate, unsure how to answer. Why isn't *he* suggesting something? Why is he asking me?

And then I finally get it. He wants *me* to be the one who finds a way for us to be together. Because if *he* does it, he knows I won't be as committed to whatever he suggests. I'll come up with an excuse for why it won't work. Damn, he's good. He knows me way too well.

The old Jade would be stubborn and refuse to admit what she wanted. But now, my stubbornness is losing out to my strong desire to be with Garret.

"I was thinking we could share an apartment this summer." There I said it. For once I finally asked for what I want. "We could test out living together. If we decide it isn't working, we'll just stay in our dorm rooms next fall."

He sits up, forcing me to sit up with him. "That's an interesting idea." He acts like he needs to consider this, totally

121

getting me back for all the times he's asked me to do stuff and I've turned him down.

"Never mind. It was a stupid suggestion." I wait for him to protest and tell me how it's a great idea and that we should definitely do it.

"Then forget the apartment. I'll just try to fit in a couple trips to Iowa this summer."

He starts to lie down again, but I yank on his shirt.

"Garret, what the hell? Are you saying you don't want to spend the summer with me?"

He's trying not to laugh. Seeing me work this hard to be with him is apparently funny.

"Jade, are you asking me to get an apartment with you this summer? Because I really can't tell."

I take a deep breath, setting aside my tough girl, doesn't-need-a-guy attitude. "Yes. I'm asking you to get an apartment with me this summer. Are you happy now?"

He pulls me into his chest and kisses the top of my head. "Very happy. And my answer is yes. I would love to get an apartment with you this summer."

My heart practically leaps for joy. Like it actually skips a beat I'm so happy. What the hell is wrong with me? I never in a million years thought I would act this way over some stupid boy and now here I am, asking said boy to share an apartment with me for an entire summer.

"So do you want to get a place close to Frank's house?"

Garret's question knocks me out of my euphoric high and back to reality. "Well, no, I wasn't planning on going back to Des Moines. I mean, I'll go visit Frank and Ryan in May when school's out, but I don't want to live there."

"Really? Why not?"

"That's my old life. I want to try something new. I never planned to go back there after college. Frank and Ryan know that. They'll understand if I don't spend the summer there."

"Then where do you want to live? Here in Connecticut?"

"I don't know. Maybe we should pick an entirely new place. Maybe a town near a beach. Some place that attracts tourists. I'll get a waitressing job. People always leave big tips when they're on vacation."

"You don't have to get a job. You have the rest of your life to work. Let's just have fun this summer."

I lift my head off his chest and look at him. "I'm getting a job, Garret. I need money."

He shakes his head but moves past the topic. "West Coast or East Coast?"

"What do you mean?"

"You said you wanted to live on the beach. Do you want to live on the Atlantic or the Pacific?"

"I wasn't saying we'd live *on* the beach. Just near the beach."

"You can't be that close to the ocean and not live on the beach. We're living on the beach. I'm deciding that right now."

"I can't afford a place on the beach. I need someplace cheap."

He flips me on my back and hovers over me. "We're living on the beach, Jade. I want to wake up every morning with you in my bed and the cool ocean breeze blowing through our window. I want you to fall asleep in my arms every night listening to the waves crashing against the shore."

I laugh. "Are you writing a romance novel here?"

"We're not getting some shitty place miles from the beach. If we're doing this, we're getting a place on the ocean."

His cheesy romance novel description did sound appealing. I could almost see it in my head. Why fight him on it? I've always dreamed of living on the beach, never once thinking it would actually happen.

"Okay. Let's do it. Let's get a place on the beach." Just saying the words out loud has me smiling so much my cheeks hurt.

"I'll start looking this week." Garret's smiling, too. I'm sure he thought I'd never agree to this. "Beach rentals fill up fast. Tell me which coast you want and we'll go from there."

"Um, I don't know. You pick. I've never actually been to a beach. I've never even seen the ocean, so I really shouldn't be deciding that."

He stares at me. "You've never been to the ocean? How did I not know this?"

"I grew up in Iowa. When would I have gone to the ocean? Coming here to college was the first time I ever left the state."

"Shit, I didn't even think about that. Why haven't I taken you to see the ocean? We're less than an hour away from the damn ocean and I've never even taken you to see it." He gets off the bed and holds out his hand. "Get up. We're going."

"Going where?"

"I'm taking you to see the ocean."

"It's winter. The weather's crappy. I don't want to see it right now."

He glances out the window at the icy rain. "Classes don't start until Tuesday. We'll get on a plane and fly down to Florida."

I yank him back under the blanket with me. "We're not going to Florida. The ocean can wait. It's not going anywhere. Now let's figure out this summer. I think West Coast. California. Maybe we could go see Harper while we're there."

Garret considers it. "California, huh? I like it. Maybe an hour or so up the coast from LA. They have some great beaches and it's not as crowded. My dad has a real estate agent out there. I'll call her and see if she handles summer rentals."

"I want input, Garret. Don't just pick a place."

"She'll give us options and we'll pick the place together."

I wrap my arm around his chest and squeeze him. "I'm so excited about this. I just want the semester over so we can go right now."

"You see? It's better to just say what you want instead of trying to make me guess. Or pretending you don't want something when you really do."

"But I didn't know I wanted this. I just knew I didn't want to be away from you all summer."

"And you never would've told me that if I hadn't forced you to."

"Well, you almost had me convinced you didn't want to see me this summer."

"You know there's no way in hell I'd go four months without seeing you. I love you, remember?"

"I love you, too." I shiver, burrowing deeper under the blanket.

"Let's get out of here. It's too cold. I hear the heat running now, but it'll take forever to warm up. Let's go eat and come back later."

I get up, keeping the blanket wrapped around me. "Maybe we could go to your house and watch a movie in the theater room."

"You're not worried about seeing Katherine?"

"I'm done worrying about her. I don't care if she hates me. She'll have to get used to me because I'm not going anywhere."

Garret smiles. "It's good to hear you finally say that."

It's good to finally *think* it, too. With our recent plans to live together, I feel even more secure in my relationship with Garret.

And it certainly didn't hurt to hear him tell Sadie that he planned to marry me someday.

Katherine can try to break Garret and me apart all she wants, but it won't work. So let her try. I'm not afraid of her anymore.

CHAPTER THIRTEEN

As we drive to Garret's house, I mentally prepare myself to see Katherine. I've come up with all kinds of good comebacks if she tries to insult me or tell me I can't see Lilly.

When we get there we walk up to the front door, and just as Garret's about to open it, Katherine does. She's wearing a long black coat, her purse hung over her shoulder and a set of keys in her hand.

"Oh, goody, Pearce," she says, keeping her eyes on me. "Look who's back. Your little charity case." She darts past me, purposely bumping my shoulder as she goes by.

Wow. She's not even trying to hide how much she hates me. At least before she tried to fake being nice.

"What the hell, Katherine?" Garret reaches for her arm but she's too quick. She's already in the circular driveway headed to her silver Mercedes. The rain has stopped but the wind has picked up, blowing her long blond hair around.

"Katherine, get back here!" Mr. Kensington steps between Garret and me to the driveway. "You need to take Lilly. You know she can't be here."

"She's your daughter, too," Katherine says as she gets in the car. "You really should spend more time with her. I'm sure she'd love to attend your little meeting."

Mr. Kensington's face is red with anger. "When are you coming back?"

She doesn't answer. Instead, she slams the car door in his face, starts the engine, and speeds off down the long driveway.

He storms past us into the house. "Garret, I need you to watch Lilly. Keep her quiet and up in her room."

We follow him into the house.

"Dad, what's going on?"

"Your stepmother's out of control. That's what's going on." He goes in his office and shuffles through a stack of papers. Garret goes in there, too. I wait outside the office door, not sure if I should be listening in on this.

"What are you two fighting about?" Garret asks him.

Mr. Kensington lets out an angry laugh. "What are we NOT fighting about?" He sits down at this desk and types something into his computer.

Garret glances back at me, then back at his dad. "Why do you need us to watch Lilly? Are you going somewhere?"

"No, but some very important people are coming over any minute now and I can't have a 6-year-old girl running around while I'm trying to do business."

"Who's coming over? Clients from work?"

Mr. Kensington looks up at Garret and notices me standing just outside his office door. "It's not work. It's some other business I need to take care of. Now please just deal with Lilly, will you?"

"Yeah. Sure. How long do you need us to stay?"

"It shouldn't take longer than a couple hours. I'll come up and get you after they leave." He checks his watch, then gets up and stands in front of Garret. "They'll be here soon. You need to go upstairs."

"Um, yeah. Okay." Garret walks out and we both head to the staircase.

"Oh, and welcome back you two," Mr. Kensington says from his office doorway. "It's good you stopped by." He shuts the door.

"That was weird," I whisper to Garret as we're walking up the stairs.

"Welcome to my family. There's always plenty of drama to keep you entertained."

When we get to Lilly's room, I go in first. As soon as she sees me she bursts up from her little chair and runs over to me.

"Jade!" She holds her arms up like I'm supposed to pick her up. Why not? She can't weigh that much. I pick her up and her little legs and arms wrap around me. "You came to play with me! I knew you would. I missed you."

"Hey, what about me?" Garret acts offended. "You didn't miss me, too?"

She smiles and reaches her arms out to him. He takes her from me. "I missed you, Garret." She buries her head in his shoulder.

It's so cute to see them together. He's really good with her. He'll make a great dad someday. What am I saying? I don't want kids! If he wants kids he'll have to marry someone else.

"Mom and Dad were yelling." Lilly's voice goes from happy to sad. "They were fighting. Are they gonna get a divorce?"

How does she know about divorce at that age? Do they talk about it with her? Maybe she heard about it on TV.

"Sometimes moms and dads fight," Garret tells her. "It doesn't mean they're getting divorced."

She lifts her head. "But if they do, will you still be my big brother?"

He smiles. "Yes. I'll always be your big brother." He sets her down. "Let's watch a movie, okay? You can pick out one of your cartoons."

She shakes her head. "Tea first. Then a movie."

I look at Garret, smiling from ear to ear. I've been dying to see him attend one of these tea parties and now I'll finally witness it.

"Come on, Lilly," he says, trying to get out of it. "We do the tea party thing all the time. Let's play a game instead."

"Please?" She gives him her sad face and tilts her head.

Garret lets out a long sigh and I can't help but laugh.

"This never leaves this room," he says as he walks past me to the tiny white table set with little pink tea cups and pretend cupcakes. It makes me laugh even more.

After the tea party, Garret helps Lilly get a movie going while I go to the bathroom. As I'm heading down the hallway, I hear Garret's dad talking downstairs.

"Don't worry about Iowa. It's too late to get votes there now. You don't need to win that state anyway. You need to focus on New Hampshire. My guys have everything set up. You just need to smile and read the teleprompter."

"My numbers are way down in New Hampshire. A smile and some scripted speech isn't going to get me where I need to be. I told them that at the meeting last night."

"Let us worry about getting you there. The convention is still months away. We have plenty of time to make you the nominee. The public hated Sinclair in the beginning and he ended up the frontrunner."

"Sure, but he had—"

"Stop comparing yourself to other candidates. Just do as we say and you'll have nothing to worry about. We've got this thing locked away. You're the one, Kent. You're the next President of the United States."

I haven't moved from my spot in the hallway. I hear footsteps on the tile floor in the foyer and glance down the stairwell to get a glimpse of the man Mr. Kensington is talking to. I've seen the guy on TV. He's one of the remaining six candidates trying to win the nomination for president. What is he doing here? Does Garret's dad know all of these guys? First Sinclair, and now this guy? Kent Gleason. That's his name. Mr. Kensington seems awfully sure this guy is going to win. Not just the nomination. But the presidency.

He opens the front door and four men in suits walk in. One man is holding a laptop.

"How did the video turn out?" Mr. Kensington asks him.

"Excellent. You'd think Kent was really there. You gotta love CGI. Makes things so much easier."

"Let's go in my office and you can show us." He leads the way and the men all follow him into the office.

I hurry down to the bathroom. When I come back out I see Garret walking down the hall. "There you are."

"Yeah, I'm coming," I say. "Did you start the movie?"

"No. Lilly insisted we wait for you."

We only get halfway through the movie when Mr. Kensington comes in. "If you two need to go, I can watch Lilly now."

"No, Daddy," Lilly says. "Don't make them leave." She's wedged between Garret and me on her tiny twin bed.

"I think we can stay." Garret looks at me for confirmation.

"We *have* to. We can't leave in the middle of the movie."

"You're welcome to stay for dinner as well." Mr. Kensington notices our hesitation. "Katherine won't be joining us."

"I do miss Charles' cooking," I say to Garret.

"Then I guess we're staying for dinner."

"Yay!" Lilly gets up and jumps on the bed, nearly knocking Garret and me off.

Mr. Kensington seems pleased as well. "I'll tell Charles. And Garret, I need to speak with you downstairs."

Garret gets up and follows him out. Lilly scoots up next to me and holds my hand. The poor girl is in serious need of some friends and a normal mother. It's odd how much that sounds like me at her age and yet my environment was so much different than hers. Rich or poor, I guess you can have the same problems.

When Garret and I leave later that night, Katherine still hasn't returned. The second we're in the car, I start quizzing him.

"What's the deal with Katherine? Did your dad tell you anything?"

"Yeah. They're separating." He almost seems sad about it.

"So she's moving out?"

"They haven't decided the living arrangements yet. She might still live in the house for Lilly's sake. It's a big enough house. They could live there together and not even see each other."

"Why aren't you happy about this? You hate Katherine."

"Because I feel bad for Lilly. I told her they weren't divorcing."

"Separating isn't divorcing."

"Yeah, but it's the first step."

"How's your dad handling this? Or did he ask for the separation?"

"I don't know who asked for it. The way the two of them fight all the time they probably should divorce, but it's going to be hard on Lilly."

"So is that all your dad said?"

"Yeah. Why?"

"Well, when I was on my way to the bathroom, I overheard your dad talking to Kent Gleason."

"The guy trying to win the nomination?"

"Yeah. We just saw him on TV. He was in Des Moines last week while we were there. Is your dad friends with him?"

"Not that I know of. But my dad latches onto politicians all the time. He throws money at them, hoping they'll do stuff that benefits our company if they ever get into office."

"Your dad acted like the guy was actually going to win. He told him it was a done deal. That Gleason would be president."

Garret shrugs. "He's just boosting the guy's ego. That's all."

"So you don't think it's odd that he was involved with Sinclair and now Gleason?"

"No. He does this every four years with presidential candidates. Now that Sinclair's gone, he had to find someone else to throw money at. He must think Gleason has the best chance of winning."

"Have any of the guys your dad gave money to actually become president?"

"Yeah. Most of them. My dad seems to be able to pick the winners."

"Are you saying you've met the President?"

"Several of them. Last summer when I was interning in DC, I had dinner at the White House. My dad and grandfather were there, too." Garret says it like it's no big deal.

"And the President was there?"

He presses the buttons on the dashboard that control the heat. "Well, yeah, along with some other people. The senator I worked for arranged it. All his interns were invited and then we each got to bring two family members."

"And you never thought to mention this to me?"

"You said you're not interested in politics." Now he's messing with the vents. "Are you warm enough? This air doesn't seem very warm."

"It's the freaking President! I'm interested in knowing that my boyfriend had dinner with the President!"

He gives up with the vents and turns the heat on high. "The dinner wasn't that great. You sit there and listen to a boring, old, rich guy with way too much power talk about himself."

"He's the President of the United States. You're not impressed by that?"

"When I was younger I was. But then I learned about all the bribes and backroom deals and I lost faith in the whole system. It's a joke. I don't have any respect for those guys. And you shouldn't either after finding out about Sinclair. That guy could've been president, Jade. And he was crazy."

"He never would've been president. He wouldn't have even gotten the nomination."

"He was ahead in the polls. It could've happened."

"I can't believe you met a president. Or more than one." I turn the heat down because now it's starting to get too hot.

"Hey." Garret nudges my arm. "Are you staying over tonight?"

"I always stay over on Saturday."

"Okay. Just making sure you didn't change the rules for a new semester."

And just like that he changes the subject. Like he has nothing else to say about meeting the President of the United

134

States. He starts talking about a movie that just came out, but all I can think about is him eating dinner at the White House. With the President!

Back on campus, it's total chaos. It's like everyone arrived in the brief time we were gone. Cars are double parked in front of the dorms. Music is blaring from stereos. Drunk people are stumbling down the sidewalk.

"Kensington!" We get out of the car and see Garret's friend Decker approaching us. "Hey, Jade. When did you guys get back?"

"Earlier today. How about you?"

"This morning." He removes a silver flask from his coat and takes a swig of whatever hard liquor it contains. He sees me watching him. "Sorry, Jade. I forgot about the no-alcohol thing."

"It's fine." I don't really care if he drinks around me. It's a college campus. Everyone's drinking around me.

He puts the flask back in his jacket. "There's a party down on Maple Street if you guys are interested."

"Not tonight," Garret says. "You go ahead."

"Okay, see you later." He starts to walk away, then stops. "Oh, and just so you know. Blake hasn't left for California yet so you might see him around. Anyway, welcome back."

My stomach knots just hearing Blake's name. I'd put the attempted rape incident out of my mind ever since Frank got sick. I was trying to forget it.

Our luggage is still in the trunk, so Garret grabs the bags and we go to my room.

"Why is that asshole still in town?" Garret sets my suitcase by the closet. "He should be gone by now."

"Garret, relax. I'm not worried about Blake." It's not entirely true. I *am* worried, but I don't want to admit it.

"Do you still have the taser and the pepper spray I gave you?"

"Yes. But Blake's not going to come after me." I go over to my drawer and grab some pajamas. "Let's go upstairs and start our sleepover."

He smiles as he pulls me against him. "What's with the pajamas? You planning on actually sleeping at this sleepover?"

I smile back. "For part of the time."

"I think we should institute a pajama-free option this semester."

"I could go for that. But given how cold your room was earlier, I'm taking the pajamas."

He leans down and gives me a slow, sexy kiss. "You won't be cold when I'm finished with you."

"I'm already feeling a little warm."

He kisses my neck just under my ear. "Warm's not good enough. I wanna make you hot. Now let's go upstairs."

I don't tell him, but he's totally making me hot—so hot I could do him right here and now, but we somehow make it up to his room.

Later that night as Garret sleeps next to me, I think back to last semester and how I felt when I arrived at Moorhurst. The Saturday before classes began was the first day that Garret and I spent together. I was so mean to him. I never thought I'd date him, so I didn't see a reason to be nice to him. Now I'm in love with the guy, who of course took it upon himself to try the pajama-free option tonight and sleep naked.

I decide to give it a try myself. I slip my t-shirt off and scoot back into his chest until I feel his warm skin pressed against mine. I gently lift his arm up and place it around me. He wakes up briefly and kisses my shoulder as he notices me there, then falls asleep again.

I love our sleepovers.

I can already tell. This is going to be a great semester.

CHAPTER FOURTEEN

Harper gets back to campus late Sunday night. We've been calling each other over the break, but not as much as we said we would. I haven't talked to her for a week now.

Classes don't start until Tuesday so we agreed to spend Monday morning together before she devotes the rest of her day to "catching up" with Sean, which I'm sure is code for having as much sex as possible. They haven't seen each other for almost four weeks.

"Tell me everything, Jade. What's been going on since I saw you last?"

We're sitting in her room with the coffees she insisted we drive to town to get.

"There's not much to tell. I already told you what I did when I was in Des Moines. And I told you about going to New York." I take a moment to sort through what things I can tell her and what I can't. I can't tell her anything about Garret's family. I might let one of their many secrets slip out.

"Anything happen last week?" she asks.

"Garret's ex-girlfriend tried to get back together with him."

Her eyes bug out. "And it took you this long to tell me? I need details, Jade."

138

I recap the story for her. "I don't think Sadie will be calling him again anytime soon."

"Did Garret really tell her you two might get married someday?"

"Yeah, but I'm sure he was kidding. He just said it to get rid of her. And it worked." I take a sip of my coffee. "Oh, and Garret and I decided to get an apartment together this summer."

She almost spills her coffee. "What? That's major news! Why didn't you call and tell me?"

"We just decided it the other day. We're going to rent a place on a beach in California. I was thinking we could come see you once or twice."

"Once or twice? If you're gonna live in California this summer I want to see you guys all the time. This is crazy. I can't believe you two are doing this. I mean, it makes sense that Garret would. He's totally in love with you. But I can't believe you'd agree to live with him. You always act like you're afraid to get serious with him."

"No, I don't."

"Whatever. It doesn't matter. So where in California?"

"Garret thinks we should go somewhere north of LA. He's going to ask his dad's real estate agent to help us find a place."

She picks up her phone and starts tapping on the screen. "Tell him not to. I know people who could get you a better place and a better deal, not that Garret cares about the price."

"We need a good deal because I'm paying for half the rent. I need to find a job out there. I was thinking of waitressing."

She puts her phone down and looks at me funny. "Waitressing won't get you enough money to afford a place on the beach. Not even enough to pay for half of the rent."

"How much are these places?"

"Depends on where you go and how big of a place you want. Like a one or two bedroom beachfront condo could be anywhere from $2000-$6000 a week. More if it's new or really nice. I'd plan for around $4000."

"A week? So $16,000 a month?"

"Yeah. That's about average."

"I didn't know they cost that much! That's completely insane. Who has that kind of money?"

"Most people just rent them out for a week, not the whole summer. But you could probably get the price down since you're staying for the summer."

Suddenly all my excitement about the summer is gone. I knew a place on the beach would be expensive but not *that* much. Why didn't Garret tell me this? Because he knew I wouldn't go. That's why.

"Are places that much on the East Coast, too?" I ask her.

"Some are more than that. Garret would know. He said his family rented a house on Martha's Vineyard last summer. Ask him how much that cost. I'm sure it was a fortune. What do you care? His family is loaded. A few thousand dollars a week is nothing to them."

"I don't want Garret paying for everything. I wanted to at least pay for half of the rent. But there's no way I can afford that."

"Jade, just let him pay for it. You guys are gonna have so much fun. I should try to talk Sean into living in California this summer. He keeps telling me he wants to learn to surf."

Harper spends the next hour telling me everything she did over break. Then she tells me what's new with her family. Her dad's a Hollywood director and just started work on a comic book superhero movie. Her sister, Kylie, is an actress and Harper's mom is now managing Kylie's acting career. Kylie got a side role in a teen vampire movie which is supposed to be huge. According to Harper, Kylie has been hanging out with the lead actress in the film and now has paparazzi following her around everywhere. Harper's other sister is a model and travels all the time for photo shoots, but she was home over the holiday.

"Jade, here." Harper tosses me a small wrapped box she took out of her suitcase, which is still unpacked and sitting on the floor.

"What's this?"

"A Christmas gift. I saw it and thought it would be so cute on you."

"Harper, we said we weren't exchanging gifts. I didn't get you anything."

"Just open it." She stands there waiting for me.

I unwrap the box to find a denim mini skirt. I usually don't wear skirts. In fact I don't even own one. But if I were to buy a skirt, this is the one I'd buy. The denim has that worn look and the back pockets are frayed a little. I recognize the designer label. A pair of jeans from that designer is easily $300, so I know the skirt cost a lot.

"Thanks, Harper. This is exactly my style."

"It's from the spring collection." Harper's totally into fashion. Whenever she talks about clothes or shoes her eyes light up and she gets this eager tone to her voice. "I've never seen you wear a skirt, but when I saw this I thought it would be perfect for you."

I hold it up. At least it's not too short. Harper tends to wear really short skirts.

"I got you some other stuff, too." She starts pulling more clothes from her suitcase. "And don't say I spent too much because I didn't buy any of this. It was all sent to my sister by companies that want her to wear it. It's like free advertising. If the paparazzi get photos of her, these designers want her wearing their clothes. Anyway, this stuff was too big on her and too small for me. But I think it might fit you."

She hands me a slightly longer, fuller skirt made from a thin, almost sheer fabric. "How small is your sister?" I ask, holding it up.

"She's tiny. Like 90 pounds tiny. Anyway, that skirt would be great with a tank top and some sandals." She hands me a stack of t-shirts. "You can toss these if you don't want them. My sister gets way too many t-shirts. She already gave a ton away but I saved these for you."

"You're giving me all of these?" I flip through the stack, noticing all the colors. Harper knows I only wear black or white shirts, so I'm guessing this is her attempt to get me to wear different colors. And maybe I will. Garret always says he's tired of seeing me in black or white. I'm kind of sick of it myself.

"And these, too." She hands me a couple sundresses. "These will be perfect for your summer in California. If I'd known you were doing that, I would've got you some bikinis." She gets her phone out. "I'll text my sister and have her save some for you."

I don't bother stopping her. She's getting me those bikinis whether I want them or not, and it *would* be good to have some for the summer.

"I need to get over to Sean's. Do you need help taking this stuff to your room?"

"No, I can handle it. Thanks again for all this. It's like I've got a whole new wardrobe."

"Free stuff is one of perks of having a celebrity in the family."

Back in my room, I start trying stuff on. It's fun getting new clothes. Growing up, I never had any. All my clothes came from the thrift store.

I try on the denim skirt first along with a red fitted t-shirt.

"Jade, are you in there?" Garret knocks on the door.

"Yeah. Come in." I adjust my skirt as he walks in the room. "Hey. You want to go have lunch or something?"

His eyes drift over my body as he closes the door. "Or something sounds good. Where did you get the new clothes?"

"Harper's sister was getting rid of them. But the skirt was a Christmas gift from Harper. Do you like it?" I spin around.

"Do I like it? Are you kidding? I love it." He leads me to the bed, sits down, and places me on his lap. "Skirts are freaking awesome." He runs his hand up and down my bare legs.

I laugh. "I didn't know you liked them so much. She got me another one. Do you want to see it?"

I start to get up but he holds me down and kisses me as his hand continues up my leg under the skirt and straight to my panties. Now I get why he likes skirts.

"Garret, don't you want to see my other skirt?"

"Surprise me with it next time. I'm liking this one right now."

He kisses me again as he lays me down on the bed. His hand brushes my thigh as it heads right back under the skirt.

"Damn, Jade," he says, his breathing heavy. "I can't believe you never wore one of these for me before."

From the way he's reacting, I think he might like this skirt thing as much as I like doing it in the shower. Who knew a simple skirt could have such an effect on him? It makes me wonder what else he likes.

After we're done with what Garret is now referring to as "skirt sex" I put my regular clothes back on.

"I'm definitely buying you more skirts," he says as he watches me put away my new clothes. "Be sure to thank Harper for me."

"She got me some sundresses, too." I take one out and show it to him. It's short and has tiny straps at the top.

Garret's smiling. "You should let Harper pick out all your clothes."

I hang the dress back in the closet. "She's having her sister send me some bikinis for the summer. I don't think I've ever worn a bikini."

"When you get them, I expect a fashion show."

"Hey, did you call that real estate agent yet?" I go and sit next to him on the bed.

"No, but I got the number from my dad. He actually thought it was a good idea that we live together this summer. He didn't even care that we're going to California. Can you believe that? I was expecting a lecture when I told him."

"About that. I think we should pick somewhere else to go. Do you know how much beach rentals cost?"

"Yeah. My family rents a place on the beach every summer."

"Harper said summer rentals in California are like $4000 a week. That's way too much. I can't make enough money to pay for that."

"You're not backing out on this, Jade. We both want to do this and I'm not letting your stubbornness prevent us from going."

"But it costs a fortune. And that doesn't even count food and—"

He kisses me while I'm still talking and keeps kissing me until I stop.

"We're done talking about money. We're going to California this summer and we're getting a place right on the beach. And we're getting a good place, not a cheap, run-down place."

"Yeah, but—"

"Jade, I don't want to hear it. You don't get many opportunities like this. Once we graduate and get jobs we won't be able to do stuff like this anymore. Now is the time to just have fun and not worry about shit. We're going. And I don't want to hear one more word about how much it costs, now or when we're there. I have it covered. Rent, food, and anything else we need."

"You know I can't just go there and not pay for anything."

"Why not? I swear, I don't understand you and this money thing. Just let it go."

"I can't. I still feel like I owe you when you keep buying me things. Like I have this huge mountain of debt to pay back."

"You don't owe me anything. Stop thinking that. And stop saying it."

"What if we broke up? Then I'd owe you."

"We're back to this now? Dammit, Jade. I thought you were done with this breakup shit."

He's mad because I spent all of last semester telling him I was sure we'd break up. We'd had several fights about it.

"I'm not planning on us breaking up, but that doesn't mean it won't happen. And if it does, I'll have to spend the rest of my life paying you back. I already owe you a ton of money for those plane tickets."

He takes a deep breath and lets it out. "Okay. This is the last time we're talking about this. Just so you're clear. If we break up, you will not owe me anything. You will not owe my family anything. You can leave free and clear with no debt. Do you need that in writing? Because I can have something official drawn up by my dad's lawyer."

I smile. "No. I believe you."

"So you promise you won't bring up the money issue ever again? And you'll let me pay for stuff?"

"I can't promise you that."

"Then I'll withhold sex until you do."

The comment along with the stern look on his face makes me laugh.

"I'm serious, Jade."

"There's no way in hell you wouldn't have sex with me. All I have to do is put on a skirt."

He thinks about it. "Nope. I could resist you. That's how tired I am of this money discussion. I just want it to end."

I consider testing him and seeing if he actually *would* hold out on me. But I really don't want that. And I did secretly make a New Year's resolution to stop worrying so much about money.

"Okay. I promise."

"Wow, that was easy." He kisses me, then stays close to my lips. "Guess you're not willing to give up sex. I must be good."

"You're okay," I say, taking his ego down a notch. "I was really just trying to avoid arguing about it. That's all."

His cocky grin appears. "Yeah, I'm sure that was the reason."

"Whatever."

He backs away. "I don't think you can do it."

"Do what?"

"I don't think you can go even a day without talking about how much stuff costs or complaining about how much I'm spending. I think there needs to be consequences for you breaking your promise. Otherwise, you'll just keep breaking it."

I cross my arms across my chest. "Consequences? Like what?"

He takes a moment to consider it. "Like if you talk about money, you have to wear a skirt. Or some lingerie. Or you have to strip for me like you did in New York."

I relax my arms. "I'd do those things for you anyway. That's not a punishment. But if you want to say it is, then fine. I'll agree to that."

"Then we've got a deal." He throws his hands in the air. "Finally. No more talk about money."

I hug him. "I love you, Garret."

"Really? I thought after that you'd be mad at me."

"Nope. You piss me off with the money thing, but I still love you."

"Ha! You brought it up again. You owe me a striptease. My room. Tonight."

"But it was just a comment, not a complaint!"

"I heard the word 'money.' Enough said."

I sigh. "Okay. Your room. Tonight. Did I tell you I'm not very good with keeping promises?"

"Yeah." He smiles. "That's why I made the consequences. I have a feeling you'll be stripping a lot for me now."

CHAPTER FIFTEEN

Tuesday morning, the first day of class, I wake up in Garret's room to bright sunshine seeping through the curtains. I check the clock. 7:40. Shit! I have class at 8.

"Garret, get up." I shove the covers off us and climb out of bed.

"What time is it?" he asks, still groggy.

"I overslept. I have class in 20 minutes. I gotta go. I'll see you later." I throw my sweatshirt on over my pajamas, then yank my shoe on but lose my balance and fall back on the bed.

Garret leans up to kiss me. "See you at lunch?"

"Not on Tuesdays and Thursdays, remember? You have class at noon and I have chem lab at 1."

I hurry downstairs to my room and quickly change into jeans and a long sleeve t-shirt. I haven't even packed my backpack for class. I'm so unprepared this semester—a side effect of spending all my time with Garret. Last semester, I was early to my first class and my backpack was neatly organized. Today I'm a total disaster. I'm not even clean. I probably smell like sex.

I need to get focused again. This semester I'm trying to get serious and figure out what I want to major in. I'm considering biology, even though last semester's biology class wasn't my favorite. But that's because my idiot lab partner stuck me with all the work.

I'm still thinking of going to med school, but I haven't told anyone this yet and I don't plan to until I decide for sure. To help make that decision, I'm taking the classes my advisor said are typical of pre-med students; chemistry, physics, and microbiology. Those three classes will be tough, so I added some easier electives; sociology and European history. It's a full schedule that will keep me buried in homework.

When I arrive at the science building at 8:05, my chem class has already started. Moorhurst is a small college so the classes never have more than 30 people. From my quick count, this one has about 25. Everyone turns and stares at me as I walk in. Luckily the professor is writing something on the board and doesn't notice.

There's an open seat in the last row so I quickly take it, quietly setting my backpack on the floor. Some guy I've never seen before is sitting next to me. I thought I knew everyone at this school, but this guy doesn't even look familiar.

The professor picks up a thin booklet from his desk and holds it up. "Before we begin, open your lab books to page 10."

I search my backpack for the lab book. It's not in there. Of course, because I'm not prepared! That's it. As soon I get back to my room, I'm getting organized.

"Do you want to share?" The guy I don't recognize holds his lab book out opened to page 10.

"Sure. Thanks." I scoot my desk closer to his.

"No problem." He smiles before returning his eyes to the book.

I glance at him quick. He's really cute, bordering on hot. His wavy, dark brown hair matches his intensely deep brown eyes and I noticed a dimple in his cheek when he smiled.

He must be new. If this guy was here last semester, I definitely would've remembered him.

"The lab experiment you'll be doing later today is listed on page 10," the professor says. "Review the instructions before you get to lab and make sure you get there early to pick up your supplies, which are listed on page 12. And if you don't have a partner yet, find one before you arrive." He returns to the board and starts writing again.

Partner? Who already has a partner? Class just started. I see the people in front of me whispering to each other. So we're picking partners right now? Shit! Now I'm going to be paired up with whoever's left. I'm going to get another loser like I had in biology lab.

"Do you have a partner?" new guy asks, leaning over so close I can smell the minty gum he's chewing.

I back away slightly. "No. I don't."

He's clearly hinting he wants to be partners, but I don't even know this guy. What if we don't get along? I don't want to be stuck with him all semester. I scan the room. Everyone is facing forward again as if they all now have partners.

"Would you mind being my partner?" new guy asks. "I promise I'll always do my share of the work." He smiles again, showing off his perfect white teeth and that seriously cute dimple.

"That already makes you better than my last lab partner, so, yeah, we can be partners."

"I'm Carson, by the way." He holds his hand out.

"I'm Jade." I shake his hand, which is very large. He's a big guy. Wide shoulders and chest. Muscular forearms. He definitely works out.

The professor is speaking again. "Now turn to page 8 in your textbooks and we'll begin."

After class, Carson follows me into the hallway. "Do you want me to get the lab supplies?"

"Sure, if you don't mind. And I'll definitely be on time for lab. I'm usually not late to class like that. In fact, that's probably the first time I've ever been late to class. I'm usually early."

"Me too. Except today I got there way too early. I wanted to make sure I went to the right room. I'm new here, in case you didn't know that already."

"Did you transfer from somewhere?"

"Um, no. I had some family issues last fall, so I couldn't start until this semester."

He seems uncomfortable, so I don't ask him about the "family issues." I skip to the basic questions that I'm sure he's already been asked a hundred times.

"Are you from Connecticut?"

"No. Illinois."

I smile. "A Midwest boy, huh? Finally. Someone else from the middle of the country. I used to be the only one here."

"You're from the Midwest?"

"Des Moines, Iowa."

"Oh yeah? My grandma lives in Des Moines. We go there all the time to visit her."

"How did you end up at Moorhurst?"

"My dad found this college a few years back when he was out here for a conference. He liked the area and did some research on the school and suggested I check it out. We came for a visit and I liked it. But now that I'm here I'm feeling a little out of place. So nobody else at this school is from the Midwest?"

"Just me. Everyone else is from the coasts, mostly the East Coast."

"Then it's a good thing we met." He flashes the dimple again. "So far I haven't found the people here to be very friendly."

"They're kind of cliquey, especially the ones from Connecticut. Some of them went to the same high school. Oh, and you should know that these people have no idea what's in the middle of the country. If you tell them where you're from, they'll look at you all confused. I've told people a million times I'm from Iowa and half of them still think I'm from Ohio."

He laughs. "That explains it. I was telling some people in my dorm that I'm from Illinois and they keep asking me if I liked growing up in Indiana."

"See? And it's no use trying to correct them. I tried and they still think I'm from Ohio." I hoist my backpack onto my shoulder. "Well, I should get going. I'll see you at lab."

He follows me out of the building and walks with me across the open quad. "Hey, um, I don't mean to bother you, but do you think we could maybe have lunch and you could tell me more insider secrets about the school?"

I stop walking and turn to face him. Wow. He's really good looking. And he's tall. Maybe 6'4 or 6'5? He seems desperate for someone to be friendly to him. I'm usually not very friendly, but I know how much it sucks to not know anyone and I feel like I should be nice to the only other Midwesterner on campus.

"I could do lunch. Are you free at noon?"

"Yeah, but I was gonna get the lab supplies at 12:30. Could we meet earlier than that?"

"Let's say 11:30. Which dorm are you in?"

"That one over there." He points to the one next to mine.

"Okay, I'll meet you in your dining hall at 11:30."

"Great. See you then."

When I get back to my room I realize that I just agreed to have lunch with a really cute guy who isn't Garret. Is that bad? It shouldn't be, so why do I feel guilty? And why did I purposely arrange to eat at Carson's dorm and not mine? It's not like the girls from my floor would see me with Carson and assume I'm interested in the guy, would they? That's ridiculous. It's just lunch. Am I not supposed to eat a meal with a guy ever again? That doesn't seem right.

At 11:30 Carson is waiting for me at the entrance to the dining hall. As we get into line, I feel like everyone is staring at us, gossiping about how I'm cheating on Garret. But I'm not cheating. I'm just having lunch. And nobody is staring. It's just my guilty conscience telling me they are.

We take a seat at a table in the corner. I'm starving because I never ate breakfast.

"You must really like fries," Carson says, noticing my plate.

Despite my resolution to eat better, I still haven't done it. Today's lunch is a plate of waffle fries, a dish of chocolate ice cream, and a soda.

"Everyone likes fries." I reach across the table for the ketchup. "And why are you picking on me? You have a pile of fries, too."

"Yeah, but I also have a chicken sandwich."

"So what questions do you have?" I ask as I tap the ketchup bottle on my plate.

Carson quizzes me about some of the professors and what to expect in terms of homework and tests. Then we talk briefly about the social scene and I explain how everyone goes to parties off campus on Friday and Saturday nights and how it's a social sin to have a party in your dorm room.

"Do you know if there are any trails around here?" he asks. "I like to run, but I don't like running on a track."

"Same here. But I don't feel safe on the trails by myself, especially at night, so I usually end up on the track. Anyway, to answer your question, there's a trail that starts in the woods behind the science building."

"How far do you run?"

"Nine or 10 miles. Sometimes less if I'm in a hurry."

"I usually go 8 or 9. We should run together sometime."

"Yeah, maybe." Guilt is creeping into my conscience again. What am I doing with this guy? First lunch. Now plans to go running? I haven't even mentioned Garret's name yet. I didn't even tell Carson I had a boyfriend. No wonder he keeps asking me to do stuff with him. Just as I'm about to bring up Garret, Carson starts talking again.

"So what's your major?"

"I don't have one. I'm undecided. What's yours?"

"Biology. I'm planning to go to med school."

"What kind of doctor do you want to be?" I take a big bite of my ice cream.

"I want to be an oncologist."

I cringe as the ice cream causes a moment of brain freeze. When I recover, I say, "So you want to be a cancer doctor. Any reason why?"

"Yeah, because um . . ." Carson sets down the french fries he was holding and wipes his hands together, shaking the salt off. "My sister had cancer."

I'm confused by his use of the past tense. She either beat cancer or is dead. I'm too afraid to ask.

He moves his tray to the side and leans forward, resting his forearms on the table. "I don't like to talk about it, but since I already brought it up I'll tell you. My sister died of cancer last month. She was 16."

So that explains the past tense.

154

"Oh. I'm sorry. That's awful."

"Yeah. She wasn't doing well last summer, so I didn't start school in the fall because I wanted to spend time with her. She passed away the week before Christmas."

I never know what to say when people tell me sad things. I just sit there looking lost and feeling like an idiot.

"Anyway," he continues, "seeing her go through that made me want to be a doctor. Plus, my dad's a doctor and so was his dad, so it kind of runs in the family."

"I'm thinking of going to med school, too." I had no intention of that little secret spilling out, but I was so flustered from the dead sister story that I wasn't even thinking.

"Really? Do you know what you want to specialize in?"

"No. I haven't even decided for sure if I want to be a doctor. I'm just thinking about it."

Now I totally regret telling him that. I haven't even told Garret. I can't tell a stranger what I plan to do with my life when I haven't even told Garret.

"Well, if you ever want to talk to a doctor about med school or different types of medicine, you could talk to my dad. He has a private practice and also teaches a class at a university."

"Yeah, okay, I'll let you know."

"I should probably head over to the lab." Carson gets up from the table. "Are you busy now or do you want to come with me and help get the supplies?"

"I might as well go with you, but I have to stop at my room quick and get my lab book."

Carson follows me back to my room. Some girls on my floor see us together, but they don't give me any strange looks, so maybe I'm making too big a deal out of this. I can hang out with a guy friend. Why not? Other girls do.

The girls walking past us are really checking Carson out. The way he looks, he'll have a girlfriend by the weekend.

"I'll just be a minute." I hurry into my room and start searching for my lab book.

"You don't have a TV?"

"What?" I look up and see Carson sitting on my bed. "Um, no. I don't watch much TV." I kneel down and sort through the stack of books on the floor by my desk. "I swear someone stole my lab book. I remember buying it, but now I can't find it."

"Hey, Jade. I got out of—" Garret walks through my half-open door, but stops when he sees the hot new guy sitting on my bed.

Damn! This is not at all how I pictured my first day of the new semester.

CHAPTER SIXTEEN

"Looks like you have company," Garret says to me.

I give up trying to find my lab book and go stand next to Garret. "This is Carson. He's new here. Carson, this is Garret."

"Hi." Carson gets up and holds his hand out. He's taller than Garret, but only by an inch or so.

"Hi." Garret looks at him suspiciously. "I'm Jade's boyfriend." He shakes Carson's hand, then puts his arm around me.

Carson keeps his eyes on Garret. "Jade didn't mention she had a boyfriend."

What the hell did he say *that* for?

"She didn't, huh?" Now Garret's looking at *me* suspiciously.

I try to explain. "Carson had all these questions about Moorhurst, so we were just talking about school stuff."

This is so awkward. I hope I'm not blushing. I feel like I am. Either that or this room is getting really, really hot.

"Did you two just meet?" Garret asks.

"Jade's my partner for chem lab," Carson answers. "We met at class this morning and then she was nice enough to have lunch with me."

"Yeah, Jade's friendly like that," he says, knowing it's a lie.

Garret looks at me again and I scramble to find some words to fill the awkward silence. "Carson's from Illinois. His grandmother lives in Des Moines."

Carson smiles and the dimple appears. "Small world, right?"

Garret doesn't smile back. "I guess it is."

"Why are you back from class so early?" After I ask Garret the question, I realize it sounds like I was hoping he wouldn't be home. Like I was hoping to hide Carson from him.

"The professor gave us the syllabus and assigned some reading, then let us go."

"I need an easy class like that," Carson says. "What's your major?"

"Business," Garret replies, annoyed. "It's a finance class. I'm sure it won't be easy. What's your major?"

"Carson and I really need to go." I break free from Garret's arm and grab my backpack. "We have lab at 1 and we have to get our supplies."

"I guess I'll see you later," Carson says to Garret. He follows me to the door, then looks back at Garret. "Oh, and biology. That's my major. I'm pre-med. Just like Jade."

I freeze, my heart stopping along with the rest of me. Garret's asked me numerous times what I want to do for a career and I always tell him I don't know. And now Carson's telling him. Shit! This is bad.

"Jade?" I turn back to see a confused and somewhat hurt look on Garret's face.

"We'll talk later." I kiss him quick, then pull him into the hall so I can lock my door.

I can't concentrate at all during chem lab. Carson is likely regretting picking me as a partner. I already screwed up the first experiment.

"I'm sorry, Carson. I didn't sleep much last night. I promise I'll be a better lab partner next time."

"Don't worry about it." He places his hand on my back. It's completely innocent, but it still feels wrong. "Not every experiment turns out."

The lab is almost over, so I start gathering my things. "I guess I'll see you Thursday."

"Are you taking physics?"

"Yeah, why?"

"Wednesdays at 3? With Professor Bryce?"

I nod. "So I'll guess I'll see you tomorrow then."

It makes sense we would have similar classes if he's pre-med and I'm considering it, but I hadn't thought about that until he mentioned it. At this rate, I'll see him more than I see Garret.

"Can I get your phone number?" Carson calls after me as I'm leaving.

My phone number? He just met my boyfriend. Why is he asking for my phone number?

I turn back and see him holding his phone. "We should exchange numbers in case one of us has to miss lab or needs help with the homework."

I give him my number, then race off to European history, my next and last class of the day. Afterward I go back to my dorm and collapse on my bed, wondering how to handle the Garret situation. It's 4 and Garret should be back from class by now. He hasn't texted or called me since I saw him last. I decide to go up to his room and talk to him.

It takes him forever to answer the door. He finally does, but he's on the phone. He motions me to come inside.

"Yeah, Thursday at 3. Got it." He hangs up. "Physical therapy appointment," he says, dropping the phone on his desk.

"Garret, you don't have to explain every phone call you get. I'm over the thing with Sadie. I'm not monitoring your calls. And you don't have to report back to me every time you talk to someone."

"Are you sure you're not saying that for your own benefit?"

"What's that supposed to mean?"

"Seems like you didn't want to tell me about that guy you met today."

"Carson? I just met him this morning. If you hadn't stopped by earlier I would've told you about him now or at dinner tonight."

"So whose idea was it to have lunch? Yours or his?"

"His. He wanted to ask me stuff about Moorhurst. That's it." I go up and give Garret a hug, but he doesn't hug me back. Not a good sign. I pull away. "Why are you mad at me? I just had lunch with the guy."

"I wouldn't be mad if you'd told him you had a boyfriend. But according to Carson, you didn't even mention it. Why is that, Jade? Did it just slip your mind?"

"It wasn't relevant to the conversation. We talked about school, not our relationships. I didn't talk about you and he didn't talk about his girlfriend."

"Because he doesn't have a girlfriend. If he did, he wouldn't be trying to date mine."

"He's not trying to date me."

Garret shakes his head. "A guy doesn't ask you to lunch and then follow you back to your room if he's not interested in dating you."

"It's not like that. He's just looking for a friend. And I could use more friends."

"That guy is *not* going to be your friend."

160

His forceful tone pisses me off. "You can't tell me who to be friends with. I'll be friends with him if I want."

"Really? Because if that's how this works, then I'll go back to being friends with Sadie. How would you feel about that, Jade?"

"Yeah, like that's comparable. Sadie made it clear she wants to date you. Carson has shown no interest in dating me. Besides, the girls on my floor couldn't take their eyes off him. If he doesn't already have a girlfriend, I'm sure he'll have one by the end of the week. I'm telling you, he only sees me as a friend. And we have a lot in common, so I'd like to be friends with him. I'd like the three of us to be friends."

"I don't think that'll be happening." Garret crosses his arms over his chest. "What exactly do you have in common with this guy anyway?"

"Well, he's from the Midwest, which you already know. And he likes to run. He does 10-mile runs like me. He was asking me about the trails around here and wanted to know if I'd go on a—" I stop.

"On a what? On a run? He invited you to go running with him?" Garret rolls his eyes and laughs to himself.

"What? It's just a run."

"You're considering this? You're kidding me, right?"

"You know I don't feel safe running on the trails by myself and you'll never run that far with me. So now I'll have a running partner."

"Jade. He's asking you out. The running thing? It's a date."

"It is not. You get all sweaty and gross when you run. That's not a date."

"How did we meet?"

"You know how we met. You helped me unpack the car when I got here."

"That doesn't count. What happened the next day?"

"You met me out on the track and we raced. But you didn't plan that."

"No, but when I found out you liked to run, I kept asking you to go running with me. I hate running, especially at your insane pace. I only did it so I could spend time with you. It was the first step in getting you to go out on a date with me."

"Okay, but that was you. Not Carson."

"That's a trick *all* guys use. Find something the girl likes to do, then casually offer to join her in that activity, and go from there. It's a classic first move. And it has a much higher success rate than taking a girl out to dinner and a movie. You're on her turf so she feels comfortable. You're showing interest in something she likes."

"If Carson goes on 10-mile runs, then he obviously already likes running. He's not pretending to just to date me."

"Then why does he want you to run with him? He doesn't need a running partner. You always say running is a solitary sport. And we know he's not using you to feel safe when he's on the trails."

"Okay, fine. Maybe there's a tiny chance he's interested in me. But he's not now that he knows about you."

"Did he act different after he met me?"

"No. He just acted normal."

"Normal as in he kept asking you out? So he just ignored the fact that you have a boyfriend."

"He didn't ask me out." I slip my arm around Garret's and tug on him until he sits down with me. "Are you seriously jealous of this guy? A guy I don't even know?"

He takes his arm back. "You know him well enough to tell him your major, which apparently you've decided is something I don't need to know."

"I'm sorry about that. It just came out because he told me something and I didn't know what to say."

"What did he tell you?"

"He said he wants to be a cancer doctor so he can help people like his sister. His sister died of cancer last month. She was 16. That's why he didn't start college until now. And you know I never know what to say when people tell me sad things. So I just blurted it out."

"You just blurted out that you want to be a doctor? This just occurred to you at lunch?"

"No. I've been thinking about it for a while. I just haven't made a decision yet. But I'm taking some of the courses I would need if I decide to go to med school."

"Why haven't you ever told me this?"

"Because I wasn't sure that's what I wanted to do."

"It doesn't matter. You still could've told me. You know how shitty I felt today when some guy I just met knows more about my girlfriend than I do?"

"He doesn't know anything about me. And I didn't mean to tell him about the pre-med thing, but I can't take it back, so can we just move past this?" I sneak my arm back around his. "You know I love you, Garret. I'm not interested in Carson. I'm only interested in you."

"It's not that I don't trust you. I just don't trust other guys. As a guy, I know how we think. And I don't want you hanging out with Carson outside of class."

"We'll have to get together for the homework at least a few times."

"I get that, but I don't want you doing other stuff with him."

"Then *you* can't be friends with other girls."

"I stopped being friends with girls the day we met. Because they weren't friends. They were girls I was trying to sleep with."

"Garret!"

"I'm just saying. That's how guys think. It may not be right, but that's how it is. If you don't believe me go ask any guy on my floor."

"Let's not talk about Carson anymore. In fact, I don't feel like talking at all right now." I turn Garret's face to mine and kiss him. "I missed you today."

"Oh yeah?" He kicks his shoes off and scoots back on the bed. "Just exactly how much did you miss me?"

"Let me show you how much." I climb on top of him, straddling him as I take my t-shirt off.

He cups the sides of my face with his hands and brings my mouth to his, skipping the gentle kiss he usually starts with and kissing me in a way he's never done before. The kiss is aggressive, powerful, possessive. It's as if the idea that some other guy wants me has changed the dynamic between us.

He wastes no time undressing the rest of me and then himself. He flips me on my back and in an instant we're together. But it's different. Good different. It's fast and urgent. His hand grabs hold of my hip, keeping me firmly in place as he moves in and out. His other hand tangles in my hair and lifts my head, crashing his lips to mine. I reach around and dig my fingers in the taut muscles of his back. He seems to like that because he gets an even firmer hold on me and speeds his movement, his hips driving, determined. My body explodes with pleasure before I'm even ready for it and continues on this feel-good high as Garret does one last thrust before his body collapses on mine. He lifts his head to kiss me, then rolls off me onto his back.

We take a moment to catch our breath. And *I* take a moment to replay what just happened. Because, wow. It's not like I don't like his usual mix of slow, sweet foreplay mixed with a hot, fast ending, but this all-fast, all-urgent version was really hot. Steamy hot. Molten lava hot.

"Let's go out to dinner," Garret says. "I'm craving a steak. A good steak."

"Did you work up an appetite just now?" I turn on my side and give him a kiss on the cheek.

"I must have, because I'm starving." He's also sweating. We both are. We look like we just got back from the gym.

"You know I hate giving you compliments, but I think you're getting even better at that. Have you been taking classes or something?"

He laughs. "Yeah, Jade. I've been taking sex classes every Monday and Wednesday morning. It was supposed to be a secret, but now you know."

"I'm just saying, it was good."

"Thanks." He turns on his side, facing me. "Now can we go eat?"

"We should shower first. Come downstairs in 10 minutes."

"Hey." He keeps hold of me as I start to get up. "I think it's really great that you're going to med school."

"I told you. I haven't decided for sure."

"I know. But I think it's a good idea. You'd make a great doctor." He leans over and kisses me. "I'd definitely go to you."

"Just so I'd touch you while you're naked."

"You already do that." He smiles, then his face gets serious again. "Jade, I want you to tell me this stuff. I don't know why you didn't, but it kind of worries me that you thought you couldn't tell me. I want to know what you want out of life. Your

165

dreams for the future. I want to help you make them come true. But I can't do that if you don't share them with me."

"That's why I didn't tell you. I don't want you helping me. I want to decide this for myself. I want to figure out how to make it happen by myself. That includes paying for it." I sigh. "I guess I'll have to wear a skirt now."

"You didn't say money, so maybe I'll let it slide." He pauses like he's thinking about it, then smiles. "Nope, I want the skirt."

I roll my eyes and laugh. "Yeah, I figured you would."

"Seriously, though." He sits up on his side. "If we're even considering taking this relationship beyond just dating, then you need to include me in big decisions like this."

"I'm not used to thinking that way. I'm used to making decisions on my own."

"They're still your decisions. I'll never tell you what to do, but I'd like to at least know what you're thinking. And I'll do the same. Because these decisions affect both of us. Maybe not right now, but they will in the future."

"Yeah, I know." As I say it, Garret's stomach growls really loud. I rub my hand over his abs. "As your future doctor, I think you're suffering from hunger. I think you need that steak."

He flips me on my back again and hovers over me. "This doctor thing is totally turning me on. Want to do a little role playing? I'll be your patient. You can do whatever you want to me."

"Maybe later. You need to eat." I push on him but he doesn't move.

"I'm not hungry anymore." He kisses me. "At least not for food."

"You're hungry. And you're sweaty. We both are. Let me up so I can shower."

He shifts to the side. "Fine. But I'm making an appointment with Dr. Taylor for later tonight."

"See? This is why I didn't tell you." I get up and put my shirt on. "Now you'll keep calling me a doctor when I haven't even decided if that's what I want to do."

He yanks me back on the bed. "I was just having fun."

"I know." I kiss him quick, then jump up and put my jeans on and hurry to the door.

"I'll meet you downstairs in 10," he says as I leave.

I laugh as I walk back to my room. Dr. Taylor. It sounds so important. And although I'm laughing at the sound of it, I actually think I really could be a doctor someday.

One of the few good things about my mom was that she never said I couldn't do something. Probably because she showed no interest in my life and didn't care what I wanted to do. But because of that, I didn't grow up thinking I wasn't smart enough or determined enough. Money was my biggest obstacle. It still is. If I go to med school I don't know how I'll pay for it, but I know I could get through it and be a doctor someday.

Dr. Taylor. It still sounds funny.

CHAPTER SEVENTEEN

Wednesday at physics class, Carson comes and sits down right next to me. I arrived early and Carson and I are the only two people there.

Thanks to Garret I now see Carson as less of a friend and more like a guy trying to sleep with me, which I still don't think is a fair assessment.

"Hi, again." Carson shows off his dimple as he reaches into his brown leather messenger bag. "You like chocolate?"

"Who doesn't?"

He pulls out a handful of candy bars and sets them on my desk.

"My mom sent me a care package. She sent way too much, so I thought I'd share with my lab partner."

Is giving out chocolate a sign he's trying to sleep with me? I'm sure Garret would say it is, but I think Carson's just being nice.

He digs in his bag again and drops more chocolate bars on my desk.

"Thanks, but you don't have to give me so much."

"I'm trying to make friends and food usually helps with that."

See? The poor guy is just trying to be my friend. And here I am taking his chocolate knowing we'll be nothing more than lab partners. That's just mean.

"Did you meet anyone at dinner last night?" I ask him as I stuff the candy in the front pouch of my backpack.

"I sat with some guys on my floor, but they didn't say much. Then they left and some girls came over and we talked for a few minutes."

"You should go to one of the parties this weekend. You'll meet a ton of people."

"Maybe we could go together."

That definitely sounded more date-like and less friend-like. Unless the "we" included Garret.

"I don't do the party thing. I don't drink."

"Really? I mean, I think it's good. I'm just saying that it's probably hard to be in college and not drink. Does your boyfriend drink?"

At least Carson remembered I had a boyfriend. I was starting to think he forget all about him.

"Garret used to drink, but he cut way back when we started dating. He hardly drinks at all anymore."

"Then what do you guys do on weekends when everyone's partying?"

"Go out to dinner. See a movie. Hang out in his room."

"And he's okay with that?"

I find the question somewhat rude but answer him anyway. "If he wasn't we probably wouldn't be dating."

"Hmm. Okay." He sits back.

"What? Are you trying to tell me something, Carson?"

"It's just that I was talking about you two last night to those girls I met and they said Garret was kind of a legend around here as far as his performance at parties. So I was surprised when you said he didn't go to them anymore."

"When Garret used to drink, he got a little out of control. At least that's what I heard. But that was back in high school. He's not like that anymore."

"Isn't he on some reality show with a girl who goes to school here?"

"No, the producers are just trying to get ratings and they're using this fake story about Garret to hook viewers. It's completely unethical. I don't even know how they get away with it."

"How long have you two dated?"

"A few months. We were friends first. I met him the first day I got here, and after that we just started hanging out." I glance back at the door, wondering why our classmates aren't showing up. "So do you have a girlfriend back home?"

"I did, but she broke up with me right before I came out here. She wouldn't do the long distance thing."

"Do you two still talk?"

"She called me last week just to see how school was going, but other than that we haven't talked." He takes his phone out and swipes the screen. "This is her."

He shows me her photo. She's gorgeous. Like model gorgeous with bright blue eyes and long blond hair.

"She's pretty. She looks older than you."

"She is. She's graduating from college this May and starts law school in the fall."

"You like older women, huh?" I kid.

"I like mature women," he clarifies. "Not necessarily older."

The way he's looking at me, it almost seems like he's indicating that I'm mature and am therefore someone he might date. But I'm sure he's not doing that at all. It's just my skewed view of him thanks to Garret. Seeing the hot blond on his phone, I am most definitely not Carson's type.

He puts his phone back in his pocket. "Did you look at the syllabus for chem lab? Because I was thinking we should get together this weekend and divide up the assignments."

"We can just do that after class. It shouldn't take long."

He nods and his smile disappears. "Yeah, okay."

"Is something wrong?" I ask him.

"I was hoping we could be friends, not just lab partners. Grab a coffee sometime. Maybe go for a run. You're the only person who's been friendly to me since I got here. But I get the feeling you're not interested."

Damn. I feel really bad for this guy, but I can't mess things up with Garret over it.

"I'd like us to be friends, but it doesn't seem right for you and me to hang out when I have a boyfriend. I should be spending my free time with him, not some other guy."

"He doesn't let you have friends? That's kind of possessive, isn't it?"

"Female friends are fine, but male friends are a different story."

"I'm not trying to date you, Jade. I just want to be friends."

"You'll make other friends. It just takes time. Hey, I know who you should meet. This guy, Decker. He's really nice. He's one of Garret's friends. He'll be at the parties this weekend. Just look for a short guy with light brown hair and black-rimmed glasses. Sometimes he wears a bow tie."

"Would you and Garret mind going with me to one of these parties and introducing me to some people?"

"We could probably do that. Let me ask Garret and I'll let you know tomorrow."

171

"You really have to ask him? You can't just make a decision?"

His question really pisses me off, but I let it slide. "Garret might have plans for us. We haven't talked about the weekend yet."

"So he can make plans without telling you, but you can't do the same?"

Okay, that's just plain rude. He knows nothing about Garret or me and yet he's making all these assumptions about our relationship. I glance at the door. "Where is everyone? Class should be starting now."

"We're not having class. Didn't you see the sign? It's cancelled. The profs sick."

I turn to see a piece of paper taped to the glass on the door. I saw it when I walked in, but didn't bother reading it.

"If you knew class was cancelled, why did you come in here?'

"To say hello and share my chocolate. You want any more?"

"No, thanks. I have plenty." I shove my book in my backpack and get up to put my coat on.

"Since we don't have class, do you want to show me around town? I haven't even been off campus yet."

"I don't have a car." I start walking out. "I'll see you later."

Carson catches up to me. "I have a car. We can take mine."

Okay, maybe Carson *is* trying to date me, given his repeated insistence that we spend time together.

"That's probably not a good idea," I say as we leave the building.

"Why? Because your boyfriend would get mad?"

"It's just not a good idea. Besides, this is a really small town. It's easy to find your way around."

He walks with me across the open quad toward the dorms. He's quiet now and I'm sure he's thinking Garret is a controlling jerk. But if it were the other way around, I wouldn't want Garret showing some girl around town.

"Jade."

I turn back and see Garret walking up to me, with Carson standing right beside me. Great.

"Why aren't you in class?" Garret asks me.

"The professor was sick so it's cancelled."

"Hey, Garret," Carson says. "Good to see you again."

"Yeah." Garret nods at him, then focuses back on me. "Are you two headed somewhere?"

Before I can answer, Carson does. "Jade's going to show me around town."

Garret looks at me, waiting for me to deny it, but I'm too stunned to say anything. I can't believe Carson just lied like that!

"Then I guess I'll see you later." Garret takes off across the quad.

"Garret, wait." I race after him. "He's kidding. I'm not showing him around town. I don't even have a car."

"We're taking my Jeep." Carson is next to me again. This guy is really pissing me off. "You want to come with us, Garret?"

"Nope. I'm busy." Garret stares straight ahead, walking so fast it's practically a run.

When we get to the dorms, I follow Garret to ours while Carson goes to the building next to us.

"We'll just do the tour another time," Carson calls out to me. "See you guys later."

I follow Garret up to his room and try to explain. "I swear I was not going anywhere with him. The guy is crazy. He made all of that up. I told him I couldn't show him around."

Garret sets his backpack down. "Couldn't or wouldn't?"

"What's the difference?"

"Couldn't implies you won't go with him because I won't let you. Wouldn't implies it's your choice. That you didn't *want* to go with him."

"I *didn't* want to go with him, so stop making this into something it's not. I had a talk with him and told him how my free time should be spent with you, not some other guy."

"And what did he say?"

"He thinks you're being a possessive boyfriend. And he said that he's not trying to date me. He just wants to be friends."

"I really don't like that guy." Garret strips his jeans and t-shirt off and starts sifting through his drawers.

"He's not that bad. I think he's just lonely. His girlfriend dumped him. He's at a new school. He's really far from home." I go over and stand behind Garret while he tries to find whatever he's looking for in his dresser. "I was thinking we could introduce him to some people. That way he'd make new friends and leave me alone."

"What are you suggesting?" He turns back, wearing only his tight, black boxer briefs. He's so damn hot. Broad shoulders. Strong arms. Ripped muscles running the length of his v-shaped torso. How could he even think I'd be interested in someone else?

I rub my hands along his abs. I can't help it. They're begging to be touched. "I was thinking we could go to a party on Friday night. Introduce him to some people, like Decker, and some of the other guys you know."

Garret takes my hands off his abs and holds them in front of him. "You hate parties."

"I was thinking about that and I think we should go to a few this semester. I mean, it's part of the whole college experience,

174

right? And you like parties. You used to go to them all the time. It's not fair you don't go anymore because of me."

"I don't need to go. I've been to plenty of parties in my life. They're pretty much all the same. It gets boring after a while. Plus, you hate being around all that alcohol."

"I'm better with it now that I know what really happened to my mom. I'm not saying I'll drink, but I'm not afraid to have it around me, especially if you're with me."

He lets go of my hands and sighs. "So you're making us go to a party because of Carson. A guy who's trying to date you. A guy I can't stand."

"You don't even know him. And it's just one party. We'll introduce him to people and then we'll leave." Garret looks so freaking good I just have to touch him again. I wrap my arms around him and kiss his bare chest. He smells good, too. "Plus once Carson sees us together and realizes how in love we are, he won't even consider trying to date me."

"Yeah, right."

"So will you go?" I look up at him and smile.

"You seem to really want to do this, so yes, I'll go."

"Do you know where the parties are this weekend?"

"Decker's been texting me asking me to go to the one on Beech Street. I'll text him back and tell him we're going. But that guy, Carson, is driving himself. We're not taking him."

"That's fine. I'll tell him. Thanks for doing this." I reach up and kiss him. "By the way, why are you undressed?"

"I'm going to the gym to work out. I was trying to change clothes, but someone's making it very difficult." He kisses me. "It's like that someone doesn't want me to get dressed."

"I think you're right." I tug his boxers down. "I have to get ready for my next class, so can we do this in 10 minutes?"

"Ten minutes, huh? That's not much time."

175

"Then I guess I'll see you later." I turn and start to walk off.

He grabs my wrist, laughing. "Get back here. Ten minutes is more than enough time."

The next few days go by with far less Carson drama. When I see him at class I consider confronting him over that stunt he pulled with Garret but decide to let it go. He's been walking around campus with some blond girl, so maybe he's found someone to date.

Friday night, Garret and I go to the party on Beech Street. We get there around 9 and the house is already packed with people. It's an old house with cracked plaster walls and scratched-up wood floors and it smells like a mix of beer, sweat, and cologne.

As we walk through the living room, drunk people keep bumping into me and a guy almost spills his drink on my shirt. Now I remember why I don't go to parties.

"You okay?" Garret says in my ear as the music blares around us. "Because if you're not, we'll leave right now."

"I'm okay," I tell him, taking his hand.

"Kensington!" A guy from Garret's floor comes stumbling up to us holding a plastic cup filled with beer. I think his name is Dean. I see him in the hall when I'm going to Garret's room. He always wears a polo shirt with the collar up and khaki pants instead of jeans. He's got the whole preppy look going.

"Hey, Dawson," Garret says.

So I guess his name is Dawson, but he looks more like a Dean.

"It's about time you showed up at one of these things," Dawson says.

"What are you talking about? I went to parties all last semester. Almost every Friday night. You saw me there. We talked. Played pool."

Dawson thinks for a moment. "Oh, yeah. Whatever. You never stayed very long. And I don't think you drank either. Shit, I don't even know why you went."

I know why. Because that asshole, Blake, blackmailed Garret into going, threatening to tell Mr. Kensington about Garret and me if Garret didn't party with him. I'm glad that's over. Blake's long gone and Garret's dad has finally accepted us dating.

Dawson notices our empty hands. "You guys need a drink. There's a keg over there in the corner." He turns to me. "They've got some fruity punch for the ladies. But just a warning. That shit's strong. A girl your size will feel it after one drink." He takes a big gulp of his beer. "That's the point, right? Get you girls drunk as fast as possible. Makes it easier on us guys." He takes another gulp of his beer.

Garret puts his arm around my shoulder and leads me away. "You sure you want to stay here?"

I scan the room. "There's Carson. Let's go over and talk to him."

Carson's wearing jeans and a black polo shirt that accentuates his huge shoulders and muscular arms. He's built like a football player. I bet he played in high school.

"Hi, Carson. Did you just get here?" I keep hold of Garret's hand and scoot closer to him.

"I got here a few minutes ago." He looks around. "This place is packed. Are these things always this crowded?"

"Yeah, usually. There isn't much else to do in this town."

I nudge Garret to join the conversation.

"So you ready to meet some people?" Garret gets right down to business. He has no interest in making small talk with Carson.

"Sure. Can I grab a drink first? You guys want anything?"

"No, we're good," I say.

Carson goes over to the keg.

Garret leans down. "The guy drinks, Jade, and you want to be friends with him? When we met, you refused to speak to me after I had a couple sips of beer."

"I'm trying to loosen up a little. If you want a beer, go ahead and have one."

He waits, anticipating the "but" which he knows is coming.

"I won't kiss you with beer breath, but you can still have one."

"I'd rather have the kiss." He says it next to my ear, his lips brushing my skin while his hand rests on my lower back. He's barely touching me and it still makes me want to take him into one of the bedrooms so we can be alone. Even after all these months, he still affects me this way. It's crazy.

"Okay, I'm ready." Carson's back with a plastic cup filled to the top with light-colored beer. The smell is so disgusting. I back away but the stench of it still lingers in the air.

My alcoholic mother didn't drink beer that much. She usually stuck to hard liquor. But when we were really low on money, she had to settle for cheap beer. She'd buy that before she'd buy food. To this day, when I smell beer, it brings back memories of being hungry. School lunch would be my only meal of the day and those meals weren't very filling.

I'd never tell Garret that story. If I did, he'd never drink beer again and I don't want him to do that for me. I know he likes it and he should be able to have one now and then. Plus I hate it when he feels sorry for me.

Garret leads Carson over to a group of guys from his floor, including Dawson, who comes over and hangs his arm off Garret's shoulder. He's even drunker than when we saw him a few minutes ago.

"Kensington!" Dawson likes yelling Garret's last name. He does it when I see him at the dorms, too.

"Finally decide to come out of your room, Kensington?" Some guy I only know as Shafer yells it from a few feet over. I think Shafer is his last name, but I've never heard him called anything else.

Garret ignores him. "I wanted you guys to meet Carson. He just started at Moorhurst."

Shafer stumbles over to Carson, holding a shot glass in the air like he's trying not to spill even though the glass is empty. "Carson. That's a stupid name. What's your last name?"

Carson swigs his beer before answering. "Fisher."

"Fisher, huh? I can work with that." Shafer smacks him on the back and some of Carson's beer splatters out. "Okay. Everyone listen. This is our new friend, Fish." Shafer turns to him. "Got a girlfriend, Fish?"

Carson shakes his head, then drinks again.

"Fish needs to get laid tonight," Shafer announces. He turns to Garret. "Kensington, you've slept with half the girls here. Pick one for our buddy, Fish."

"Good luck with the friend thing," Garret says to Carson. He grips my hand and drags me away from them. "You see why we don't go to these?"

"What was he talking about? Why would he say that about you?"

"Just ignore him. He's totally wasted."

"Kensington, get your ass back here," Dawson calls after us.

I turn back to find Carson following us. "Wait up. You can't leave me with those assholes."

Garret turns around, annoyed. "Most of the guys here are assholes, especially when they're drunk."

"Decker's not," I say, "but I haven't seen him yet."

"Who's this?" I hear a girl's voice behind Carson and see that it belongs to Sierra, my least favorite person after Ava. They're best friends, so it makes sense that I don't like her.

Sierra curls her hands around Carson's massive bicep. "Hi. I'm Sierra. I'm a friend of Garret's." She looks at me as she says it.

"I'm Carson," he says, not bothering to remove her hands from his arm. "I just started at Moorhurst."

"He's from Illinois," I say, waiting for the confused look to appear on her face. It does and I almost start laughing, but Garret squeezes my hand signaling me to be nice. Forget that. I hate Sierra. "Illinois is in the middle. It's next to Iowa."

Garret squeezes my hand again. I don't know why he insists I act nice to her. He doesn't like her either.

"I know where Illinois is, Jade." From her expression I know it's a lie.

She smiles at Carson. "Are you on the football team? Because you look like a linebacker with these big muscles."

I almost gag at her attempt to flirt.

Carson smiles back at her. "I played football in high school. I don't play anymore." He drinks his beer. "So how do you know Garret?"

Sierra's in a daze, staring up at Carson, noticing the dimple and those deep brown eyes. She snaps out of it and glances over at Garret. "We went to high school together. Garret played football, too. He was quarterback."

Garret played football? He never told me that. I thought swimming was his only sport.

"Quarterback, huh?" Carson nods at Garret. "So finding a date must've been easy."

"I don't remember. That was a long time ago." Garret doesn't like talking about high school. In fact, we've never talked about it, which explains why I didn't know he played football.

"Garret and I went to homecoming together senior year," Sierra says. "We were homecoming king and queen. Garret, you should show Jade the pictures from that night."

"I didn't know you two dated," I say, glaring at Garret.

"We didn't," he says, keeping his eyes on Sierra.

"We just went to homecoming together." She smiles at me with her glossy pink lips. "But we should've dated. Everyone said we'd make a great couple."

Garret clears his throat. "Jade and I need to get going. Carson, just hang out with Sierra all night. She knows everyone here. She can introduce you to Decker if he ever gets here."

"You sure you have to leave?" Carson asks, directing the question only to me.

"Yeah, we have plans. I'll see you at class on Monday."

"Bye, Garret," Sierra says, as if I don't exist.

We inch our way toward the front door. It's so crowded now it's hard to move. Garret's ahead of me and I'm stuck behind a wall of bodies unable to get past.

And then I smell it. The familiar yet horrid smell that surrounded me on that awful night. I can still feel his heavy body holding me down. His giant hand shoved over my mouth so tight I could barely breathe.

My legs become numb and heavy and I can't move forward. I have to know where that smell is coming from. It's not from him. He's gone. He's in San Diego. That's what everyone said. Someone else is wearing his cologne. It's not him. It can't be him.

CHAPTER EIGHTEEN

"Hey, shithead!"

It's him.

I know that voice all too well. I still hear it in my head when I remember what he did to me.

The smell of him surrounds me now. I seriously think I might throw up. Right here. Right now. Stuck in a crowd of people.

I try to call Garret's name but I can't. My throat is so dry I can't swallow, so I definitely can't scream. And the music is so loud Garret would never hear me anyway.

"Kensington! I'm talking to you!"

The voice is getting closer. It's like it's right next to me. Shit, I think it is!

"Hey. What's up, Ohio?" I feel his long fingers on my shoulder and jerk away from him, banging hard into the girl next to me.

"Watch it, bitch!" she yells at me.

I spin around and see Blake right in front of me, leering at me with that sick grin. The same one he gave me that night.

Someone yanks me back. It's Garret and I can feel his anger as he shoves himself in front of me.

"Get the fuck away from her!" Garret screams it so loud that everyone around us stops and stares, their chattering quieted to a low murmur while the music continues to blare from the speakers.

"What? You're not happy to see me?" Blake yells out, his voice rich with sarcasm. "I thought we were friends."

Blake and Garret are now face to face. This is not good. It's really, really not good. Garret ended up in jail last time he fought with Blake. He got out thanks to blackmail and backroom deals, but if he beats Blake up again Garret will serve time. Blake's dad will make sure of it. He's attorney general for the state of Connecticut and I'm sure by now he's figured out a way to avoid being blackmailed again.

"Come on, Garret. So I slept with Ohio. The bitch asked for it."

Shit! That's the absolute worst thing Blake could've said. One, it's a complete lie. Two, he's implying I'm a slut. Three, he called me Ohio, which Garret knows I hate. And four, he called me a bitch, which makes Garret even more enraged than it makes me. He's told Blake repeatedly to never call me that again.

Blake isn't as dumb as he looks. He knows exactly what he's doing.

"Garret, stop!" I yell it as I watch him take a swing at Blake who steps back to avoid being hit.

Decker suddenly appears, putting his short, stocky body between Blake and Garret, his arms stretched out on each side. "You know you can't do this, Garret. Just stop before you do something you'll regret."

Blake shoves Decker aside like he's swatting a fly. "Get the fuck out of the way, Dek!"

Garret's fist goes up again. Then out of nowhere, Carson appears behind Garret, grabbing hold of his arms as two other guys work to hold back Blake.

I move in front of Garret and talk directly into his ear. "Just calm down. Don't do this. You'll go to jail. You won't get out this time. Please don't do that to me. To us."

Garret relaxes his arms, then yanks them from Carson, his eyes still locked on Blake. He grabs my hand and heads toward the door, his shoulder colliding with Carson's as we leave.

I hear Blake laughing above the music. The crowd noise returns to a low roar.

When we get to the car, Garret opens my door and slams it shut. Then he gets in the driver's side, slamming that door shut. He says nothing, his jaw clenched, his breathing heavy.

There's a tapping sound on my window and I look out to see Carson standing there. The car's not turned on, so I can't get the window down.

I crack open the door and Carson takes hold of it, opening it more as he leans down to talk to me. "Are you okay? Do you need a ride?"

"No, she doesn't need a fucking ride," Garret says. He's now gripping the steering wheel so tight his knuckles are white.

Carson pokes his head into the car. "Hey, man. You seem a little out of control. I'm just trying to make sure Jade is safe."

Garret glares at him. "Are you serious? You think she's not safe with me? You don't even know me. All I do is worry about her safety."

"I'm fine, Carson," I reassure him. "You can go back inside."

He doesn't. He just continues to stand there.

I turn back toward Garret, who's shaking his head side to side. He notices me watching him and looks at me. "You're not even gonna explain what happened? You just want this guy accusing me of being some psychopath? Like I get in fights every day?"

"It doesn't matter. Let's just go."

Carson opens my door even farther. "I don't think you should ride with him."

Garret jumps out of the car, slamming the door again. He storms over to Carson, getting up in his face. "Maybe you should get your fucking facts straight before you go accusing me of shit." He points to the house. "A few weeks ago, that guy in there almost raped my girlfriend. Did you hear me asshole? He almost raped her. And just now, he had his hands all over her again. How the fuck is a guy supposed to react to that? Just stand there and do nothing?"

Carson backs away. "Um, yeah, man. I get it. I didn't know."

I'm so embarrassed. The attempted rape is not something I want people to know about, especially my chem lab partner. Now every encounter I have with Carson is going to be awkward. He'll always be thinking about this. About me. With Blake.

"You can leave now." Garret goes back around the car to the driver's side. He gets in and starts the engine. Carson stands there, still looking concerned for my safety. I close the door and we drive off.

"I fucking hate that guy," Garret says as he turns onto the main road.

"I hate Blake, too, but you can't beat him up again."

"I wasn't talking about Blake."

"You mean Carson? Why do you hate Carson? He just stopped you from going to jail."

"He shouldn't have interfered like that. It was none of his fucking business."

We drive past the college and continue down the winding road.

"Where are we going?"

"I don't know. I don't want to go back to Moorhurst right now. Let's just drive. Unless you have a place you want to go."

"Can we just sit and talk for a minute? I think you're too angry to drive."

"So now you're agreeing with Carson?" Garret shakes his head. "That's just fucking great."

"Why are so jealous of him? We're lab partners. That's it."

Garret pulls into an empty parking lot and stops the car, leaving the engine running. "He wants you, Jade. It's so damn obvious. He's been trying to make me look bad since I met him. And then tonight he tries to come in and rescue you, like he's some fucking superhero saving you from the evil villain. How are you not seeing this?"

"It doesn't matter. He can do a million things to try to impress me, but I'll still end up with you. Don't you get that? You don't need to be jealous. I want to be with you and only you. Nothing is going to change that."

"Yeah, right," he mumbles.

"What's that supposed to mean? You don't think I'm committed to this? Is that what this is about?"

He looks straight ahead into the darkness. "You're always telling me this won't last. That something or someone will break us apart. And as much as I tell you that's not true, you continue to think it."

"I used to. But not anymore. I'm the one who suggested we move in together. That's a huge commitment."

"I suggested it first. And you turned me down. You suggested the summer rental because it's temporary. You said if it doesn't work out, we'll still have our dorm rooms in the fall. Like you're already planning on it not working."

"That's not what I meant."

He turns to me. "Then why say it, Jade? Why do you have to put all this negative shit out there like that? Why can't you just leave it at 'I want to get an apartment with you, Garret' and forget whatever thoughts you have about it not working?"

"I don't know. I just say that stuff without even thinking."

We sit quietly for a moment.

Garret turns the car off and lets out a long sigh. "I'm sorry about tonight. Things got out of hand. It started when I saw Carson looking at you that way."

"He wasn't—"

"Let's just agree to disagree on that, okay? And then Sierra had to start bringing up all that high school shit again."

"About that. Did you really play football?"

"Yeah. Why?"

"And you were the freaking quarterback?"

"Yeah." His tone softens and he smiles just a tiny bit.

"That's really hot. Why didn't you tell me I was the dating the high school quarterback?"

"I went to a small private school. It's not like we had a good team."

"I still think it's hot. And you were homecoming king?"

"That's just embarrassing. I can't believe Sierra brought that up."

"Garret, you're like a movie cliché. The quarterback who wins homecoming king and is also rich and super hot. I'm dating a teen movie cliché."

It makes us both laugh.

"I never thought about it that way. I played football because I liked it, not to be popular or get girls. And I wasn't trying to

188

be homecoming king." He gets serious again and reaches over for my hand. "Jade, did Blake do anything to you tonight? Did he say anything?"

"Not really. He put his hand on my shoulder. That's about it."

"He never should've touched you. We had a deal. He's not allowed to come near you."

"Well, you knew he wouldn't listen."

"So are you okay?"

I shift in my seat and gaze out the side window at the dark woods that line the parking lot. "I guess."

"Jade. Are you okay?" He asks again, more forcefully this time.

I turn back to him and shake my head no. A tear runs down my face as I think about Blake and what he did to me that night. Dammit! I will not let that bastard make me cry. He's not worth it.

Garret places his hand on the side of my face. "Talk to me, Jade."

I take a deep breath, trying to get control over my watery eyes and shaky voice. "I could smell him. And then I heard him. And that's all it took. It was like I was back in my room, reliving the whole thing all over again. I could feel him on top of me. I could feel the weight of him pushing me down. And I couldn't move. I tried. I did everything Ryan taught me, but I couldn't get Blake off me."

Now I'm full blown crying, which doesn't make sense. I'm angry, not sad. So why the hell am I crying?

Garret gets out of the car and comes around to open my door. "Back seat."

We both sit in the back, just like we did at the hospital when I broke down after seeing Frank in the ICU. Garret holds me against him and my body finally starts to relax.

"I'm fine." I wipe the tears from my face. "We don't need to do this."

"You've never talked about it. You haven't said a word about it since you talked to my lawyers. And even then, you described it like it happened to someone else."

"It doesn't matter now. I'm over it."

"If that were true you wouldn't have felt that way when he approached you tonight. And you wouldn't be reacting like you are now."

He's right. I'm not over it. I still have nightmares about it. I just don't want to admit it. If I do, people will think I'm weak. And I'll be giving Blake too much power.

Garret holds me closer and threads his hand with mine. "Jade. Just talk to me."

There's something about this moment, just the two of us sitting in the back seat of the car, that makes me want to tell Garret everything. So I do. I tell him how scared I was that night. How helpless I felt. How I felt like it was somehow my fault. And how I keep reliving the whole thing, thinking I could have done something different.

"Jade, you should've told me this sooner. Why were you keeping all this to yourself?"

"Because I don't like feeling shit. And I especially don't like *talking* about feeling shit. And now you've got me doing both, you big idiot."

The way I say it makes him laugh which makes me laugh. "Sometimes you're really funny when you're yelling at me."

"I wasn't yelling. I'm just annoyed that you've turned me into this crying, feeling, hugging mess."

190

"I'm sorry." He lifts my head off his chest. "Forgive me?"

"I guess. I do feel better finally saying all that."

"So don't keep stuff to yourself anymore. If I made you this way, the least I can do is always be here to listen. And give you one of those hugs I taught you." His arms tighten around me.

"Can we go home now? It's starting to get cold in here."

"Yes, we can go."

When we get back to campus, he walks me to my room as he always does.

"I know it's not sleepover Saturday, but can I stay with you tonight?"

He leans down and kisses my forehead. "You never have to ask me that. You can stay with me every night if you want."

"I think I'll just add Fridays for now."

When we get in bed we kiss, but he doesn't take it any farther. He knows I don't want that tonight. I just want to be near him, tucked inside his warm, safe arms.

Leave it to Blake to ruin yet another evening. But as awful as it was, the night ended with Garret and me having a really good talk in the car. A talk which took our relationship to an even deeper level. That happens a lot with us. Bad stuff happens and each time it does, we seem to grow closer, not farther apart. It's another thing I love about us.

CHAPTER NINETEEN

The rest of the weekend we stay on campus. I don't want to risk going into town and running into Blake. Decker texted Garret and said Blake was only home for the weekend and was flying back to San Diego on Sunday night. I assumed Blake wouldn't be back here until spring break, but I guess when you're rich you can fly home as much as you want. And apparently you can get away with whatever you want, too. Attempted rape. Selling drugs. I'm sure Blake's done even more bad things and yet he gets to go on living his life without any type of punishment. Sure, he got kicked out of Moorhurst, but now he's at some private college in San Diego. It's hardly a punishment.

On Monday I see Carson at physics but I manage to avoid him. On Tuesday at chem class I realize I can't keeping avoiding him, so I sit next to him like I always do and try to act like last Friday night never happened. He doesn't say much, but he looks at me differently now. Like he feels sorry for me because of what he heard and saw at the party. And I hate that he looks at me that way.

When class ends I race out of the room and down the stairs, not putting my coat on until I get outside. I don't want a lecture from Carson about how Garret is dangerous and aggressive and violent—all things I know he's thinking after seeing Garret try to beat up Blake.

After lunch, I go to lab and arrive just as it's starting. Carson's already there setting up the equipment.

"Do you want to get the reactant or do you want me to?" Carson's holding up a beaker that he's already filled with one of the chemicals in the experiment.

"I'll get it."

He watches as I go to the table that has the other chemical we need, then continues to watch me as I walk back to our station and start the bunsen burner. Why is he watching me so closely? Is he thinking about the attempted rape?

I really wish Garret hadn't told him about that. I know Garret didn't say it to embarrass me. He was mad and he was trying to explain his behavior that night. I get that. But I still wish he hadn't said it.

"So how did things work out with Sierra the other night?" I ask, hoping to take Carson's mind off whatever he's thinking that's causing him to look at me that way.

"Good. She introduced me to some people. Mostly friends of hers from high school. That prep school Garret went to."

"Yeah, a lot of people from that school ended up going here."

"I heard some interesting stories about him."

I pour the reactant into the beaker and start stirring our chemical mixture. "People shouldn't talk about him when he's not around. It's rude. And just so you know, Sierra has a history of lying. She makes up stories that aren't true."

Carson checks the lab book. "We need to let this sit for 5 minutes. We're not supposed to stir it."

"Oh. Oops." I take the stirrer out and set it on the counter.

"I'm sure Garret's already told you everything anyway, so it's not like you don't already know that stuff, right?"

The way he says it, it sounds like he's implying Garret has these deep dark secrets from high school that I don't know about. He acts like I'm this naive little girl who has no idea what she's gotten herself into by dating Garret, which totally pisses me off.

Talking about it will just cause us to fight so I change the subject. "What did you think of Sierra?"

"I don't want to date her, if that's what you mean. She's not my type. She seems superficial. All about her looks and money."

"That pretty much sums her up. Did you meet any other girls at the party?"

"Nobody I'd want to go out with. But I did meet a girl last week. We went out to dinner Saturday night. She's on the tennis team. Kerry Mitchell. Do you know her?"

That explains the girl I've seen walking around campus with Carson. I only saw her from a distance so didn't recognize her.

"Yeah, I know her. We're friends. Or, I guess, more like acquaintances. I'm friends with this girl, Harper, who is also on the tennis team, so sometimes we have dinner with Kerry."

"Maybe we could double date sometime. Unless Garret doesn't do that type of thing."

Another dig at Garret. What is with this guy? Why does he keep putting Garret down like this?

When lab is done, he walks back to the dorms with me and I confront him. "Listen, Carson. I don't know what your problem is with Garret, but I need you to stop saying bad things about him. What happened at the party is not how he normally acts. He never gets into fights. He only got in one last Friday because he was trying to protect me. That's it."

"How well do you know him?"

"What type of question is that? You're basically implying that I don't know my own boyfriend or that he's hiding stuff from me." I walk faster.

Carson holds on to my jacket, forcing me to stop. "What do you know about his family?"

"I'm not dating his family, so it doesn't matter."

"That chemical company they own is always in trouble for stuff, but they never get charged with anything. It just goes away. Doesn't that concern you?"

"No. It doesn't. And why are you so interested in their company?"

"I'm into that type of stuff. Company cover-ups. Conspiracy theories. My uncle got me into it a couple years ago. He's a reporter in Chicago. Anyway, he's followed Kensington Chemical for the past few years and when I told him I was going to school with Garret Kensington, he sent me some stuff to check out online about the company and the Kensington family."

"So you're some conspiracy nut? You really believe that stuff? I have to tell you, Carson, I'm thinking less and less of you the more we talk."

"You think less of me because I want to know the truth? So you think people should just go around believing whatever lies some company PR rep says? Lies the media tells us on the news? Kensington Chemical and companies like them pay people to spread their lies. To cover up stuff they don't want people to know about. Or they get their rich, powerful friends to help them cover it up. Garret's dad is already doing this. And soon Garret will be doing it, too, if he's not already."

"Garret has nothing to do with the company." I rip my jacket from Carson's grasp and start walking again. "I'm not talking to you about this. And I don't want to hear anything else about Garret or his family. Just keep it to yourself."

He steps in front of me. "Okay. I'm sorry. I didn't mean to piss you off. I just really like you and I don't want you to get hurt."

"What do mean you really like me? Like me how? Like a friend? Like a girlfriend? Because I'm telling you right now that I'm not breaking up with Garret."

"I told you before that I wasn't trying to date you. I'm just looking out for you." He pauses. "You just remind me of someone. That's all."

"Who? An ex-girlfriend?"

"My sister." He says it quietly as he leads me over to a bench to sit down. "You remind me of my sister. You talk like her. You sound like her. You have similar mannerisms."

I remind him of his dead sister? Wow. I wasn't expecting that. How do I respond to that? I'm not sure, so I sit there not saying anything.

"You remind me of her so much that I've felt this urge to protect you ever since I met you. Just like I used to protect my sister. Now that I say it out loud, it sounds crazy." He lets out a nervous laugh and stares down at the ground. "Maybe I need to see a therapist. I didn't realize I was so fucked up."

"Carson, don't worry about it. It makes sense now." I lightly kick the side of his foot. "And I don't think you need a therapist. You're just a good older brother who misses his sister. There's nothing wrong with that."

"Yeah, but now you want nothing to do with me."

"That's not true. I like you, but I don't like it when you say bad things about Garret. You barely know him, so it's not fair for you to judge him like that. And as for Friday night, Garret only reacted that way because of Blake." I lean forward,

196

wrapping my fingers around the bottom of the bench and swinging my legs back and forth. "I didn't want you to know what happened with Blake, but now that you do I hope that doesn't make things weird between us."

"Why would it make things weird?"

I shrug. "I don't know. It's just that I feel like you look at me differently now. Like you wonder how I ended up in that situation. And then I feel like I have to explain what happened and I don't want to explain. I just want to move past it."

"You don't have to explain anything, Jade. That guy should be in jail for what he did. When Garret told me what happened I wanted to go back inside and beat that guy up myself. I understand why Garret reacted like that. I would've done the same thing."

"Then why do you keep picking on him?" I sit up and start to lean back but notice Carson's arm is now behind me on the bench so I lean forward again.

"I'm just worried about you. It's that protective instinct like I had with my sister. I don't want someone like you getting involved with people like the Kensingtons."

"You don't know anything about them, Carson. You're just believing stuff you read on the Internet."

"I still think you should be careful around them."

"Let's just agree not to talk about Garret or his family again, okay?" I stand up, slinging my backpack over my shoulder. "And you need to stop trying to protect me. I can take care of myself."

"So are we still friends?" He smiles and even though I'm still mad at him, that freaking dimple makes me soften up a bit.

"Yes, we're still friends."

We walk back to our dorms and go our separate ways. It was a good talk. At least I understand him a little better. But I'm worried about his obsession with Garret's family and their company.

The Kensingtons, and people like them, do all they can to keep their dark secrets buried. I know Garret's dad has at least one dark secret he wants to keep hidden because I witnessed it. I watched him kill Sinclair and cover it up. But I get the feeling he's done other things he doesn't want people to know about out.

If Carson keeps prying into the sins of the Kensington family, he'll end up in trouble. Big trouble. He doesn't realize this and I wish I could tell him. But I can't. Besides, he wouldn't believe me unless I told him what I know and what I've seen and I can't do that. Those are secrets I'll keep for the rest of my life.

When I see Garret later, I tell him about my conversation with Carson, but only parts of it. I leave out the part about Carson's interest in Kensington Chemical. Garret doesn't need to know that. It would just make him hate Carson even more.

"He's trying to gain your trust, Jade," Garret says. "That stuff about you reminding him of his sister is bullshit."

"You don't know that. And you should really be more respectful. The girl is dead."

"Yes, and I'm sorry he lost his sister, but I'm not letting him use that to get my girlfriend."

"I'm telling you. He doesn't think of me that way. He's dating Kerry Mitchell now. And he knows you're my boyfriend. I remind him of that all the time."

"Yeah, and he doesn't care. You said yourself that Carson lied that day he told me you were going to show him around town. Why would he do that?"

"To make you jealous," I say quietly. "Make you think I was cheating on you."

"Yes. Exactly. That's why you can't trust that guy."

It's no use arguing with Garret. No matter what I say, his mind is made up. He doesn't trust Carson and probably never will.

Several weeks pass and things start to get back to normal. Carson stops making rude comments about Garret and doesn't act interested in me at all, at least in a romantic sense. He's dating Kerry and the two of them are together all the time. Harper gives me updates on them, not that I need to know, but from what she says it sounds like they really like each other.

Garret and I haven't had a single argument since Carson backed off. And we haven't gone to any parties. Instead, we've been going to Sean's place with Harper. The four of us get along great. Sean and Garret are becoming really good friends. Garret's even starting to hang out with Sean's friends, none of whom are rich. I like that he's finally hanging out with regular guys instead of the elitist jerks his dad forced him to be friends with in the past.

I haven't been back to Garret's house since witnessing the fight between Katherine and his dad. Apparently, Katherine's living in a different section of the estate now, somewhere on the first floor. That place is so big I haven't even seen all of the rooms.

I feel bad that I haven't been over to see Lilly, but I've talked to her on the phone a few times. She says she has all these pictures she made for me and that I have to come pick them up so I can hang them on my walls at school. She doesn't sound as happy as she used to. Garret's been home a couple times to see her and said she keeps asking if I'll come over, but

I don't think I should. Doing so would just cause Katherine and Garret's dad to fight even more.

It's now almost the middle of February and for the past week, Garret's been dropping hints about Valentine's Day. The hints are not helpful at all. I'm starting to think they're just meant to confuse me. When I try to guess what we're doing, he won't tell me anything. All this secrecy is making me nervous. I hope he isn't planning something huge, like a proposal, because I am not at all ready for that. I think he knows that, but still, I worry about it after the ring discussion we had on our New Year's trip.

Valentine's Day is on a Sunday this year. Today is the Friday before, and I still have no clue what Garret has planned.

After my last class of the day I go back to my room and find a dozen red roses sitting in a vase on my desk. A light fluttery feeling tickles my insides and I catch myself smiling in the mirror. *It's just flowers, Jade. Don't get all girly.* I tell myself that, but I'm still smiling like an idiot because I've never received flowers before.

I smell each rose, then open the little card sitting next to the vase. *"Happy Valentine's Day. I'm making the day into a weekend. Pack a bag. We're leaving at 4. Garret"*

CHAPTER TWENTY

Garret's note implies we're going out of town, but I have no idea *where* we're going which means I have no idea what to pack. I grab my suitcase from the closet and start to put the basics in; underwear, socks, pajamas. Seeing everything laid out in my bag, it all looks wrong. This is Valentine's Day. I can't bring my boring pajamas and everyday underwear. I toss them back in my drawer and find the lingerie Garret gave me on New Year's Eve. Then I pull out my sexiest panties and start picking out bras.

"You ready yet?" Garret is standing there, leaning against the door frame. I didn't even hear him open the door. I probably forgot to close it after I saw the flowers.

"How long have you been standing there?" I ask, bras dangling from my hand.

"Not long." He's laughing. "You need some help with those?"

"No." I look down at the five bras in my hand. "I mean, maybe. I couldn't decide which one. Do you have a preference?"

"The black one with the lace."

I yank him into my room and shut the door. "Would you please tell me where we're going? Your clues have been completely useless."

"That was the point. I didn't want you guessing." He glances at the roses. "Do you like the flowers?"

"I love the flowers. It's the first time anyone's ever given me flowers."

He thinks for a moment, then says, "What the hell is wrong with me? Why have I never given you flowers before? I should've been sending you flowers every week." He shakes his head. "I'm a terrible boyfriend."

"You're the best boyfriend ever. Flowers or no flowers." I wrap my arms around him, breathing him in. He smells like he just showered and put on the great cologne I love. "We better get out of here before I attack you."

"You can attack me. I'm not in any rush." He gives me a slow, deep kiss he knows will lead somewhere.

"You said to be ready at 4 and it's almost 4 now." I kiss him back, not really caring about the time. He feels good. He smells good. We can be late to wherever it is we're going.

He lets me go. "You're right. We should get on the road."

"Hey! I was enjoying that!"

He smiles. "There's a lot more where that came from. Trust me. We have all weekend."

"Are we going to a fancy hotel?"

"Maybe. Maybe not. Now come on. Get packed." He starts going through my drawers. "On second thought, let me pack for you." He tosses a couple of the t-shirts Harper gave me into my suitcase along with the dark red cashmere sweater his parents (or really he) gave me for Christmas.

"Garret, I can pack my own suitcase."

"You're taking too long. Plus I'm banning the black and white thing this weekend. It's an all-color weekend."

"Last I checked black and white were both considered colors."

"Yes, but I'd like to see you in something other than the same two colors."

"Fine. Just don't make me wear pink."

He stops for a moment. "That's a problem. I might've gotten you something pink."

"What did you get me? Did you buy me clothes again? I asked you to tell me first, remember?"

His eyebrows raise. "Not for certain types of clothing."

Lingerie. I guess that makes sense. It *is* Valentine's Day after all.

"Okay. What else do I need?"

"A dress for dinner." He takes two dresses from my closet; the black one he gave me at New Year's and the red one that Katherine gave me to wear for Christmas. "Which one?"

"You just said I couldn't wear black."

He laughs. "That's true. I did. Well, since you don't have many dresses I'll have to make an exception. Do you want to bring the black one?"

"I don't know. The red one is more appropriate for Valentine's Day, but it reminds me of Katherine."

"Jade, I got you that dress. Katherine just said it was from her because I knew you'd get mad if I told you *I* bought it."

"Oh. No wonder I like it. But I like the black one, too."

"Just take both of them."

He hands me the dresses and I place them in the suitcase along with my heels. Then I toss my makeup and hair stuff in a bag and tuck it on the side. "Anything else?"

"Swimsuit. You don't have one, do you?"

"I do. I just got it. But it's black, so you won't let me wear it."

"If it's all you have, black is fine."

I pull out the bottom drawer of my dresser and grab the black bikini Harper gave me last week. It's another designer freebie her sister got and couldn't wear. It's incredibly sexy without being slutty. I tried it on and couldn't believe how good it looked. I was waiting to surprise Garret with it and I guess now's the time. I stuff it in the bag.

"Hey, was that a bikini? Let me see that." He reaches in to get it but I yank his hand away and shut the suitcase.

"You have to wait. I don't have money to get you a gift, so seeing me in a bikini will have to be it."

"Works for me." He picks the suitcase up. "My stuff's already in the car so just go out to the parking lot."

Before we leave I take a whiff of my flowers again. "The roses are going to die while we're gone."

"They'll be fine. It's only a couple days. And if they die, I'll get you new ones. I made a mental note to buy you more flowers." He sets my suitcase down and takes his phone out. "I'll even write myself a reminder."

I push him out the door. "You don't need to do that. Let's go." I grab my winter coat, but I really don't need it. It's been unseasonably warm the past few weeks, even getting into the sixties yesterday. I miss the snow, but it's nice to not freeze to death every time you walk outside.

After we've been driving for an hour I still can't figure out where he's taking me. "Are you ever going to tell me where we're going?"

He picks my hand up off the seat and kisses it. "You don't like surprises, do you, Jade?"

"I do, but I can't wait any longer. How long before we get there? Are we staying in Connecticut?"

"Nope."

"Just tell me." I tilt my head. "Please."

"We're going to the ocean."

"We are? Really?" I say it like a little kid who's just been told she's going to the greatest amusement park in the whole wide world.

I'm embarrassed, but my reaction has put a huge smile across Garret's face and I love to see him smile, so I guess it's okay I sounded really stupid just now.

"We're staying at a hotel on Cape Cod that overlooks the ocean. I got us a suite on the top floor. I've never been to the place, but my dad has and he really liked it. And he's picky about hotels. Oh, and there's a spa there so schedule whatever you want."

"That's okay. I'd rather spend time with you. I'm not really into spas."

"Have you ever been to one?"

"No, but I don't need to go."

"We're at least getting a massage. We'll get a couple's massage. How's that sound?"

"I've never had a massage, but I guess I could try it."

We arrive at the hotel around 7. It has a traditional New England exterior with dark gray shingle siding and bright white trim. The entrance is lined with tall black lanterns.

Garret leaves the car with the valet and a man in a white uniform takes our luggage while another man ushers us inside.

"Welcome," he says. "Check in is right over there. Enjoy your stay."

205

As he says it I check out the lobby. It has dark wood floors and a massive stone fireplace in the center surrounded by leather chairs. The back wall is mostly windows and beyond that are more lanterns and then pure darkness.

The ocean. It's right there.

I nudge Garret. "I have to go see it."

"Let's check in first."

"You do it. I'll be outside." I head out the double doors and hear Garret following behind. We're greeted by the sound of the waves crashing on the sandy shore.

Garret's arms envelop me from behind and he rests his chin on the top of my head. "Happy Valentine's Day, Jade."

We stand there for several minutes listening to the roaring waves. I could listen to that sound for hours and not get tired of it. I finally get why people buy those machines that play wave sounds.

"Sir, are you checking in soon?" A man peeks his head out the door. "We usually don't bring the luggage up until the guest has checked in."

"Yes. We're coming."

We go back inside and Garret checks us in. The guy at the desk gives him the key, then looks at me. "Would you like a key as well, Mrs. Kensington?"

I turn my head to see if Katherine might've walked in behind me, but then realize he's talking to me. Garret's smiling, waiting to see if I'll correct the guy.

"No, I don't need a key," I say.

He nods. "Enjoy your stay."

Garret puts his arm around me and leads us away from the desk. "You didn't want your own key, Mrs. Kensington?"

"Yeah, I should've corrected him but I was just trying—"

Garret leans down and kisses me right in the middle of the lobby, and not a quick kiss either.

I give him a strange look as he walks us over to the bellhop area.

"What?" He laughs. "I just wanted to kiss my wife."

I shake my head. "I knew I should've corrected that guy."

"Mr. and Mrs. Kensington?" the bellhop asks.

"Yes," Garret says, smiling at me.

"Right this way." The bellhop shows us to our room and gives us a brief tour of the suite before he leaves.

The suite is even bigger than the suite we had in New York. It has a kitchen with bright white cabinets and light-colored granite countertops. Three light fixtures that look like lanterns hang over the kitchen island which is lined with four tall barstools. The living area has a big couch covered in a light blue denimlike fabric and on each side of it are oversized blue and white striped chairs that look really comfy. There's a fireplace across from the couch with a flat screen TV hanging above it.

"Garret, I really love this place. It's great." I don't tell him, but I almost like this room better than the one in New York. It feels more homey than the Times Square hotel, which was nice, but ultra modern which made it feel a little cold and stark. Plus this room has a beach feel with all the light colors and I'm really into the beach thing right now.

"Come check this out." Garret opens the drapes in the living room. It's dark out, so he turns the outside lights on and I see that we have our own private balcony complete with reclining chairs and a small hot tub.

We go outside and I lie down on one of the chairs. "Can I sleep out here?"

He laughs. "No. I wouldn't be able to sleep next to you."

There's a knock on the door to the room. Garret leaves to answer it, but I stay outside, breathing in the salty ocean air.

"Close your eyes." Garret's outside again, but he's standing behind me so I can't see him.

"I'm afraid to. What are you doing?"

"You don't trust me? That hurts, Jade." He's kidding, but I play along.

"I'm sorry. I totally trust you. My eyes are closed."

"Now open your mouth."

"Why? What are you feeding me? Is it green? Because I don't eat green foods."

He's laughing again. "It's not green. God, I swear you're the worst person to surprise. You need to relax and just go with it."

I open my mouth and he puts a small square of something in it. Chocolate. The creamiest, richest chocolate I've ever tasted.

"Good, right?"

I open my eyes and see him sitting in the chair next to me, unwrapping his own piece of chocolate.

"Really good. Where did you get these?"

"They're from Belgium, from a really small store in Brussels. My dad was there a few years ago for business and he brought a box of these back. I'd never had chocolate that tasted that good. I thought you might like it so I ordered some."

"This is definitely the best chocolate I've ever had."

"Try this." He holds up a tray of chocolate-covered strawberries.

I take a bite of a ripe, sweet strawberry dipped in that same Belgian chocolate.

"Those are so good. I need to have another."

He hands me a strawberry. "I just realized I'm being a total cliché. The guy who buys his girlfriend chocolate and flowers for Valentine's Day and takes her to a fancy hotel. Is that lame?"

"It's not lame. I love it. This is my first Valentine's Day. I want all the clichés."

"Well, next year I'll do something completely different."

"So no flowers and chocolate? Because I kind of like those things, especially the chocolate."

"I agree. The chocolate must remain. But the rest will be different."

"You know you didn't have to do all this. The flowers in my room would have been enough."

He slips his hand into mine and says simply, "I had to show you the ocean."

We sit there quietly, the cool night air washing over us. It's times like this that I have to remind myself that this isn't a dream. That it's really happening to me. I don't know how or why, but for some reason I got lucky and finally got something good in my life.

"I love you, Garret."

He gets off his chair and comes over to kiss me. "I love you, too." He offers his hand to help me up. "Let's go inside. It's getting cold."

The room is much warmer and I peel off my sweater and plop down on the comfy couch.

Garret hands me the room service menu. "I thought we'd order in tonight, unless you want to go out. But there aren't many restaurants in this town."

I glance over the menu quick, then set it aside. "I'll just eat chocolate for dinner."

He picks the menu back up, forcing me to take it. "You need real food. You can't just eat chocolate."

"Why? Do I need to fuel up for something?" I smile as I crawl across the couch and onto his lap.

"Maybe." He grips my hips, pulling me closer as he kisses me. The room suddenly feels even warmer. I break from the kiss to take my t-shirt off.

Garret's smiling. "You can distract me, Jade, but you're still eating dinner." He brings my mouth to his and whispers, "Just not right now." He kisses me again and I part my lips to let his tongue past. It's warm and tastes like chocolate and feels so good that I hear myself softly moan.

Garret slowly pulls back. "What was that for?"

I'm usually really quiet when we're making out, so I was hoping he didn't hear that, but of course he did.

"It's nothing. Sorry about that."

"Don't be sorry." He gives me just the slightest smile, his gorgeous blue eyes gazing back at me. "I liked it. I want to know how to make you do it again."

His voice is so freaking sexy, especially when he's talking just above a whisper, which he does whenever he's this close to me.

"Tell me what you like, Jade."

I feel my face heating up. "I just really liked the kiss. You taste like chocolate."

"So the chocolate made you do that?" His smile widens.

I nod.

"Should I go get some more? Because I'd really like you to do that again."

"No. Just kiss me."

He does and his tongue still tastes like chocolate and has me moaning even more as it explores my mouth. I can tell the sounds I'm making are driving Garret crazy. Minutes later, he stands up, still kissing me, his hands under my thighs holding me up. I wrap my arms around his neck as he walks us to the bedroom.

He lays me down on the bed, then reaches behind his neck and yanks his shirt off. As I look at his arms, his chest, his abs, I still can't believe I'm with a guy this hot. I strip the rest of my clothes off while he takes off his. Then I jump off the bed quick and shove the comforter to the floor because I just saw a news story that said those things are covered in germs.

When I get back in bed Garret's giving me this odd look like he can't figure out what I was doing but he doesn't bother asking. He joins me in the bed and instead of kissing me or getting on top of me like he normally would, he lies beside me and slowly moves his hand along my skin. When his hand travels up the inside of my thigh I try not to moan again, but it slips out.

"You like that?" he whispers against my neck.

I nod, keeping my eyes closed.

"Let's see what else you like."

And so begins his quest of finding every place on my body that makes me moan in pleasure. All my secret spots. For a moment it concerns me because it's yet another thing that will bring us closer, and that scares me. But I quickly forget about it because I'm loving this way too much. And I love Garret, and if anyone's going to know this stuff about me, I want it to be him.

Everywhere he touches leaves behind a tingling heat that builds and teases and aches for more of him. When he finally moves on to the actual sex part, we're both so turned on that it ends up being really quick, but beyond amazing. It's like the sex just keeps getting better the more we do it. I guess that's why we do it all the time.

We're both sweaty so we shower off, then Garret suggests we try out the hot tub. "I know it's cold out there, but what do you think?"

"I'm up for it. I'll be right back." I go in the bathroom and put on the black bikini. When I come out, Garret's waiting in his swim trunks.

"Okay, I'm ready."

His eyes drift up and down my body, lingering at my breasts, which look even bigger than normal because the bikini top pushes them up and creates a lot of cleavage.

"Holy, shit, Jade. That is hot. Where did you get that?"

"Harper's sister." I spin around to show him the back.

"Remind me to thank her."

When I turn back around he's standing right in front of me.

"Yeah, it'll be great for this summer."

"I don't think I can let you wear that in public. You'll have guys all over you. You'll definitely have *me* all over you." He leaves kisses along my shoulder and starts untying the strings of my top.

"Garret. The hot tub, remember?"

He pulls away and looks at me again. "Yeah. I don't think we'll be in there very long."

And we're not. The bikini leads us right back to the bed.

The next morning, we sleep in, eat a late breakfast, then have our couple's massage. I don't like to be touched by strangers, so at first I'm a little on edge, but as soon as the woman begins rubbing the tension out of my shoulders I totally relax. By the time she makes it to my back I'm almost asleep.

After the massages we have lunch, then walk on the beach. It's crazy how warm it is for February—65 degrees, although it feels cooler than that with the ocean breeze.

Garret takes photos of me on the beach to send to Frank and Ryan. Then I collect shells and colored stones to take back to my dorm room.

"Ooh! Look at this one." I reach down and pick up a silvery blue shell.

"Lilly does the same thing when we go to the beach," Garret says.

I laugh. "Are you saying I'm like a little kid?"

"No." He stops to kiss me. "I just like seeing you happy. You're happy, right, Jade?"

I kiss him back. "I'm very happy."

"Good." He looks down at my shells. I've collected so many I had to curl up the bottom of my shirt to use as a make-shift bag. "I can hold those for you if you want to get some more."

"That's okay. I have plenty. Let's go inside so I can clean them off."

Back in the room, Garret watches TV while I rinse the dirt and sand off my shells in the bathroom sink.

"I guess my dad won't be home for Valentine's Day," I hear Garret say from the living room.

"How do you know that?" I go in the living room and join him on the couch. "Did he call?"

"He's on TV. I just saw him at a fundraiser in Florida for Kent Gleason." He points to the screen. "Right there. You see him? He's standing off to the side."

"Your dad didn't tell you he was going there?"

"He travels all the time. I never know where he is." Garret leans back and puts his feet up on the leather ottoman in front of the couch. "I wonder if he's meeting that woman. Maybe that's why he wanted to get away this weekend."

"Where does she live again?"

"She lives in DC, but she travels just as much as he does, so it wouldn't surprise me if—" He stops and watches as the camera scans the crowd. "Yep. I just saw her. So I guess we know what he'll be doing for Valentine's Day."

I back myself into the pillows at the end of the couch and rest my feet against Garret's leg. "Does it bother you that he cheats on Katherine? I know you hate her, but still."

"I don't really care." His eyes remain on the TV, which shows Kent Gleason shaking hands with people in the crowd. "It's none of my business. Besides, Katherine's probably cheating, too."

His answer makes it sound like cheating isn't that big a deal. I don't think he meant it that way, but then again, I'm not really sure.

"Garret, would you ever cheat? Like if you got tired of your wife? Or if you didn't like her anymore?"

He picks up my feet, placing them across his lap. "I'd never cheat on my wife. If I wasn't happy in my marriage, I'd get a divorce, not have an affair. Why are you asking me this?"

"No reason. I was just making conversation."

He reaches for the remote and shuts the TV off. "You're such a horrible liar. Just admit it. You think I'll be like my father someday."

"I didn't say that."

"You didn't have to. I can tell you're thinking it." He holds his hand out. "Come over here."

I grab his hand and scoot over on the couch. He lifts me up and sits me on his lap, facing him. "I'd never cheat on you, Jade. Not as your boyfriend. Not as your husband. I'm not my father and I'm not my grandfather."

"But they probably didn't think they'd cheat when they got married and look what happened."

214

I glance down, but he tips my chin up with his hand and locks his eyes on mine. "I'm not like them. Cheating's not an option. It's not even on the table."

"What about divorce? You just said you'd get a divorce if you weren't happy in your marriage. But you're not going to be happy all the time. Nobody is."

"Divorce is the absolute last option. If things weren't working between us, we'd fix them. We'd do whatever we have to do. I'm not taking the easy way out."

"Well, you might—" He puts his finger to my lips.

"Listen, Jade. I love you more than anything in this world. And if I'm ever lucky enough to get you to be my wife, there's no way in hell I'm letting you go."

Did he just come up with that? Because what he just said was perfect. In fact, I'd like to frame what he said and hang it on my wall so I can read it over and over again.

It's one of those times when I'm so blown away by his sweet words that I can't seem to find any of my own. So I just wrap my arms around him and hug him. I love him so much right now that if he got down on one knee and proposed, I'd say yes. It would be completely crazy and I know it's too soon, but I know for sure now that this is the man I want to be with forever.

CHAPTER TWENTY-ONE

"You're good with words, Garret." I shift off his lap and sit next to him on the couch.

He looks surprised. "I am? Why? What did I say?"

"It's just a general comment."

Why do I have such a hard time with this? Why can't I tell Garret how much he means to me or how much I appreciate the little things he does or says, like that statement he just made? What is wrong with me? He pours his heart out to me and I just sit there, afraid to tell him how I feel.

"It sounded like a compliment," he says. "So I'm taking it as such because I don't get many of those from you."

See? Why don't I give him more compliments? I'm a crappy, crappy girlfriend. And I can't seem to fix myself.

"I made dinner reservations for 7, so we should probably get ready," Garret says. "We're eating here at the hotel. People come from all over just to eat at this restaurant, so it must be good."

"I'm sure it is. Everything at this place is great."

"And since we have to drive back tomorrow I made reservations at a restaurant that's close to my house. It's a nice place so they make you dress up. I was planning to stop by my house to change so I don't have to wear my suit in the car. You can change there, too, if you want."

"When did you plan all this? Because it had to have taken a ton of time."

"I wanted it to be special. And special takes time."

"Well, thanks for doing it. All of it. I'll never forget this."

"Then it was worth all the planning." He gets up from the couch and goes in the bedroom. He returns with two wrapped packages; one big, one small. "Even though it's not technically Valentine's Day until tomorrow, I'm giving you your gifts now. You may want them for tonight."

He hands me the larger box first. It's covered in pink and white paper and looks like it was professionally wrapped.

"Garret, I feel really bad that I didn't get you anything. I seriously need to find a job."

"You're not getting a job. My gift is having you here with me. Plus that black bikini, which I want to see you in again before we leave. Now are you going to open that or what?"

I open the box and inside is the pink lingerie he hinted at back in my room. It's a silk and lace camisole with matching panties. The pink is a very light pink, not a hot pink or a kid-like pink.

"I like it," I say, holding it up. "I even like the pink. Did you actually go and pick this out like last time?"

"I did," he says smugly.

"And you weren't embarrassed?"

"I have no problem picking that stuff out. The first time I went into one of those stores I felt a little uncomfortable, but I'm good now. I've got it figured out."

I roll my eyes. "Oh, really? And what did you figure out?"

"It's all about confidence. You can't be intimated by those sales girls. And let me tell you, they try to intimidate you. They come at you with all these questions. But the trick is to tell them you don't need help and then just pick something out. It shocks them. They don't know how to react. They're so used to guys wandering around looking lost."

His story has images forming in my head of him strutting into a lingerie store, pulling stuff off the rack, and flashing that famous cocky grin at the stunned sales girl ringing him up at the register. It's hilarious and it's so Garret.

"Now open this one." He hands me a tiny blue box. As in Tiffany's robin egg blue. This box could hold something that would change my life forever. And although just minutes ago I confessed to myself my desire to marry him, I'm not ready for that. Not right now. Not this minute.

"Are you going to open it?"

I swallow hard, finding it difficult to speak. I nod, then slowly lift open the top of the box.

Relief washes over me when I see that it's not a ring. It's a pair of diamond stud earrings. And they're gorgeous.

"Garret, these are beautiful. I love them. I really, really love them."

"Those other earrings I got you seemed kind of fancy for every day, so I got you these because you could wear them with anything. At least that's what Harper said. I got her opinion before I bought them."

I hold them up to the light, noticing how much they sparkle.

"They're each a half carat." He leans over and whispers by my ear. "If you marry me someday, I'll get you ones twice that size."

I turn my head to kiss him. "These are plenty big enough. I'm sure these cost a fortune. You spent way too much money." I realize what I said and cover my mouth with my hand.

"Yes! I knew the earrings would make you say that." He laughs. "Striptease for Garret tonight."

"I'm more than happy to take my punishment." I kiss him again. "Thank you for the gifts."

"You're welcome." He pulls me up from the couch. "Let's get ready for dinner."

We have a candlelight dinner at the restaurant followed by a night of bedroom fun that includes a lingerie show and my promised striptease.

In the morning we order room service and have breakfast next to the window looking out at the ocean. The weekend is so perfect I hate to see it end.

Early afternoon, we leave the hotel and drive until we get to Garret's house. Nobody's there when we arrive.

"Katherine must've taken Lilly out for dinner," Garret says. "I should call her quick and tell her Happy Valentine's Day. Lilly will love it and it'll totally piss off Katherine. It's a win-win."

"You're calling Lilly? Does she have a cell phone?"

"It's a kid phone. She can only call the numbers programmed into the phone. And it only accepts calls from family. But Katherine doesn't like it when I call Lilly without telling her first." He dials the number. "I'll put it on speaker so you can talk to her."

Lilly answers in her tiny kid voice. "Hello?"

"Hi, Lilly. It's Garret and Jade. We wanted to say Happy Valentine's Day."

"Hi, Lilly," I say. "Happy Valentine's Day."

"Guess what?" She answers before we can guess. "I got candy and a pink bear from grandma!"

"So you're over at Grandma Kensington's?" Garret asks.

"Nope. Grandma Jacobs."

"You're in New York? I didn't know your mom was taking you there."

"Mom's not here. Just me. I made you a picture, Garret."

"Okay, I'll see it when you get back. When are you coming home?"

"I don't know. I have to go. Grandpa's taking me for ice cream. Bye."

She hangs up.

"That's strange," Garret says. "Katherine never leaves Lilly like that. Not even with her parents. She always stays with her." He puts his phone away. "Let's go upstairs and change."

Being in his room again brings up memories of us together in his bed.

"I can't be in here without thinking about—you know."

He laughs. "What, Jade? Say it."

"I don't need to say it. You know what I mean."

He stands in front of me and walks slowly forward, forcing me to walk backward until I fall back onto the bed. Then he lies over me, his face hovering over mine.

"You mean sex? This room reminds you of the first time we had sex? And all the other times after that?"

I feel my cheeks getting hot. "See? You knew what I was saying."

"Yeah, but I think it's funny how you never say it. Like it's some dirty word even though I've heard you curse plenty of times. I think I've only heard you say the word sex like three or four times."

"Whatever. I just don't like the word. They should come up with a better one."

"Like what? Make love?"

"Ugh. No. That's even worse."

"Say it, Jade. Just say the word. It's not a big deal."

"I can't just say the word without it being attached to something."

He's laughing again. "Okay. Say 'I'm dying to have sex with Garret right now, but I'm too afraid to ask for it.'"

"I am not saying that." I try to squirm away from him. "Let me up."

"Not until you say it." He kisses the ticklish part of my neck, right in the back under my hair.

"Stop! Please," I say, laughing as I try to push him away.

The tickling stops, but he won't let me up. "I'm waiting."

"Fine." I sigh. "I'm dying to have sex with Garret right now, but I'm too afraid to ask for it. There. Can I get up now?"

He doesn't move. "But you're dying to have sex with me. And I can't disappoint you, especially on Valentine's Day."

I smile. "We'll be late for dinner."

He puts his lips just above mine and whispers. "I know the owner. We can be late."

And we are. What can I say? I can't resist him.

The restaurant is on the top of a hill overlooking a lake. It's very elegant with white tablecloths, red velvet curtains, and chandeliers. Classical music plays in the background. We're seated at a table near the window. Even though it's dark out we can still see the lake because it's surrounded by torch lights and trees decorated with white lights.

"I'd suggest the steak, but get whatever you want." Garret says as he looks at the menu.

"Steak sounds good, actually. Is that what you're getting?"

He looks up. "Yeah, I think I'll get that and—" He stops and I notice him staring at something behind me. I turn around, and walking out from what looks like a private dining room is

Katherine and some man. They're both dressed up and appear to be trying to sneak out a back entrance.

"Katherine." Garret says it loudly causing the people around us to stare. I watch as she turns back. I wish I could get a picture of her face. It's a mix of embarrassment, horror, regret, anger, and confusion. The woman's face never shows emotion, so this is a real treat.

Garret stands up. There's no way he's letting her leave without talking to him. She walks over to our table and Garret sits back down. The man who's with her follows, his hands stuffed in his pant pockets and his eyes darting to the floor, to the sides of the room—anywhere except our table.

Katherine's lips quiver as she struggles to maintain her fake smile. "Garret, what a lovely surprise." She glances at me but doesn't say anything.

"Out celebrating Valentine's Day?" Garret asks her. Before she can answer Garret looks at the man standing next to her. "Stephen, didn't you and my dad just attend that financial conference in Dallas? How was it? Did your wife go with you?"

No way! Garret knows this guy?

The man clears his throat. "The conference was good. And no, Sheryl wasn't able to attend."

"Stephen and I were actually just meeting to go over the company's financial reports," Katherine says. "With your father out of town, I stepped in to help out."

"I'm sure you did," Garret says, smiling. "So anyway, I talked to Lilly earlier."

Katherine's fake smile disappears. "I really wish you wouldn't phone her without talking to me first. You know it disrupts her schedule."

"She didn't seem to have a schedule today. She was getting ice cream with your father."

Katherine is trying to remain calm, but I can tell she's pissed as hell. She's breathing fast, her lip is still quivering, and she's looking at Garret like she wants to strangle him right here at the table.

Garret sits back and reaches in his pocket for his phone. "You know what? We should call Dad right now. It would be a nice surprise."

He's really pushing Katherine over the edge. And I love it!

Katherine puts her hand over his phone. "We really shouldn't disturb him, Garret. Your father's a very busy man."

"Not too busy to talk to his loving wife and son." He grins as he pushes her hand away from the phone.

Katherine turns to the man. "Stephen, wait outside. I'll be right out." As she says it, I notice that her hair doesn't look as stiff and perfect as normal. She has it up, but it's falling out in places. And her dress is wrinkled. Holy crap! Did they just have sex in that private room?

"Garret, stop this," Katherine snaps at him, bringing my focus back to the table. She's sitting next to him now, angled toward him with her back to me. "What you saw was nothing. Just two people having dinner. Do NOT tell your father about this."

"Why? You're separated. You're practically divorced."

She sits up straighter and smooths her hair back in place. "We're not getting divorced."

"You're not? Then why are you separated?"

"We're not separated. We're back together now." She starts fidgeting with the tablecloth, running her long, skinny, manicured fingers along the crease.

"Why didn't Dad tell me about this?"

"It just happened. Now I need you to promise me you won't say anything to your father about tonight."

"Sorry, Katherine. If you wanted me to cover for you, you shouldn't have been such a bitch to me all these years. And you definitely shouldn't have been a bitch to my girlfriend."

Wow! Who knew I'd get so much entertainment at dinner?

Katherine lowers her voice even more. "Don't you dare speak to me that way! I am your mother."

He rolls his eyes. "You are NOT my mother." He takes a sip of his water. "Could you leave now? Jade and I are trying to have dinner."

"What do you want, Garret?" she hisses. "Just tell me what you want to keep quiet. Another car? New golf clubs? A trip?"

Garret looks at me. "What do you think, Jade? What do you want?"

I'm taken aback by the question. I don't want to be part of this. I'm just observing the scene. I'm already more involved with his family than I want to be. I don't want to be part of their family blackmail.

"I don't care. You decide," I blurt out.

He looks at Katherine again. "You have to be nice to Jade. And not your usual fake nice. You have to actually be nice. No more rude looks. No more rude comments. You'll make her feel welcome when she stays at the house. And she gets to see Lilly whenever she wants."

Katherine glances at me, then back at Garret. "That's it?"

"You also have to apologize to her for the way you've acted."

This is totally unnecessary. I don't need Katherine to be nice or apologize. I've accepted she's a bitch and moved on.

Katherine turns to me and forces out another smile. "Jade, I'm terribly sorry if you felt that I was treating you poorly in the past."

"Katherine?" Garret says, calling her on her sarcasm.

She sighs and tries again. "I'm sorry, Jade. I was rude and unwelcoming to you. I will do my best to be kinder to you in the future."

"Are you satisfied with her apology?" Garret asks me.

"Yes," I say keeping my eyes on him and not Katherine. Truthfully, her apology wasn't that great, but I just want the woman out of my face.

"Goodnight, Katherine," Garret says, not looking at her.

She quickly gets up and exits out the back door.

And here I thought this Valentine's Day couldn't get any better.

CHAPTER TWENTY-TWO

"Well, that was interesting," Garret says, looking at the menu.

"Interesting? That was like watching a soap opera played out live at our table."

The waiter cautiously approaches us. He'd stopped by a few minutes ago when Katherine was there, but she gave him her famous death stare and scared the poor guy away. We order and Garret acts extra friendly to put the guy at ease.

"So who was the man she was with?" I ask Garret after the waiter leaves.

"Stephen Reinhart. He's the CFO at our company."

"CFO. What's that?"

"Chief Financial Officer. The money guy. He lives in New York and works out of our office there. He and his wife have been at our house a bunch of times for dinners and parties. My dad's going to be so pissed when he finds out."

"I thought you weren't going to say anything."

"I won't have to. Katherine's not that smart. She'll screw up and say or do something that will give it away. Plus, my dad's already suspicious of her. He's probably having her followed."

"Why would he be mad that she's cheating? He's doing the same thing."

"Doesn't matter. He'll still be furious. Especially since it's with his CFO. A guy he plays golf with. The guy he trusts with the company finances." Garret puts his phone away. "Stephen better start looking for a job. Did you see his face when he saw me? I thought the guy was gonna have a heart attack."

"Why do you think your dad and Katherine called off the divorce? She said they're not even separated anymore."

"I guess they don't want the social embarrassment of a divorce or the bad publicity. Or maybe they're actually being decent parents for once and thinking about Lilly."

I run my finger up and down the stem of my water glass. "You didn't need to make Katherine apologize to me. It was kind of a waste. She would've bought you another car, or a trip, or what was the other thing?"

"Golf clubs. Like I need any more of those." He reaches over and takes my hand from the water glass and holds it in his. "It was important to me that she apologized to you. I can't promise you she'll follow through on the being nice part, but she might at least make an attempt now."

"Well, thank you for doing that." I smile. "But next time go for the car. Then you can loan it to me, so I can actually drive places."

"Do you seriously want a car? Because you know I'll buy you one. I just didn't think you'd let me."

"I'm kidding, Garret. Do not buy me a car. I don't need one."

"What kind of car should I get you?" He lets go of my hand and sits back in his chair, pretending to contemplate this while I shake my head. "I think you'd like a convertible. What color do you want? White? Red?"

"Real funny. Let's talk about something else."

"I didn't even think of that. We totally need a convertible. We'll be living in California all summer. We have to get one."

"I think your current car will work just fine."

"No, it's all wrong for California. It's black for one, so it's too hot in the sun. We should get a white convertible. Or red."

"Are you done yet?" I give him my fake annoyed-at-him face.

The waiter brings our salads. He seems much more relaxed now.

"Jade, you really need to start using the BMW. It's ours, not mine. If you need to go somewhere, just take it." Garret picks up a roll from the basket and spreads it with butter that's been molded to look like a rose.

"That car is too expensive. You'd kill me if something happened to it."

"No, I wouldn't." He sets his butter knife down with a now deformed butter rose stuck to it. "Why would you even think that?"

"Because that's how guys are with their cars. You get one scratch on it and they go crazy."

I look down at the salad that came with my meal. I rarely eat salad, but I decided I'd eat this one because it's just lettuce and it's really small. But there's no dressing on it. They didn't even put any on the side. And there's no way I can eat lettuce unless it's drowning in dressing.

"First of all, you're a very cautious driver," Garret says as he eats his roll. "And second, I don't care about the car. If something happens to it, I'll get it fixed. It's no big deal."

"Then maybe I'll take it sometime. If you're sure it's okay." I spot a silver serving dish next to Garret that looks like a gravy boat but contains something white with black flecks. I pick it up and drizzle what I hope is dressing over my salad.

"If you don't take it, I swear I'm going to get you your own car," he says, completely oblivious to my salad conundrum. "Can I have the dressing?"

I notice that I'm still holding what he's now confirmed is dressing. "Yeah. But why is it in a gravy boat?"

"They always put it in one of those." He takes it from me and pours some dressing over his salad. "A lot of restaurants do."

They do? I really need to get out more.

We finish our salads just as our meals arrive. I'm glad I went with Garret's recommendation. The steak looks really good.

When we're finished eating, Garret puts his napkin on the table and leans back in his chair. "So for dessert, we could either order one of the fancy desserts here or we could go to the diner and have that sundae we ate on our first date."

"You're calling that a date now? That time you barely knew me, but took me to the diner and had the audacity to order for me without even letting me look at the menu?"

"Yes. That's the one," he says seriously.

"So why is that suddenly considered a date? I thought our first date was at the bowling alley."

"I was thinking about that and I think we should make the diner our first date. It sounds better for the kids."

"What kids?" I take a sip of water.

"Our kids."

I cough a little as I choke on the water. "Excuse me?"

"Let's say I were to propose to you in the next, I don't know, few months or so." He's completely casual about it, like we've already discussed this. "We wouldn't want our kids thinking we dated such a short time before getting engaged. It would set a bad example."

I stare at him, trying to process this, but also trying to see if he's serious or just doing this to get a reaction out of me. I assume it's the latter and play along.

"There aren't going to be any kids, Garret, because I don't like kids. And since you already know that, I'm pretty sure you won't be proposing in the next few months, or even the next few years, because I know for a fact that you want three kids. So I don't think you need to worry about the timing of our first date."

His cocky smile appears. "Just give me some time. I'll wear you down on the kids thing. And if three's too much, I'm willing to compromise at one and a half. A half a kid might be nice. Not as much work."

An image of that pops in my head making me laugh. "Okay, enough about kids. Let's go to the diner and split a sundae."

Before falling asleep that night, I relive the entire weekend in my head. I don't want to forget a single detail. The way the ocean sounded. The way the sand felt on my feet. The way it felt to kiss Garret as the salty breeze blew around us. It was almost too perfect.

As much as I try to ignore it, there's still that voice in my head telling me that these perfect days won't last. That something bad is just around the corner. The voice is much softer now, but it's still there. And maybe it always will be.

Monday at lunch Harper races up to me in the dining hall just as I'm setting my tray down. Her enthusiasm causes her to bump the table, sending my chocolate milk splattering all over my chicken nuggets and onto my tray. "Jade, this weekend was beyond amazing!"

"Mine too," I say, trying to mop up the nuggets with my napkin. "Go get your lunch so we can talk."

I haven't seen Harper since she left for Sean's place Friday afternoon. She, too, had a Valentine's weekend and didn't get back to the dorms until this morning.

Minutes later, Harper returns with her usual oversized salad. She sits down across from me, wearing a light pink v-neck sweater, her long blond hair held back with a sparkly silver headband.

"Well, basically we never left his apartment."

"Yeah, I probably don't need all the details. I'm trying to eat here."

"No, that's not what I meant." She dips her lettuce in her bowl of dressing. "Well, obviously we did *that*, but not for the whole weekend. Friday night he made me the best pizza I've ever had. I told him he has to make one for you and Garret sometime. And then on Saturday, he snuck out of bed and made me a cheese souffle for breakfast. He made every meal and they were all fantastic. He even started teaching me how to cook."

"So you two cooked all weekend? Did you do anything else, besides that and you know." Once again, I avoid saying the word sex. I have no idea what my hangup is with that word. Sometimes I have no problem saying it, but other times I can't. Weird.

"I know it sounds boring, but it wasn't at all." She leans across the table, keeping her voice low. "I won't go into details, but the guy uses food in ways you wouldn't imagine. It was totally hot. We'd planned to go see a couple movies, but never made it out of his apartment." She sits back again. "Anyway, Sean and I were talking about the summer and it sounds like he's going to come out and live with me in California. I mean, he has to find a job and all, but there are tons of fancy restaurants in LA he could work at."

"So you two are getting a place together?"

"That's the plan. He's flying home with me over spring break so we can look at apartments. And he's going to try to get some interviews scheduled for when he's there."

I get my phone out. "I have to text Garret quick and tell him. He keeps asking me if Sean's going out there this summer."

"Isn't it great those two get along so well? This summer is going to be so much fun, Jade. The guys can go surfing while you and I tan on the beach." She bites into a piece of lettuce. "So tell me about your weekend."

I give her a rundown of each day, leaving out the part about catching Garret's stepmother cheating on his dad. Those are Kensington family secrets and I have no desire to share them.

"Garret loved that bikini you gave me," I tell her.

"It *was* a great suit. Kylie's sending me some others this week. You can look through them and see what you want."

"Anyway, that was my weekend." I say it casually, even though it was one of the best weekends Garret and I have had together. But I don't want to brag.

"Jade, that weekend sounds amazing. It must've cost Garret a fortune. Plus he gave you those diamond earrings. I can't believe you didn't yell at him about spending money."

I shrug. "We have an agreement now. I promised not to bug him about it anymore."

"Good. Because I gotta tell you, Jade, I was getting really tired of hearing you complain about the money thing, especially since Garret's family is loaded. And if *I* was getting tired of it, I'm sure Garret was *really* tired of it."

"Yeah, I still don't like him paying for everything, but I'm trying to get over it." I push my tray away. The chocolate-milk-splattered chicken nuggets are not at all edible. "So Garret brought up the marriage topic again at dinner Sunday night."

"What did he say?"

"I'm sure he was kidding but he talked about us having kids."

"Kids? You're 19."

"I know. He wasn't talking about having them anytime soon. He was just putting the idea out there, seeing how I'd respond."

"And what did you say?"

"I told him I don't want kids. And Garret knows that, so I don't know why he even brings it up."

"So what if he asked you?" She dips a carrot in her dressing, holding it above her plate as she waits for an answer.

"Asked me what?"

"To marry him. If he's already thinking about kids, he obviously wants to marry you and he doesn't seem like the type of guy who waits for what he wants. So what would you say?"

"I'd probably say no. We're too young. People who get married this young always end up divorced."

"My parents got married in college and they're still together. And my dad works in Hollywood. He should be on his fourth wife by now."

"They really got married in college?"

"Yeah. My mom was 20 and my dad was 22. They had like no money. My dad was interning at one of the movie studios, but they didn't pay him anything. And my mom was working two jobs while going to school."

"And they, um, seem happy together?" I hope she doesn't think I'm being rude, but I'm wondering if her parents stay together for appearance sake, then have affairs on the side like Garret's dad and Katherine do.

"My parents are totally in love. And they're not afraid to be affectionate with each other in front of people. I'm telling you that now in case you meet them this summer. My dad can't take his hands off my mom. I swear, they're like teenagers."

"I think that's kind of nice they're still into each other like that."

"It is. I just don't want to see it. Anyway, I'm just saying that getting married young doesn't mean you'll get divorced. And seeing how much Garret loves you, I don't think you have anything to worry about. Maybe if you got married it would stop the—" She gets flustered and starts picking at her salad with her fork.

"Stop the what? Harper, what were you going to say?"

She sets her fork down on her plate. "Jade, do you ever read those celebrity magazines?"

"No, but I read some when I was waiting for Frank at the doctor's office over Christmas break. I told you how one of them had a photo of Garret and Ava. I was so pissed. I still am. That article made it sound like the two of them are a couple. I can't believe a magazine can just make up lies like that."

Harper quickly gets up, taking her tray with her. "Let's go. I need to show you something."

CHAPTER TWENTY-THREE

I follow her to her room. "I've got class in a half hour. What is it?"

She goes to a stack of magazines on her desk, sorts through them, then hands me four of them.

"I thought you would've already seen those, or at least heard about them, but you didn't say anything at lunch. They all came out last week. I got them to take over to Sean's so I'd having something to read while he was cooking. But when I bought them I didn't even notice what was on the covers. And then later I saw the photos and well…you'll see."

The first magazine has a photo of Ava along with some other girls. The cover blurb reads, *Inside! Sneak Peek at the Prep School Girls' Reunion Special.* I look at the next magazine which has a small photo of Ava at the very bottom. This time it's a close-up of her face and the words next to it read, *Are the romance rumors true? Find out inside!* The third magazine has just the Prep School Girls' Reunion logo in the corner with the words, *Get the latest on Ava and Garret! p. 26.* The last magazine has a photo of Ava and Garret together. It looks like a high school prom photo and the headline reads, *"Will they get back together?"*

"These all came out last week?" I ask.

"Yeah, but I wouldn't worry about it. By next week everyone will have forgotten all about it. And it's not like any of that stuff is true."

"I know it's not true, but it's still out there. And people believe it."

"On second thought, you don't need to read those." She tries to take the magazines from me but I won't let her. I have to see what lies they're spreading. "Jade, just forget it. I only showed you so you'd know what's going on in case you heard people talking about it."

I flip through the magazine that had the prom photo on it. Inside is a page-long story about Ava and Garret. There's a pull-quote from Ava in the middle of the page: *Garret was my first love. I never should've let him go.*

"First love? Garret never told me they dated. Why would he keep that a secret?"

"Jade, I'm sure it's a lie. And if it's not, then so what? They dated in high school. Big deal."

"It *is* a big deal because he should've told me. It would explain why Ava acts so possessive over him. Listen to what she said about him. 'Garret and I started dating when we were 15. From the first time we kissed, I knew that I loved him. Garret loved me, too, but he wouldn't admit it so we broke up. We dated again senior year during the filming of Prep School Girls and then he ended it, even though I knew he still loved me. But get ready Garret fans, because the Kensington boy may finally be realizing that our love is meant to be.'"

I toss the magazine on the floor. "What the hell? And she seriously thinks people will believe this?"

"I know it sounds bad, but she's just saying that to get people to watch the show. It's probably in her contract.

Everyone knows those reality shows aren't real. And Garret won't even be on the reunion episodes."

"Which means that Ava can say whatever she wants about him and he won't be there to defend himself! And the producers will make it look like she's telling the truth. Garret said that last year the show edited videos of him to make it look like he was dating Ava. But he wasn't. He said he barely talked to her in high school." I hold up the magazine with the prom photo. "But he obviously went to prom with her. I can't believe he didn't tell me that. Why would he go to prom with someone he claims he didn't even talk to? And why didn't Ava say anything? All this time she could've been rubbing it in my face."

"So there's proof she's lying. She wouldn't say that stuff in front of Garret because she knows he'd say it's not true." Harper hesitates, eyeing the stack of magazines. "Either that or she purposely wanted you to find out now, right before the show starts. Maybe she's hoping to get a reaction from you. Those shows love to create drama."

I pick up the other three magazines and flip through them. Two of them feature the other girls on the show with just a paragraph about Ava. But the last one is all about Ava and Garret, along with quotes from fans about what a cute couple they make and how Garret is super hot. There's even a sidebar with stats about Garret, half of which aren't even true.

"His major is business, not pre-law," I say, reading through the list of lies. "And he's not a surfer. He's taken a few lessons. That's it. And listen to this. It says that Garret wants to be a senator someday. He hates politics." I toss the magazine on the floor. "It's like the producers are trying to make Garret into a character for the show without his involvement."

"That's how these shows work. They're not at all reality. They just pretend to be. And they make up stuff to get ratings."

I get up to leave, taking the magazines with me. "Can I borrow these? I have to show them to Garret."

"You can have them, but Jade, don't get mad at him about this. This is all Ava's doing and the producers of the show."

"I won't get mad at him. I'm just going to ask him if any of this is true."

"You already sound mad. And if you get mad at Garret, you'll only be doing what Ava wants you to do. She's trying to break you two up. You can't let her do that."

"I'll see you later. I have to get to class."

I take the magazines back to my room, then grab my backpack and head to physics.

"How was your weekend?" Carson is already in class, early as usual, and in way too good a mood.

I drop my backpack, causing a thump as my textbook hits the floor. "It was fine."

"Doesn't sound fine. You sound pissed. Did something happen with Garret? You guys didn't break up, did you? Because that would really suck on Valentine's Day weekend."

I look at him, noticing how he almost seems happy when he says it. "No, the weekend was great. Really great. I'm just in a bad mood about something else."

"Do you want to talk about it?"

"No. Just forget it." I reach down to get my book out, wishing I hadn't come to class so early. "So how was your weekend? Did you take Kerry out?"

"Yeah, we went out for dinner Sunday night. What did you and Garret do?"

I don't want to tell him, but I know he'll keep asking until I do. "We went out of town to a hotel that overlooks the ocean."

"Did he give you those earrings?"

I feel my ears, noticing the diamond studs. "Yeah, he did give me these."

"Must be nice to have that kind of money. I could only afford dinner. But Kerry didn't seem to care. It's not like she expected a gift or anything."

"What are you trying to say? That I expected a gift? Because that's not like me at all. I tell Garret all the time not to buy me stuff. He just surprised me with these."

"I wasn't trying to imply anything. It was more of a comment about Kerry. I like that she's not all materialistic. I like that about you, too. But since you're not that way, I'm surprised that you're okay with Garret giving you those earrings. That's a really expensive gift."

Here we go again. Carson's gone weeks without putting down Garret and now here he is, trying to make me feel like Garret's a bad boyfriend for buying me diamond earrings. Like he's trying to buy my love.

"Let's not talk about this. I told you to stop saying bad things about Garret and you keep doing it anyway."

"I'm not talking bad about Garret. I'm just wondering where he gets all his money. He doesn't have a job, so does he have a trust fund? Or does his dad give him money?"

"I don't know. And I really don't care."

"I'm just saying, if I were him, I'd want to earn the money to buy my girlfriend a gift. Not use my dad's money."

"Okay, seriously? Did you not just hear yourself? That was a total dig at Garret. Why do you care so much about where he gets his money or what he spends it on? It's none of your business."

Class is starting, which is perfect timing because I was just about ready to scream at Carson. I'm finally moving past the whole money issue with Garret and now Carson's shoving it front and center in my mind again. He's hitting all my buttons today and I think he knows that which infuriates me even more.

After class, he follows me out. "We need to meet about our paper for lab. We have to turn in the outline this week and the paper is due next week."

"Yeah. I know. I read the syllabus." I walk fast and don't look at him.

"So? When should we meet? Tonight? We could meet after dinner."

"I don't think so. We should meet during the day."

"Come on, Jade. It's homework. It's not a date. I have a girlfriend. And it's the only time I can meet before the outline is due."

"Fine. We'll meet tonight at 7 at the library."

"We can't talk at the library. Why don't we just grab dinner somewhere and we'll talk over dinner?"

"Sounds like a date to me."

"Garret won't let you eat with anyone but him? I can't believe you put up with that. You don't seem like that type of girl."

Now he's really pushing my buttons. And even though I know that's what he's doing, I still go along with it. "And what type of girl is that, Carson?"

"The girl who lets her boyfriend tell her what to do."

"So you wouldn't have a problem if Kerry went to dinner with some other guy?"

"No, not at all."

We're now at my dorm and I stop abruptly when I reach the door. "Tonight at 7. I'll reserve one of the study rooms in the library so we can talk. I'll text you with the room number." I don't wait for him to respond. I just go inside and down to my room. As I fumble with my key, Garret appears.

"Need some help?" He kisses my cheek, then takes the key from me and opens the door.

"What are you doing down here?"

He laughs. "What kind of a greeting is that? Can't I stop down and see my girlfriend?"

"Yes. I just wasn't expecting to see you." I throw my backpack on the floor along with my jacket. "I thought you had class."

"Not for another hour." He reaches for my hand, but I move it away, pretending to adjust some papers on my desk.

"What was that for?"

"What? I'm just cleaning up a little. My desk is a mess."

He reaches around my waist this time, pulling me into him. "What's wrong with you? Are you mad at me or something?"

"No." I try to squirm away.

"Jade, what the hell? We just had a great weekend. Why are you mad at me? I didn't do anything."

I break free from him and pick up the magazines sitting on the floor. "This is why." I hand them to him.

"You're mad at me about some magazines?" He takes them over to my bed and sits down. "I had nothing to do with this. I told you these things are all lies."

"Then how do you explain the prom photo? Did you take Ava to prom? You made it sound like you two weren't even friends in high school."

He holds up the magazine. "This was a group photo. Ava was standing next to me and they cropped it so it would look like we were together. I didn't take her to prom."

I feel like an idiot, but then I remember Ava's comment about dating him. "So you two never dated? Even when you were 15? That was all just a lie?"

241

He sets the magazines down. "We *did* date when we were 15. But only for a month, if that."

"And you didn't think you should tell me this?"

"I didn't think about it until you brought it up. I was drinking a lot back then. I barely even remember dating her."

"You didn't . . . you know, do anything with her, did you? I mean, you were only 15 so—"

His eyes shift down to the floor.

"Garret, please tell me you didn't sleep with her."

He doesn't say anything, but he doesn't need to.

CHAPTER TWENTY-FOUR

"You slept with Ava?"

Anger is growing inside me so fast I feel like I'm losing all control over it. I need to get it out of me. I need to run. It's cold out, but I have to get rid of this anger. I go to my drawer and pull out a sports bra and my running pants.

Garret meets me at the dresser. "Jade, just let me explain."

"What's there to explain? You slept with the girl I hate more than anyone else at this school." I turn my back to him and rip my shirt off. I quickly switch bras, then yank my jeans off and try to maneuver my legs into the tiny opening of my running pants.

"Would you just stop for a second?" He spins me around and puts his hands on my shoulders. "It was a long time ago. I wasn't even the same person back then."

My tight running pants are nearly impossible to get on from a standing position and it's even harder when Garret's holding me down like this. My pants aren't even up to my knees when he scoops me up and places me on the bed, sitting me up against the headboard.

"I need to pull my pants up. I can't move my legs."

"Good. It will force you to listen." He holds my arms by my side. "You can't get mad at me over stuff from my past. I didn't tell you about Ava because it was four years ago and I only dated her for a few weeks. We had sex one time. That's it. The rest of the time we just hung out at parties and drank. I don't even remember taking her out on a real date. It was nothing. She's making it sound like more than that to create drama for the show."

"So you never took her on a date, but you had sex with her? That's great to hear."

"I was drunk when it happened. It was at a party. We went in a room and things went too far."

"Was she your first?" I can barely look at him. Just thinking about him with Ava makes my chest tighten up. "You were only 15, so I guess she had to be."

He looks down and shakes his head side to side. "No, she wasn't my first."

"I probably don't want to know the answer to this, but when exactly was your first time? Were you younger than 15? Please say no."

"I had just turned 15. I was at a summer leadership camp up in Maine. The girl was from Boston. She was 17 and we never talked again after that week."

"And Ava was after that?"

"No. There was another girl. I met her when I was with my family in the Bahamas for Thanksgiving."

"Garret! What the hell? Why were you sleeping with all these girls when you were 15?"

He finally looks at me. "Because I was 15! I wasn't exactly thinking with my head! After the first time, I just wanted to do it again, so when opportunities came up I took them. I didn't have much parental involvement back then. My dad and Katherine acted like I didn't exist. They didn't even notice when I ran off and did stuff. I didn't have a curfew. I could basically

244

stay out all night. My dad got stricter when I started drinking more, but that didn't really change how I acted. I just had to be more careful so I wouldn't get caught."

"Is that why you never talk about high school? Because you don't want me knowing about all the girls you were with?"

"I don't want you judging me for stuff that happened back then. I told you I used to drink a lot. And people do stupid shit when they're drunk. But I'm not like that anymore."

"I know you're not, but people keep talking about you, telling me these stories about you from high school, and I hate that they know this stuff and I don't. I shouldn't have to hear about it from other people, or read about it in some gossip magazine. You should tell me yourself. You know all about my past, so why won't you tell me about yours?"

"First of all, I hardly know anything about your past. You never talk about it. And as for my own past, I'm ashamed of it, okay? And normally I wouldn't give a shit because I really don't care what people think of me." Garret loosens his hold on my arms and slides his hands down around mine. "But I care what *you* think of me. That's why I didn't want you to know about it."

A sadness comes over me as I see him in front of me, wanting so desperately for me to forget about this and just move on. But I can't and I'm not sure why. Maybe because my mind is imagining Ava and Garret together, wondering if he's still lying to me. Wondering if there's more he's not telling me. Thinking about that makes my anger return, but I don't want to yell at him so I hold it inside.

"One of those articles said you dated Ava senior year, but you told me you didn't, so which is it?" I hear the anger in my voice. So much for hiding it.

"She's lying." He looks me right in the eye when he says it. "I swear to you. Ava and I did not date last year. I saw her at school, but we barely talked. She's making up stories for the show." He sighs. "Jade, I'm sorry. I don't understand why she's involving me like this. I'll talk to my dad and see if his lawyers can get it to stop." He glances down at my hands, which he's still holding loosely in his. "Just don't be mad at me."

My body is desperate to move. I yank my hands free and push on his chest. "Let me up. I need to put a shirt on."

Garret gets off the bed and I pull my pants on the rest of the way. He takes a long sleeve t-shirt from my dresser and tosses it to me.

"So are we okay?" he asks, keeping his distance.

"I don't know." I yank the shirt over my head and shove my arms in the sleeves. "I just wish you'd told me this. It only makes me wonder what else you're not telling me."

"Jade, I'm not purposely trying to hide things from you. I mean, yes, I hid the Ava thing, but I wasn't doing it on purpose. It was so long ago I hardly even remember it."

"I don't know how you can forget the fact that you slept with someone, especially when that someone was acting as your fake girlfriend last semester." I put my running shoes on and sit on the bed to tie them. "You should've told me, Garret."

"Why? So you could get pissed at me about something that happened four years ago?" I don't answer. "And how exactly was I supposed to tell you this?"

I get up and stand in front of him. "You just tell me. It's not that hard."

He raises his voice. "Are you kidding me? What the fuck? That's not something you just bring up at dinner! Oh, by the way, you know Ava, that girl you hate so much? Yeah, I had sex with her when I was 15." He waits for me to respond, but I keep quiet. "Seriously, Jade? That's what you wanted to hear?"

"I can't talk about this anymore." I go around him to my desk.

He catches my wrist. "I'm sorry, okay? I don't know what else to say."

I grab my keys and walk to the door. He follows me out into the hall, looking like he doesn't want to leave things this way. But there's nothing more to say. I know the truth and I don't like it. Now I just need to find a way to accept it.

"Where are you going?" he asks.

"I told you. I'm going running." I close my door, locking it.

"It's freezing out. You need a jacket. And some gloves."

"I'll be fine. I'll see you later." I turn to leave, then stop. "Actually, I can't see you tonight. I'll be with Carson. We have to work on our lab paper."

He tenses up hearing Carson's name, but pretends it doesn't bother him. "Stop by my room when you're done."

"It'll be too late. I'll just see you tomorrow." I go out the door to the outside and Garret remains behind. He's probably confused and a little hurt, but I feel the same way so I don't care. Let him feel that way. He deserves it after not telling me he slept with Ava.

I take off running, not sure where I'm going. I end up on the road that leads to town, which I never run on but right now I just want to get away from campus.

My mind is so consumed with thoughts of Garret and Ava that I forget all about the time. When I get back to Moorhurst, I have no time for dinner. It's not like I'm hungry anyway after hearing the Ava news. I take a quick shower, then hurry to the library to meet Carson.

"Where's Garret tonight?" Carson asks as we're setting up our laptops.

"He's in his room doing homework." I actually have no idea what he's doing, but it's the first lie that comes to mind.

"When I was at the gym earlier I saw him going to the pool. I thought he couldn't swim with his injury."

"He can swim. He just can't swim for hours like he used to." I start searching my laptop for the outline file I started so we can make this meeting as short as possible. I want to get back to the dorm and talk to Harper about the Garret situation.

"So how exactly did he injure himself? I don't think you ever told me."

"What?" I glance up, irritated by his nonstop questions. "Sorry, I didn't hear what you asked me." I open an outline file, but it's for the wrong class. I really need to label my files better.

"How did Garret hurt his shoulder or chest or whatever he hurt?"

"He was shot." I blurt it out, then freeze as I realize what I've said. "I mean, he shot himself. Cleaning his gun." I'm talking fast and I'm sure Carson knows I'm lying. I forget about my file search and focus on what Garret's dad told me to say should this topic ever come up.

Carson's watching me like one of those private detectives on TV, examining my face for any clues that I might be lying. "What do you mean he was shot? Who shot him?"

A nervous laugh comes out. "Nobody shot him. He shot himself cleaning his gun. And he's really embarrassed about it, so don't tell anyone. And don't say anything to Garret."

"What kind of gun was it?"

"How should I know? I don't know anything about guns. He was hunting, so whatever you use for those." Now I'm off script. Garret's dad didn't say what type of gun and he definitely didn't mention hunting. Why wasn't he more specific? He should know that people will ask these questions.

"Hunters use shotguns. You're saying Garret shot himself in the chest with a shotgun? So he was aiming it at himself when he cleaned it? That doesn't make sense."

"I really don't know how it happened. Maybe it wasn't a shotgun. Can we just work on the outline? I started a file but I can't find it."

"Does Garret have other types of guns? Like handguns?"

"I don't know. I don't ask."

"He has a bad temper, Jade. That night at the party he was really out of control. And if he has guns, then you never know what will happen if he—"

I grip his forearm. "Carson, trust me. Garret's not going to kill me with a shotgun or any other type of gun, so you have nothing to worry about." I finally click on the file we need.

Carson starts to ask me more about Garret, but I cut him off and talk nonstop about the assignment. I just want to get out of here.

After a couple hours we finalize the outline and walk back to the dorms together. I prepare myself for another one of his Garret lectures, but instead Carson tells me some story about this girl he went to high school with who is now in a semi-famous band. Luckily, we make it back to the dorms without a single mention of Garret.

Harper's not in her room when I get back. I consider going up to see Garret, but I don't. I'm still too pissed off at him. He left five messages on my phone and I delete all of them without even listening to what they said. Around 10 he stops by my room.

"I'm going to sleep," I say, standing at the door. "You should, too. You look tired."

"I can't sleep if you're mad at me. Let's just talk. Can I come in?"

I step aside, letting him go past me.

"Tell me what you want, Jade."

"You sound like Katherine. Are you thinking you can buy me something and I'll forget about the fact that you lied to me? Again?"

"I didn't lie. I—" He stops, knowing that I consider withholding the truth to be lying. "And no, I'm not trying to buy you anything. I'm just trying to figure out what you want me to do here. I can't go back and change the past."

"Did you sleep with Ava last October?"

He looks confused so I explain.

"That night I saw you and her coming out of that room at the Halloween party. Did something happen that night?

"No! I told you repeatedly that nothing happened. We went in there to talk because I couldn't hear with the music. You seriously think I did something with her?"

"Now that I know your history I'm not sure. You and I weren't sleeping together back then, so maybe you turned to Ava to meet your needs."

He runs his hand through his hair and stares down at the floor. "That's real nice, Jade. Good to know you think so highly of me."

"Well, I didn't think you were the type of person who would have sex at 15 either. But you did. With three different girls!" The sex word comes out just fine that time. Probably because I'm so angry.

"Yeah. And people never change, right, Jade? They never grow up? So you're the same now as you were when you were 15? Or is your logic just true for me?"

"I'm sick of finding this shit out about you, Garret! From other people instead of you. Why won't you just tell me about your past? Have you slept with other girls at this school? Like

250

Sierra? You went to homecoming with her, so I assume that's a yes."

His gaze remains on the floor. "I didn't sleep with Sierra."

"Then who else did you sleep with?"

"It doesn't matter." He says it slowly, his jaw clenched. "Just stop this."

"At that party we went to, Shafer said you'd slept with half the girls there. I thought he was kidding, but for all I know he was telling the truth."

Garret looks up. "So now you're believing a guy you hardly know who was so fucking drunk he could barely stand up?"

"He went to high school with you, so he knows more about your dating history than I do."

Garret sighs. "You need to let this go. It's the past. It's over. And I can't go back and change it."

We both get quiet. And as we stand there in silence I'm overcome with a mix of emotions and thoughts I don't fully understand. I love Garret so damn much and yet I want to punish him and that fills me with guilt and pain—emotions I know far too well and do everything to avoid. So then I get angry at Garret, because the reason I'm feeling this way is because he withheld stuff from me. Again.

I finally speak. "I want a list."

"A list of what?"

"A list of everyone you've slept with. I don't want any more surprises."

He shakes his head as he folds his arms across his chest. "No. Forget it. That won't help. It'll just make it worse."

"You asked me what I wanted and I'm telling you. I want a list. Write it up tonight and give it to me tomorrow."

"I promise you, Jade. It won't make you feel any better. You'll be even more pissed off than you are right now."

"Why? Do I know any of the girls on this list?" He doesn't answer, which infuriates me even more. "I'm not going out with you again until you give me the list."

My heart is pounding in my chest and my brain is screaming at me to stop this. To take a minute to think about what I'm asking. But all rational thought goes to hell when I'm this angry. The old Jade comes creeping back, the one who trusts no one and will do anything to just make these feelings go away. And she refuses to listen to the part of me that knows this is wrong.

Garret stands there, not saying a word. He's just looking at me with such intensity that it's like he's trying to get in my head and force me to change my mind.

When I don't back down, he storms out of my room, slamming the door behind him.

The next day Garret avoids me, which is good because we both need to cool off before seeing other again. After dinner, I go to Harper's room to tell her the Ava story. She's been staying with Sean since all this happened so I haven't been able to talk to her until now.

"So he slept with her," Harper says. "He was 15. Guys are like animals at that age. They don't think about anything but sex. And once they get it, they'll take it from anyone. If Ava offered it to him, I'm not surprised he did it with her, especially if he was drunk at the time."

"But he didn't tell me about it! I'm almost more angry about that than the fact that he slept with her. Wouldn't you be mad if Sean didn't tell you about his past like that?"

"No. I don't want to know about the other girls he's been with. And I don't want him knowing about the guys I've been with. It's the past. It doesn't matter."

"Ava's not the past. She's acting like she's back with Garret. And if I wasn't around, she probably would be."

"Garret's not interested in her. You know that, Jade. You also know that he loves you more than anything. So you need to stop being mad at him about this and just let it go."

There's a knock on the door and she gets up to answer it. Garret is standing there holding a piece of paper that's been folded in half.

"Ready to talk?" His voice lacks any kind of emotion and I don't know how to interrupt that. His body is angled in the direction of my room like he wants to hurry up and get this over with, or more likely just leave and not do this at all.

I hesitate, but Harper gives me her talk-to-him-or-else look, so I get up and Garret and I go back to my room.

We stand next to my desk and he offers me the piece of paper. As I take it, he holds onto it. "You sure you want to do this?"

I don't answer, because truthfully I'm not sure. This was probably a really stupid request and I'm sure I'll regret it later. But knowing that doesn't stop me from taking the sheet of paper.

I unfold it and find a long list of names. I quickly count them. Sixteen. He's been with 16 girls, not counting me.

My stomach knots as I review the names. Ava is third on the list and was also the third girl he slept with. I wonder if the whole list is chronologically ordered. How would he even remember the order? Sixteen girls? That's a lot to remember. As I scan the names I don't recognize any of them except Ava. Until I spot the very last name on the list. Sadie Sinclair. My half sister.

CHAPTER TWENTY-FIVE

I drop the sheet of paper on my desk. "That's a lot."

"You feel better now?" Garret's tone is a mix of anger and annoyance but mostly anger.

"No. You were right. I feel worse."

He walks past me to the door. "Let me know when this is over, Jade." He leaves, shutting the door behind him.

I'm not sure what just happened. Or what Garret meant just now. Let him know when it's over? When what's over? Our fight? Or us?

Shit! What did I just do? Did I just destroy our relationship? Over Ava? Over that list? Why did I even ask for it? Why does it matter? Harper was right. It's the past. Garret's with *me* now, not Ava. Not any of the girls on that list.

I pick up the piece of paper and notice that some of the girls don't have last names. Garret was probably too drunk to even remember their last names. Like he said, he was a different person back then. So why am I so obsessed with the Garret I never knew when the Garret I know and love is right here?

My eyes stop and stare at the last name on the list. Sadie Sinclair. I assumed he had sex with her, but this just confirms it. Did I really need to know that? What Garret said is true. Knowing this doesn't help. It hurts. He's mine now and it hurts knowing that he's been with these other girls. So why the hell did I demand to know about them?

The next couple days go by and I don't hear anything from Garret. Not a phone call. Not a text. I don't even see him in the dining hall. The ball is in *my* court now and he's waiting for me to do something, but for some reason I don't.

The longer we go without talking the more stubborn I get. He's the one who walked out on me and left me wondering what he meant with those cryptic last words. So the ball should be in *his* court. He should be coming to me.

Harper disagrees and lectures me at dinner Thursday night. "Jade, you've gotta end this. Just go up to his room and talk it out."

"I can't. I don't know what to say. And why should I have to apologize for making him tell the truth? He should trust me enough to be honest with me."

"Yeah, and he *was* honest and look what happened. You're miserable."

"But what if this is a pattern? Think about all that stuff last semester that he didn't tell me."

"So you've never kept things from him? You've told him everything about your past?"

"Well, no. Not everything." Actually I've told him very little about my past, mainly because I don't want him feeling sorry for me.

"Then you're not being fair. You can't expect him to do things you aren't willing to do yourself. That's selfish. And immature."

"What the hell, Harper? Why are you sticking up for him instead of me?"

"I'm just calling you on your shit because you're obviously too stubborn to admit when you're wrong. You never should've asked for that list. And you shouldn't be punishing him for stuff he did years ago, before he even met you. Garret's done a lot for you, Jade, and I don't think you're treating him very well."

"He lied to me about Ava! All those times he could've told me—"

"And if he'd told you, what would've changed? Nothing! He'd still be with you, not her. He didn't tell you about Ava, or any of those other girls, because he didn't want you to feel the way you feel right now. And I respect him for that."

I stand up from the table and grab my tray. "I don't need a lecture. You're my friend and you're supposed to take my side, not his."

It's our first official friend fight. Now I'm fighting with Garret and Harper, my two closest friends and it all started with Ava and that stupid reality show.

As much as I hate to admit it, I know Harper's right. Everything she said is true. And knowing that makes me even more angry—not at Garret, or Harper, but at myself. I ruined something great, something beyond great, something I never thought I'd have, and now I don't know if I'll get it back.

Even if Garret and I get past this, I'll still have that list in my head. I'll still know he slept with all those girls. I'll see their names in my head. I'll think of him with Ava. And Sadie. I can't go back and erase all that. It'll be stuck in my brain forever. I guess that's my punishment for asking for that stupid list.

It's 6:30, and even though it's the last thing I feel like doing, I have to meet Carson again to review the comments we got back on our outline. Tonight I'm meeting him in a study room that was open in his dorm.

"Hey, Jade. Did you have a chance to look at the comments yet? I was just reading through—"

"Let's get out of here." I wait at the door with my coat on.

"And go where? The library? We didn't reserve a room."

"Let's just go to a coffee shop or some other place in town."

He gets up, surprised. "Yeah, okay. There's that coffee shop just a couple miles from here that has tables to plug in the laptops. We can go there."

"That's fine. I don't really care where we go."

He stuffs his laptop in his messenger bag and we walk out to the parking lot. "What's wrong? You seem upset."

"Nothing's wrong. I just need to get off campus. It really sucks not having a car."

"I'm sure Garret would you let you borrow his. Unless he's one of those guys who doesn't like other people driving his car. If he is, then you can borrow mine."

Carson has a red Jeep that looks brand new, just like every other car on this campus. He opens the door for me. Yep, it's new. The new car smell hits me as soon as I step inside.

When we get to the coffee shop, I find us a seat at one of the long tables with outlets.

Carson gets in line. "Jade, what do you want?" He yells it back at me.

"Just a glass of water." Has he not heard that I'm poor? Surely someone at this school has told him about my background by now.

"Come on. It's on me. Do you like lattes?"

"I've never had one. I usually just get coffee." By "usually" I mean the one and only time I've ever ordered something at this place. Harper goes here all the time and sometimes I go with her but I don't order anything. Two bucks for a small coffee? I don't think so.

Carson comes back with two large cups. "Here. Try it. It's a caramel latte. Kerry loves these. I think they're too sweet, but see what you think."

I take a sip. "I like it. It's almost like dessert."

"Yeah. Way too sweet for me." Carson gets his laptop out, smiling like he's thrilled that I agreed to go somewhere with him. Maybe I shouldn't have suggested this. I don't want him to get the wrong idea. Even though he's dating Kerry, sometimes he says things that make it seem like he's interested in me.

"So are you still okay with writing the first draft of the paper?" I ask as I turn my laptop on.

"Yeah. I'll probably start it tomorrow so you can review it on Saturday."

"Sounds good."

We go over the comments we got back on our outline. A half hour into our discussion, my phone rings and I check to see who's calling. It's Garret. I actually feel nervous seeing his name pop up on the screen. Nervous but also ecstatic that he's calling me again. This silent treatment has only lasted a few days, but I miss him so much I haven't been able to think about anything else. Now I totally regret letting this go on for so long. I should've talked to him days ago and ended this fight that never should've started.

"I need to get this," I tell Carson. I take my coat and walk outside.

"Garret, I—"

"Jade, where are you?" He's talking fast, almost frantic.

"I'm at a coffee shop. Why?"

"Lilly's missing. Katherine can't find her and I'm going over there to help. Can you come with me and look for her?"

"What do you mean she's missing?"

"She was in her room and when Katherine went to get her for dinner she was gone. There were some maintenance guys there around that same time and Katherine is freaking out. She can't find Lilly anywhere and she thinks they might've taken her."

"Did she call the police?"

"You know we don't involve them in stuff like this. Anyway I told Katherine I'd search the back woods. I don't think Lilly would go out there by herself, but I have to at least look. Can you help?"

"Of course. Whatever you need."

"Which coffee shop? I'm in the car on Fifth and Main."

"I'm at Last Cup. It's right after the gas station."

"Yeah, I know where it is."

We hang up and I hurry back inside. "Sorry, Carson, but I have to go. Garret's sister, Lilly, is miss—" I cut myself off, shoving my laptop in my backpack and hoping he didn't hear what I said.

"His sister is what? Missing?"

I smile. "She's missing her favorite stuffed bear. She won't sleep without it. I told Garret I'd go help him find it."

Carson gives me a strange look. I know he doesn't believe me. "Can't his parents find her bear?"

"His dad's out of town and his stepmom said she searched everywhere and couldn't find it. Anyway, we can talk at class tomorrow. I'll try to get there early."

I hoist my backpack over my shoulder and turn to see Garret walking in. I was hoping to meet him out front.

"Jade, are you ready?" His eyes fix on Carson and I can tell he's surprised to see him there. He probably thought I was here with Harper.

"Yeah. Let's go." I tug on his coat sleeve.

"Hey, Garret," Carson says, a smug grin on his face. "Good luck finding that bear."

On the drive to his house, Garret doesn't mention Carson. He doesn't mention our fight either. It's not the time for that. We need to focus on Lilly.

"How long has she been missing?" I ask him.

"Katherine doesn't know. After the maintenance guys left she went to Lilly's room and saw she wasn't there. She started looking for her and when she couldn't find her she called me."

"Maybe Lilly's just in a different room. Has she checked the whole house?"

"Yes. The maid looked. Charles looked. Katherine. Everyone's been searching the house and they can't find her."

"Is anyone tracking down the maintenance guys?"

"Our security people are trying to find the van they were driving." Garret slams on the brakes as we approach a red light. "Katherine should've stayed with Lilly the entire time those guys were there." He bangs his hand on the steering wheel. "What the hell was she thinking leaving her alone like that?"

He picks his phone up from the area between our seats and checks it quick, then sets it back down. I reach over and put my hand around his, seeing if he'll let me. He does, so I hold it tighter, realizing how much I've missed the simple act of just holding his hand.

"I'm sorry, Garret. I'm sorry this is happening." I pause. "I'm sorry about everything."

"Forget it. We don't need to talk about it."

"Yeah, we do. Just not now."

We get to the house and run inside. "Did you call my dad?" Garret yells it at Katherine who is practically in a trance, standing like a statue in the middle of the foyer. Garret goes up and puts his hands on her shoulders, shaking her. "Katherine. Did you call my dad?"

She snaps to. "What? No. I can't call Pearce. He'll kill me for losing her. I can't—"

"Call him!" He screams at her.

She takes her phone from her pants pocket, but holds it at her side.

"You searched the whole house?" he asks. "You're sure she's not in here?"

She nods. "Yes. We've searched it several times."

"How much of the outside have you searched?"

"Charles is looking out front with Paul. Our security men left to follow the van." Katherine is talking robotically, like she's completely shut down.

"Katherine." Garret shakes her again to make her pay attention. "Jade and I will be out back searching the woods. If you find out anything, call my cell. And you need to call my dad. I'm not calling him for you. You did this, and you need to tell him yourself."

"He's staying in New York tonight. We had a fight and he left. I can't tell him about this. He'll—"

Garret grabs her phone and shoves it in her face. "His daughter is missing! You're fucking calling him! Right now!"

She takes the phone from him and swipes her fingers across the screen.

"Come on, Jade." Garret takes off down the back hallway. He stops at a door that opens to a large closet full of brooms, mops, and other cleaning supplies. He pulls out two large flashlights, testing them quick to make sure they work, and hands me one.

As we walk back down the hall, we hear loud voices echoing in the foyer. Garret holds me back and we wait off to the side.

261

Mr. Kensington is home and in an all-out screaming match with his wife. I guess he decided not to stay in New York after all.

"What the hell were you doing that was so important you couldn't watch her?" Mr. Kensington stands in front of Katherine, towering over her tiny frame.

She quickly tries to explain. "I was on the phone, but I went to check on her as soon as I hung up."

"On the phone with who?" he demands.

She looks away. "Just a friend. Nobody you know."

He grabs her cell phone from her hand and swipes through it. "Unknown caller?" He swipes the phone again. "This unknown caller seems to call a lot, especially late at night." He glares at her. "Who is it, Katherine?"

"Stop it! Give me the phone!" She reaches for it, but he keeps it high above her head.

He walks away, tapping on the phone. I'm guessing he's calling this unknown person. He holds the phone to his ear and listens, then turns toward Katherine again, his face bright red like he's about to explode. "No, Stephen! It's not your sweetheart! It's not Katherine! It's your fucking boss! And you're fired!"

Mr. Kensington slams the phone on the floor, then takes his own phone from his pocket. Garret races up to his dad. "Who are you calling?"

"Garret, what are you doing here?"

"Katherine called me to help look for Lilly. I'm going out back to search the woods with Jade."

Mr. Kensington glances at me, then back at his phone. "I doubt she'd be out there, but go ahead and look. I need to make some calls and get my people working on this."

His people? What people? Their security guys? Somehow I think he means other people. People I shouldn't know about.

Katherine has returned to her comatose state, frozen in place in the middle of the foyer, her phone shattered on the shiny, white tile floor.

Garret and I race outside past the pool to the edge of the woods. "I'll go right and you take the left," he says. "If you get lost or need me for anything, just call my cell."

"Yeah, okay." I turn the flashlight on and run down the trail that leads into the woods. It's so dark that I can't imagine Lilly coming back here. She'd be way too scared.

My heart is breaking just thinking of something bad happening to her. It makes me think of Garret's comment about kids. If he ever had kids, is this how it would be? Always having to worry they might be kidnapped? Always having to watch over them, even in their own house?

"Lilly!" I continue to yell her name as I zigzag through the trees. I hear rustling in the leaves and stop briefly to check it out, but it's just a squirrel. I wonder what other wildlife is out here. Crap! I forgot all about that. What if I run into a skunk? Or a raccoon? Or step on a snake? The thought makes me shudder. I take a deep breath and refocus on the task at hand. To find Lilly.

As I continue to search, images flash in my mind of her trapped in the back of a van, scared to death, wondering who has her and where they're taking her. I quickly wipe the images from my brain. I'm not going to believe that. She has to be here on the property. That's all I want to believe.

CHAPTER TWENTY-SIX

I've been searching for 15 minutes without any sign of Lilly. No pink mittens. No candy wrappers. No stuffed animals.

"Dammit, Lilly, give me something." I say it aloud as I scan the ground with the flashlight. "Give me a sign that you're out here. Anything."

I yell her name even louder. I'm so scared for her. So worried that someone bad has her and that we'll never see her again.

My voice is getting hoarse, but I continue to yell her name. I'm starting to lose hope as reality sets in. There's no way she'd be out here. It's way too cold, and way too dark and scary.

"Lilly! It's Jade. If you hear me, yell really, really loud!"

I can't see very far ahead, but I'm guessing I'm only halfway to the end of the property. I'll keep going, but I really don't think Lilly's tiny legs could even make it that far. I get my phone out to call Garret and see where he's at.

"Jade." I hear my name but it's very faint. The voice sounds far away.

"Jade." It's the same voice, still very faint. I put the phone in my pocket and start running toward where I think it's coming from. The crunch of dead leaves under my feet is making it difficult to hear, so I stop for a moment. I hear it again. It doesn't sound like Garret. It sounds like a little kid voice. It's gotta be Lilly. It has to be.

"I'm coming, Lilly! Keep yelling, okay?"

I hear my name again and again as I get closer. As the voice gets louder I run faster, because I know Lilly's here somewhere in front of me and I have to get to her to make sure the voice isn't just my mind playing tricks on me.

Just as I hear my name again, my foot catches on something and sends me crashing to the ground, my knee banging and sliding against a large rock and my head hitting a fallen log. I see stars for a few seconds and my knee is seething with pain that shoots up and down my leg.

"Jade?" I hear a tiny voice as a little hand touches the side of my face. The hand is icy cold.

"Lilly!" I flip over on my back and the pain in my leg grows even worse. I sit up and pull Lilly into my arms. She has a sleeping bag wrapped around her but she's shivering. "What are you doing out here? Everyone's been looking for you." I hold her close to my body, trying to give her my warmth. "Are you okay? Are you hurt?"

"I'm scared." She shivers in my arms. "It's too dark. And there's monsters out here and they—"

"There's no monsters. They all left. I told them to go home and never come back here again."

"You did?" I see her looking up at me in the light of the flashlight which landed on the ground when I fell. She looks relieved, like she actually believes my monster story.

"Why are you out here, Lilly?"

"I'm running away."

"Why?"

"Because Mom and Dad fight all the time and I don't like it."

"I know, but you can't run away like that. You can't—" I stop because it's not the time to lecture her. We both need to get inside. I lie back slightly to get my phone from my pocket, still holding on to Lilly.

"Garret, I've got her," I say when he picks up.

He lets out a huge sigh of relief. "Where are you?"

"I'm not sure." I reach over for the flashlight and move it around. A few feet away I see a clearing and the top of a small hill. "We're by the hill where we took Lilly sledding."

"Okay. Wait in the clearing. I'll meet you there."

"Hold on." I cradle the phone between my head and shoulder and reach down to my throbbing knee. My jeans are soaking wet and from the pain I'm feeling I know it's blood. "I can't meet you there. I fell and did something to my knee. And I hit my head, so I'm kind of dizzy."

"Shit! Okay, I'll go to the clearing and when you hear me just start yelling."

Within minutes he finds us, out of breath from running so fast.

"Lilly." He kneels down, taking her from me and hugging her tightly against his chest.

"I think she's okay," I tell him. "But she's freezing. She needs to get inside."

"Jade's hurt," Lilly says.

"I'll be okay," I assure her. "Garret, take her inside. I can wait here."

He shines his flashlight along my body. "Jade, what the hell happened? There's blood everywhere!"

"It's not everywhere. It's just my knee. I tripped over Lilly, but I'm fine. Just take her in the house."

"Your head is bleeding, too." He reaches up to touch it.

I wince. "Ouch! Don't do that!"

"I barely touched you. I need to get you inside. Can you put weight on your other leg?"

"I don't know." I try to get up but can't do it on my own.

"Lilly, I need to help Jade." Garret sets her beside him. "Hold the flashlight and don't you dare run off."

She nods, taking the flashlight and letting her sleeping bag fall down around her.

Garret helps me stand up on my good leg. The pain in my other leg is now excruciating and my vision fades to black.

When I come to, Garret is carrying me in his arms and walking fast toward the house, Lilly at his side.

"Did I just pass out?"

"Yes." Garret says. "You need to get to a doctor. Fast."

"No, really. I'm fine. I just need to clean my leg up."

"Your leg needs stitches, Jade, and maybe a cast. And you probably have a concussion."

"But I don't have insurance." As I say it my head feels dizzy again and my vision blurs. "I can't—" Everything goes black.

I wake up in a bed, but it's not mine and it's not Garret's. I'm wearing a hospital gown and I'm hooked up to an IV. But I'm not in a hospital bed. It's just a normal bed in what looks like a normal room with wood floors, a patterned area rug, a leather chair off to the side, and beige curtains on the windows.

"Jade." Garret appears next to me.

"Where am I?"

"You're at a private medical clinic. The same one I went to when I was shot."

"But where? Are we by your house?" I sit up, suddenly remembering what happened in the woods. "How's Lilly? Is she okay? What happened with your dad? And Katherine?"

He takes my hand. "Hey, one question at a time. And lie down. You're making me nervous."

I rest back on the stack of pillows behind my head.

"I can't tell you where we are," he says. "But it doesn't matter. What matters is that they're taking good care of you."

"But I don't have—"

"It's all paid for, Jade," he interrupts, knowing my concern.

I'm not sure what he means. Is his dad paying for this? He must be. All I have is the college health plan, which only covers visits to the health clinic on campus. I don't have insurance for any other type of medical care.

"And Lilly's fine," he continues. "She just needed to warm up from being outside for so long. It sounded like she was out there for a couple hours."

"What happened with your dad?"

"He's back at the house taking care of Lilly and keeping an eye on Katherine. I'm sure he'll have her followed now to make sure she doesn't end up back with Stephen. But Katherine was right. She and my dad aren't getting divorced and they're no longer separated. I have no idea why, but I'm not going to ask."

He rubs his thumb along my knuckles, still holding my hand. "How do you feel?"

I take a moment to figure that out. "Okay, I guess. My knee doesn't hurt anymore." I pull the blankets away and see that my knee is bandaged up and I have bruises up and down my leg.

"What happened? Did I get stitches?"

"Yeah. You really busted up your knee. They said it'll be fine. You just can't go running for a while."

"Then why am I here? Can I go home now?"

"You hit your head pretty hard. You have a concussion, so they kept you here to make sure you're okay. They said you might be able to leave later today or tonight."

"How long have I been here?"

"It's Saturday, so about a day and a half."

I sit up again. "I missed Friday classes? I had assignments due! And a quiz!"

"Jade, relax." He eases me back down on the pillows. "We let your professors know you'd be out."

"When did you get here?"

He looks confused. "What do you mean? I came here with you. I never left."

"You missed class? But, Garret, you—"

"Why are you so worried about school? It was only one day."

"Yeah, but you didn't have to sit here with me, especially if I've been asleep the whole time."

He sighs. "I love you, Jade. I'm not going to leave you when you're hurt."

I glance down, smoothing the blanket with my hand. "I thought you were mad at me about the whole list thing."

"I'm over it." He squeezes my hand to get me to look at him. "Are you?"

"Yes. I never should've asked you to do that. And I knew you weren't messing around with Ava last semester, so I never should've accused you of that. I'm sorry. About all of it."

"Jade, I only kept that stuff from you because I knew it would hurt you. I know how shitty I would feel thinking about you with some other guy, even if it was in the past, and I didn't want you to feel that way. None of those girls matter. I only want you." He picks my hand up and kisses it, his eyes never leaving mine. "I'll always only want you."

I don't know if it's the painkillers I'm on or what, but his words have me tearing up. "Come here." I pull him in for hug. "Let's not do the fighting thing again."

269

"I'm pretty sure we'll fight again. It's normal. We just can't let it go on for two days or however long that was. It seemed like two weeks."

"Yeah, I know." I let him go. "I should've talked to you sooner, but sometimes I can be a little stubborn."

He laughs. "A little?"

I roll my eyes. "Okay, a lot. Whatever."

Garret's phone rings. "Yeah, she's right here," he says when he answers. He hands me the phone. "Frank."

"Hi, Frank." I look at Garret, unsure what to say. Does Frank know what happened? Does he know where I am?

"You're finally awake," Frank says. "Feeling any better?"

"Um, yeah. I feel okay."

"Listen. No more running on those trails in the woods, especially by yourself. You see what can happen? You trip over a log and end up almost splitting your head open."

It must be the made-up story Garret told him. I'm relieved Frank doesn't know the truth. The less he's involved with the Kensington drama, the better. "Yeah, I know. I'll make sure not to go alone anymore. Or I'll stick to paved roads from now on."

We talk a few minutes more before we hang up.

Garret takes his phone back. "I've been updating him. And my dad talked to Frank, too, and told him you're okay."

"So you told him I fell when I was running on the trails?"

"Yeah. And I told him you called me on your cell and I was there right away, so he wouldn't think you were lying in pain for hours."

It's another lie and I hate lying to Frank. But telling him about Lilly would cause him to ask too many questions. I'm still trying to understand it myself. It's still hard to believe that Garret and his family just assumed Lilly had been kidnapped. Like she's not even safe in her own home.

"Garret, remember when you were talking about having kids?"

He seems surprised. "Yeah. Why?"

"I was just thinking. If you ever have kids, will you have to worry about them the way you worry about Lilly? Always worried someone's going to kidnap them? Because I think it's sad that Lilly has to be locked away in her room and can't even play outside."

"I'm not going to live my life the way my dad does. I'm not going to do the bribes and the blackmail and whatever else he does to put his daughter at risk." He smiles. "Our kids will be able to play outside."

I ignore the "our" reference and move on. "What about the company? You're not even going to be involved? Don't you have to be? Aren't you expected to take over the business some day?"

"Lilly can run it. She's only 6 and she already likes bossing people around. She'll make a great CEO some day."

"I'm serious, Garret."

"So am I. I don't want the company. I don't want anything to do with it. I've already told you that. I'm getting a business degree so I can start my own company. Something totally different."

"Does your dad know that?"

"Yes. He doesn't accept it, but that's not my problem. He can't force me to take over the business. Besides, my dad's only 48. He'll be running the company for at least the next 30 years. And in that time he can either train Lilly to take it over or find someone else."

The door opens and a man walks in wearing dark pants, a white dress shirt, and a tie, with a stethoscope around his neck. I do a double-take when I see his face. It's the doctor who's been helping Frank. The one who also helped Garret the night he was shot. This guy really gets around.

"Jade, I'm glad to see you up and alert." He comes over to my bed. "I'm Dr. Cunningham. We've met before. Do you remember me?"

"Um, yes."

Garret steps aside as the doctor takes my wrist and checks my pulse. Then he checks one of the machines next to my bed.

"Any headaches? Vision problems?" he asks.

"No. Nothing." I shouldn't be surprised seeing him there. I know he works for this secret medical group, but I still don't know what that means. I wish someone would just tell me what's going on with this guy and explain more about this group and what they do.

"Well, everything looks good. I think we'll go ahead and send you home." The man turns to Garret. "You'll keep an eye on her?"

"Yes. Absolutely."

"What about overnight? Can someone stay with her? Does she have a roommate?"

"I'll stay with her."

"Then I'll give you this." He hands Garret a sheet of paper. "Look it over and let me know if you have questions." He turns back to me. "I'll send you home with some crutches. You'll probably only need them for a couple weeks, if that. But even if your knee feels better, don't run on it. Walking only for now. Do you have any questions for me?"

"Um, am I supposed to come back here to get the stitches out?"

"No. I'll see you at a clinic near campus. Garret knows where it is. We'll call you to set up an appointment. If that's it, I'll let you two head out." He starts to leave.

"Wait. Can I ask you something?" My palms get sweaty as he walks toward me again. I'm sure I shouldn't be asking this and I consider chickening out, but I feel like I owe it to Frank. I need to know the truth.

CHAPTER TWENTY-SEVEN

"What is it, Jade?" the doctor asks.

"What are you doing to Frank?" I blurt it out.

The doctor glances at Garret, then back at me. "I'm not sure I understand the question."

"I mean, are you helping him?" I realize how bad that sounds and quickly try to fix it. "Sorry. I know you're helping him, but how? Do you have some kind of cure?"

He shakes his head. "No. We don't have a cure for MS. I wish we did. I'm just taking a more individualized approach to treating his condition. Modern medicine tends to take a one-size-fits-all approach, which is cheaper than a more personalized approach but isn't good for the patient. The medications he was taking weren't right for him. They were actually making his condition worse. He's doing much better now."

"Well, thanks for everything you've done for him."

He nods and smiles briefly, then walks briskly out the door.

"You ready to get out of here?" Garret asks.

"What did the doctor give you?" I point to the paper in his hand.

"Instructions for caretakers of people with head trauma. I'm supposed to watch for all these signs." He reads them off. "Nausea, vomiting, confusion, memory loss, slurred speech . . ."

I take it from him. "My head is fine. You don't need to watch me."

He snatches the paper back. "Hey, this is my job and I take it very seriously." He leans over to kiss my forehead. "If your head doesn't get better, it'll be all my fault. And I can't have that on my conscience. I'm going to keep watch on you every second of the day."

"Oh, really? What about Monday when you're at class?"

He thinks for a moment. "I'll make you call me every 10 minutes and I'll ask you questions to see if you're confused or losing your memory. Like I'll ask if you know what day it is. Or if you remember who I am."

It makes me laugh. "If I can't remember who you are, I definitely need medical attention."

He gets up and takes my clothes out of the closet. "Need help getting dressed?"

"No, I can do it." I smile as he hands me my clothes. "Besides, you're better at undressing me."

He smiles back. "That's true."

After I'm dressed I practice walking a little on the crutches. As we're leaving the room, he stops to kiss me.

"What was that for?" I ask him.

"For finding Lilly. I just realized I didn't thank you for that."

"You don't need to thank me."

"Lilly would've froze to death if you hadn't found her."

"You would've found her yourself if I wasn't there."

"Just accept the thank you, Jade."

"Okay. You're welcome. But if you're thanking me with kisses, feel free to keep thanking me because I've really missed your lips."

He kisses me again. "I've missed yours, too."

I hobble down the hall on my crutches with Garret walking slowly beside me. "This really sucks. I feel like I'm going to fall."

"You'll get used to it. I broke my leg when I was 8 and I was an expert with those things after just a few days."

The hallway leads to an underground parking garage where a car is waiting with a driver. As we leave, I look for any clues that might tell me where we are, but there aren't any. We drive along a tree-lined road that could be anywhere. There aren't any landmarks that even hint at our location. After almost an hour, we finally get on the interstate and I see signs that say we're in Connecticut.

When we arrive at Garret's house the driver lets us out, then takes off before I remember to check his license plates.

"Lilly wants to say hi quick before we go back to campus," Garret says, as he waits for me to make it to the front door.

As we walk in the house, Garret's dad comes out of his office. "Jade, it's good to see you're feeling better."

"I'll go get Lilly." Garret takes off, leaving me alone with his dad.

Mr. Kensington puts his hand on my shoulder. "I can't thank you enough for finding my daughter. It's a shame you took such a bad fall."

"I should've been more careful. When I heard her calling for me, I just ran. I wasn't thinking."

"Katherine and I really appreciate what you did. We got you a little something as a thank you."

"Oh, that's okay. I don't need anything."

He ignores my insistence and opens the front door. "It's right out here. Can you make it back outside?"

I turn and go back out the door, embarrassed by how slow I am with the crutches.

"I know you can't use it yet, but you'll be able to soon." Mr. Kensington points to a white BMW convertible sitting behind Garret's black BMW.

He's giving me a car? An actual car? A brand new car? I feel like I've won a game show. I just want to run up to it and get inside, then get out again and jump up and down like the people on those shows do.

But then reality hits.

"I can't take it, Mr. Kensington. It's too much."

"Nonsense. You need a way to get around. Every other student at Moorhurst has a car. You should have one, too."

I gaze at the shiny white car. "Well, I guess I could borrow it for the rest of the semester."

"It's yours, Jade. It's registered in your name. We'll take care of the insurance and maintenance."

"Jade!" Lilly comes racing outside, waving a piece of paper in her hand. She runs up to me and hugs me, nearly knocking me over.

Garret places his hand on my back. "Be careful, Lilly. She's not used to the crutches yet."

"I made you this!" She hands me a drawing that shows me lying in a pink bed with dolls lined up beside me. *Get well soon!* is written on top in her dad's handwriting.

"Thanks, Lilly."

"So what do you think?" Garret asks, nodding toward the car.

"I love it, but it's way too much."

Katherine comes out, dressed in a white suit, her dark red lips struggling to form a smile. "Jade, I'm so glad you're okay."

There's not even a hint of sincerity in her tone. It sounds like Garret's dad gave her a script to follow.

"We were all so worried about you." She steps right in front of me, her eyes full of anger and resentment as they look directly at mine, barely blinking. "Thank you for finding my daughter. Words can't express my gratitude." She puts her hands on my shoulders and loosely hugs me, making my whole body tense up.

"Can Jade have dinner with us?" Lilly asks her mom.

"No, Lilly. She needs to get back to school."

"Okay." Lilly hugs me again, not as tight this time. "Bye, Jade. I hope you get better."

"Thanks, Lilly."

She goes inside with Katherine.

I turn to Garret's dad. "Thank you for the car, but you really didn't need to do that."

"We'll keep it in the garage until you're able to drive. And if you need anything, please let us know. Garret, you have the physician's number?"

"Yeah, he gave it to me before we left."

"Good. Well, I'll let you two get back to campus." Mr. Kensington goes inside.

I stand there in the driveway, staring at the car, still not believing it's mine.

"You want to take a look inside?" Garret asks.

"Are you kidding? Of course I do." I slowly make my way over there. "I'm guessing you picked it out?"

"Hey, I tried to get you to tell me what kind of car you wanted and you gave me nothing. Not even an idea."

"A BMW, Garret? You couldn't have picked something cheaper?"

"They're good cars. And I know you like mine."

"Yeah, but it's too much. Why did they do this?"

"To thank you for finding Lilly. My dad would've done even more, but I told him the car was enough. I knew you'd get mad if he did more than that."

"What else did he want to do?"

"Write you a check. He knows you never have spending money."

"How much was he going to write it for?"

"Ten thousand."

I almost trip on my crutches. "He was going to give me ten thousand dollars? In addition to the car?"

He shrugs. "It's not that much, Jade. You did save his daughter."

"That's like a million dollars to me! I'm glad you told him no. I couldn't accept that. The car is more than enough. How much did this cost, anyway?"

"I'm not telling you. If I did, you'd never drive it."

He opens the door and helps me inside. I breathe in the new car smell as I feel the buttery soft leather seats. I wrap my hands around the steering wheel, imagining myself driving it.

"Good choice, Garret. I really love this car. But when Ryan finds out about this, he'll kill me."

"Why? He should be happy you have a safe, reliable car."

"I know. And he will be, but he'll still be totally jealous."

"We should get going." Garret holds his hand out for me, but I remain in my seat running my hand along the soft leather.

"Say goodbye to the car now," Garret says, laughing at me. "You can come visit it later."

"Why can't I drive? My right leg isn't hurt."

"Because you might pass out behind the wheel. You have to wait for your head to heal. Now come on." He pulls me out, helping me back on my crutches.

On the drive back, I check my phone and find a few messages from Harper and one from Carson.

"I forgot about Carson. I'm supposed to be reviewing our paper for chem lab. He's probably wondering what happened to me."

"I called him and let him know. I called Harper, too. I told both of them the same story I told Frank. That's the story you have to go with. You can't mention Lilly."

"I know. So what did they say?"

"Harper was really worried about you, but I told her you're okay. And Carson said he'll finish the paper and if you're able to review it before class you can, but if not, he'll take care of it."

"I should call them quick and let them know I'm back."

Garret puts his hand over my phone. "Why don't you wait until tomorrow? It's Saturday night. Harper's over at Sean's and Carson's probably out with Kerry."

"That's true." I put the phone away. "So you never asked me why I was out with Carson the other night."

"I didn't need to ask. You were working on your paper."

"I know, but we left campus. I rode with him in his car. He bought me a coffee."

"What are you doing here, Jade? I'm trying to be cool about this. Are you trying to make me jealous?"

"No. I'm just surprised you're not mad. That's all."

"I still don't like Carson, but you seem to think he's okay so I'm not going to say anything about it. It's not worth fighting about."

I feel like I should tell Garret some of the things Carson has said to me, specifically his interest in Garret's dad and Kensington Chemical. But I keep quiet. If Garret's finally accepting the guy, there's no need to stir up trouble.

"We should get some food," Garret says. "You want to stop and eat somewhere? Or get takeout?"

"Can we get Chinese and watch movies in your room?"

Garret glances over at me and smiles. "You're the sick one, so we'll do whatever you want."

"I'm not sick."

"You're injured. Same thing. And sick people get special treatment."

"They do?" Growing up I never got special treatment when I was sick. I didn't get any treatment. I had to take care of myself.

"Yes, you get whatever you want, so this is your opportunity to ask for stuff. I'll even watch that cartoon dog movie you like so well."

We stop for Chinese food and arrive back on campus around 8. I dig through Garret's box of movies and pick out a comedy to watch.

I change into my pajamas because I usually fall asleep watching movies in Garret's room. But an hour into the movie I'm still wide awake, probably because I just slept for two days.

"Do you want to watch another one?" I ask after the first movie ends.

Garret doesn't answer because tonight *he's* the one who's asleep.

"Garret," I nudge him.

He sits up, rubbing his eyes. "Was I sleeping?"

"Yeah. You look tired." I lean over and kiss his cheek. "Did you stay awake the past two days while I was sleeping?"

"Well, yeah. I had to make sure you were okay."

"Garret, you didn't need to do that." I smile. "But I love you for it. Now let's go to bed."

"But I'm supposed to be watching you." He scoots closer to me and looks directly into my eyes. "Do you know where you are?"

I laugh. "Yes. I'm in your room at Moorhurst College."

"Do you know what day it is?"

"I'm not sure. February something?"

"You don't know what day it is? That's not good, Jade," he kids. "How's your vision? Are you seeing double?"

It makes me laugh even more. "No. Now stop with the questions."

"It's my job. And you have to answer me. Do you know who I am?" he asks seriously.

"Hmm. I'm not sure. You look familiar. I could probably tell from a kiss."

He kisses me quick but it's been days since we kissed and I need more than a quick one. I return the kiss, but make it a long, deep, I-want-you-right-now kiss.

"Yeah, I think I remember you," I say, sneaking my hand under his shirt.

"Hey, don't start. You're not ready for that."

"How do you know? Did the doctor say we couldn't do it?" His abs tighten under my hand as I undo his belt.

"He didn't exactly come out and say it, but he said to hold off on any physical activity. And I'd say that's physical activity."

"Not if you do all the work." I kiss him again, lingering at his lips. "Didn't you miss me?"

"Yeah. Too much. So you're killing me right now. I'll have to go take a cold shower."

"Or we could just do it." I rub my hand along the front of his jeans.

"Not yet," he says, smiling as he gently moves my hand away. "I need to make sure you're okay first. Then we'll do it as much as you want."

I sigh. "Then let's go to sleep so I can get better faster and you won't turn me down."

He scoops me up from his bean bag chair and lays me in his bed, pulling the covers up around me. He leaves a kiss on my lips, then looks at me with those piercing blue eyes. "It's taking every ounce of strength I have to turn you down right now, so don't give me shit about it."

"Just making sure you still want me that way." I turn my back to him and adjust my pillow as he changes into his pajamas.

Moments later he slides in behind me. "You know I want you that way."

The words and the way he says it in a deep, sexy tone turns me on even more. I reach my hand back and notice that he's only wearing boxer briefs. "No pajamas tonight? Are you trying to torture me here?"

"Nope. I was just too tired to get them out."

I scoot my back against his bare chest, rubbing my butt against his boxers in a last ditch attempt to seduce him.

"Jade," he scolds.

"What? I'm just getting comfortable."

"Go to sleep." He gives me a quick kiss goodnight.

Despite Garret nagging me to take it easy, I spend all of Sunday doing homework, emailing Friday's assignments to my professors, and working on the new stuff that was assigned.

Garret stays with me in my room, asking me silly questions every hour to make sure I'm not having memory loss or confusion. Some of the questions are so funny I consider writing them down.

Harper stops by around noon to see how I'm doing. She's smiling like crazy seeing Garret and me back together again. I don't tell her about my new car because I'm not quite sure how to explain it to her, or anyone else. I can't tell people the real reason why I got it. So do I just say that my boyfriend's dad gave me a super expensive car? Will they believe that? Mr. Kensington's a billionaire so maybe nobody would think it's odd. But just in case people question it I'll have to come up with a story. But I can do that later. I don't need to tell anyone about the car until I actually have it at school.

After dinner, someone knocks on my door and Garret answers. I hear Carson's voice from the hall.

"Hey, I was just stopping by to see how Jade's doing and to talk about our paper."

"I read the paper," I say as he walks in. "It looks really good. I didn't have any changes. Sorry I couldn't help more, but I'll do the next one."

"I didn't mind writing it. My weekend was pretty open."

"Didn't you go out with Kerry?"

"We broke up." He doesn't seem that upset about it.

"Oh. Sorry."

"It's okay. It just wasn't working." Carson looks at Garret like he's annoyed that he's there, then focuses back on me. "So you tripped while you were running?"

"Yeah. I need to be more careful on the trails. With all the downed tree branches and the leaves covering them, it's easy to trip."

"You really shouldn't run by yourself. Call me next time and I'll go with you."

"I'll go with her," Garret says.

"Jade said you didn't like to run."

Garret glares at him. "I'll *learn* to like it."

"Well, I'll see you at class tomorrow, Jade. If you want me to walk with you, just call."

"I'll be okay. But thanks."

When he leaves, I can see that Garret's doing all he can not to say anything.

"So I know what you're thinking," I say. "Carson's acting too protective of me again. And maybe flirting a little."

"A little? He basically asked you out right in front of me."

"I'll tell him to back off. I've told him before. He's just persistent."

"Tell him to be persistent with someone else."

"You want to go outside quick? I could use some practice with the crutches. Otherwise it will take me two hours to get to class."

"Sure." He helps me get my coat on, then puts on his.

It takes me forever just to make it down the hall to the door. When we step outside the building, a guy yells, "It's him!"

Suddenly we're blinded by flashes of light as guys holding cameras race up to Garret.

CHAPTER TWENTY-EIGHT

The flashing lights are so blinding I can't see. Someone shoves me aside as another person knocks one of my crutches out from under my arm. I lose my balance and come crashing down on the hard concrete. Sharp, prickly pain erupts from my stitched-up knee and radiates down my leg.

"Jade!" I hear Garret calling me, but all I can see are specs of black dots as the flashing lights go off. "Jade! Where are you?"

"On the ground!" I find my crutches and try to get up, but one of the photographers bumps into me, knocking me down again. Then someone's foot hits my head and I feel dizzy and disoriented. Seconds later, I feel Garret's arms pulling me up from behind.

"Go back inside," he says. "We'll get the crutches later."

I hold onto Garret and hop on one leg back to the door until we're safely inside the building again.

"What the hell was that?" I ask, trying to catch my breath.

"It's Ava's fucking reality show and the photographers trying to make money off it. Are you all right?"

"I don't know. I need to get my pants off and see if I tore the stitches open."

"That guy hit you that hard? I'm gonna fucking kill him!" Garret turns to go outside again.

"Wait! I need help getting back to my room."

"Yeah, of course." He picks me up and carries me there, setting me on the bed and carefully sliding my jeans off. I peel the bandage back. There's blood oozing out around the stitches but they're still intact.

"You're bleeding!" Garret whips out his phone. "I'm calling the doctor."

"No, I don't want to go back there for this. It's just a little blood."

He hesitates, the phone still in his hand, staring at me with this worried look on his face. "How's your head? Did you hit it when you fell?"

"No, but when I was on the ground some guy kicked it when he walked past."

"Shit!" Now Garret's panicked. He calls the doctor and explains what happened. A few minutes later he hangs up. "The doctor wants to see you tomorrow morning at 8. We'll meet him at a clinic here in town. If you have any symptoms at all you have to tell me and he'll find someone locally to take a look at you tonight."

"Garret, calm down. I'm fine."

"You're not fine. You're hurt and it's all my fault. First you get hurt finding Lilly. And now you're hurt because of the paparazzi."

"So that's the paparazzi out there? I thought they all worked in LA."

"They go wherever they need to go to make money and they don't care what they have to do to get it. I can't believe those assholes knocked you down like that. Which guy hit your head?

I need to go out there and kick his fucking ass." He starts to get up but I grab his shirt.

"Garret, don't. That will just make things worse."

He sighs, looking down at my knee. "What can I do? Should I go get something, like some more bandages? I could run to the drugstore."

"The bleeding's already stopped. And the doctor gave me extra bandages. They're in the top drawer." Garret goes over to my dresser. "Could you get me some sweat pants, too? I probably shouldn't put tight jeans on again."

He comes back over and sits next to me on the bed. He unwraps the bandage and carefully places it over my knee.

I smile as I watch him secure the edges. "I could've done that myself, you know."

He looks up, annoyed. "Would you just let me take care of you?"

I lean down to kiss him. "Sorry. Go ahead."

He puts my sweat pants on me, being extra careful around my knee. I'm perfectly capable of putting them on myself but he wants to do it so I let him. I've never had anyone take care of me the way he does.

Someone knocks on the door and Garret goes to answer it. "Hey, Jaz. Did you see what's going on outside?"

"Yeah, they got here about an hour ago." Jasmine, my RA walks in. "Hi, Jade. I heard you fell when you were running last week. Did you break anything?"

"No, I just have some bruises."

"She has stitches on her knee. And a concussion," Garret tells her. "And it just got worse thanks to those assholes outside."

"I checked, and it's legal for them to be here," Jasmine says. "They just can't come into the dorms."

"How could it be legal?" Garret asks. "This is a private college. It's private property."

"I'm just telling you what the dean said. If you're outside, you're out in public and that means they can photograph you."

"And harass us? And cause physical harm? That's legal?"

"You'll have to ask an attorney how all that works. I really don't know."

"Okay. Thanks, Jaz."

"I hope you feel better, Jade."

"Thanks. Hey, would you mind getting my crutches? I left them outside."

"Sure, I'll be right back." She leaves.

Garret was starting to calm down but now he's fuming. "I can't believe they can get away with that shit! I need to call my dad and have him ask his lawyers." He calls him, but his dad doesn't answer so he leaves a message.

Jasmine drops off my crutches and says the photographers are still there. We check out the window and it looks like half of them have left. Probably the ones who got photos that are good enough to sell.

"Maybe I should just go out there," Garret says. "That way they'll get the photos and leave us alone."

"You can, but I think they'll keep showing up. They'll probably follow you everywhere you go now. The show starts in a few weeks and you seem to be the star."

We stay inside the rest of the day and night. In the morning, the photographers are gone. Garret takes me to see the doctor, who ends up adding stitches to a section of my knee that split open overnight.

Garret's so worried about me. He wants to do everything for me. I swear he'd carry me to class if I let him. He doesn't even want me to go to class, but I insist on going. I already missed a day and I hate falling behind.

"You sure you don't want me to walk with you?" he asks when we're back in my room.

"Yes. I'll be fine. Besides you have to get to your own class."

"How are you going to carry all your stuff?"

"I'll use my backpack like I always do. Now stop worrying about me and get to class."

He sighs. "Your refusal to let me help is really annoying."

"You've already helped a ton, but I have to learn to get around on my own. Now give me a kiss in case I die on the way to class."

"Jade!"

"I'm kidding. Geez, relax."

He kisses me. "Call me when you there so I know you made it."

"You're worrying way too much, but yes, I'll call you."

"Thank you." He shakes his head as he watches me wobble on my crutches.

"Goodbye, Garret," I say, urging him to leave. He finally does and I make my way slowly across campus.

By the afternoon, I'm already better with the crutches. I even arrive at the science building ten minutes before physics class starts. Carson is standing outside talking on his phone. He hangs up when he sees me approaching.

"Jade, you should've called me. I would've walked over here with you and carried your backpack."

"I need to do it myself. I need to practice getting around campus with the crutches."

"I'm surprised Garret didn't walk you to class."

"He wanted to, but I wouldn't let him. So is our chem paper ready for tomorrow?"

"Yeah, I just need to read over it once more." Carson holds open the door to the science building. As soon as I'm inside he steps in front of me, blocking my path to the elevator. "Jade, can I ask you something?"

"Yeah, what?"

"Are you lying about how you got hurt?" Carson has this serious look on his face, like he's really concerned for me.

"No. I told you. I fell when I was running."

He puts his hand on my arm. "So Garret didn't do this to you?"

"What?" I almost laugh it's so ridiculous. "Of course not! Why would you even say something like that?"

"Because I don't trust that guy, or anyone in his family. They're bad people, Jade. I've been doing some more research and I really think you need to stay away from them."

"I assume you're doing this research online? You know that most of the stuff on the Internet isn't true, right?"

"I'm serious. These people are dangerous. You don't want to be involved with them."

"And how are they dangerous?"

He glances around as if someone might be listening in. "The people around them seem to keep coming up dead."

"Like who?"

"Royce Sinclair."

I freeze, wondering if Carson somehow knows what really happened to Sinclair. But that's impossible. He can't know.

I'm taking too long to respond and I have to say something to get his suspicious mind from pursuing this theory any further. "That guy killed himself. And Garret's dad gave Sinclair's campaign a ton of money. He wanted the guy to be president, so why would he kill him?"

Carson looks down at the floor, scratching his head like I've confused him. "Okay, so maybe that's not the best example." He looks up again. "But other people Pearce Kensington knew, or had business dealings with, have turned up dead."

I roll my eyes. "That doesn't mean he killed them. People die all the time."

"They're freaking loaded, Jade, which doesn't make sense because Kensington Chemical doesn't make enough money for them to be that rich."

"Maybe they're good at investing their money." I start to move but he grabs my arm.

"Every politician Pearce Kensington has supported for the past 20 years has ended up winning."

"Yeah? So?" I yank my arm back.

"Don't you find that suspicious?"

"No, I really don't." I go around him to the elevators.

"I'm not giving up on this. I'm going to keep digging until I find out the truth about these people." He holds the elevator door open for me.

As we ride up to the third floor, I hear Garret's warnings in my head. The warnings he gave me last semester when I was determined to learn the truth about my mother. He told me to never dig up the past. That it could be dangerous and could get me killed. That people like his family will do anything to keep their secrets buried. And after what I've seen, I know that it's true.

"Carson, you really need to let this go. If you think doing this is going to get me to break up with Garret, you're wrong. I love him, and nothing you say is going to change that."

"Garret is a Kensington. Do you really think he's not involved in whatever it is his family is doing? Or doesn't at least know about it?"

I turn to face him. "We're done talking about this. Garret is not doing whatever bad things you think he's doing and neither is his family." I step off the elevator with Carson right next to me. "And if you want us to still be friends, you'll drop this. Otherwise, our friendship ends right now. I won't even talk to you anymore outside of class."

He holds my backpack strap so I can't move forward. "I have a whole file of stuff about the Kensington family and the people they associate with. If you'd just look at the file, you'd see. There's something strange going on with them. If you only consider a single incident, then no, you wouldn't suspect anything. But when you look at everything together, things look much different. Just come to my room tonight and I'll show you."

I tug on my backpack, but he keeps hold of the strap. "I'm not going to your room. I told you, I'm not interested in dating you. And this is the last time I'm going to say it."

"Jade, I just want you to see the file. If you don't want to come to my room, then we'll go to the library. Or we'll go to that coffee shop again."

"I don't care about your stupid file! Now let me go. I mean it."

He finally lets go of my backpack, then walks ahead of me to open the door to the physics classroom. He keeps quiet as he waits for me to walk in.

When I'm in my seat I send a text to Garret letting him know I made it, then I flip through my physics book refusing to look at Carson sitting beside me. I've had it with him. I'm sick of his accusations and his attempts to get me to break up with Garret. And now he's got me wondering what exactly he has in that file, which pisses me off because I'm finally starting to like Garret's dad. I even trust him a little.

Mr. Kensington saved my life when he killed Royce Sinclair. And he's been kind and generous to me ever since then. He's supportive of my relationship with Garret. He stuck up for me with Katherine. He's paying for my tuition. He bought me a car. He paid for my medical care. Plus he's paying for that doctor to help Frank. How bad could the guy be?

It just takes one seed of doubt to wipe all that away. And that idiot Carson has done just that. Now, as I think back to what Mr. Kensington has done for me and the timing of it, part of me wonders if he's paying for my loyalty. Paying me to keep quiet. Making me so enmeshed with his family that I can't ever get out.

That night when I overheard Garret's dad fighting with Katherine, he said I'd seen too much. That I was one of them. So is his kindness only due to the fact that I know their secrets? Am I being rewarded for keeping those secrets?

Carson's accusations have me so flustered that I can't concentrate and I miss most of physics class. Afterward he insists on walking me back to my room, but I lie and tell him I have to go to Student Services. He heads back without me.

The Student Services building is a few buildings down from the science building and the opposite direction from my dorm. Carson walks across the open quad, looking back to check that I'm really going where I said I was going. He's walking super slow and I actually reach Student Services while he's still only halfway to the dorms. Tired of having him check up on me, I walk to the side of the building by the parking lot so I'm out of his sight. I take a seat at a picnic table and rest for a moment. The sun is really warm today and it feels good soaking into my black coat.

As I sit there, I notice that I don't feel very good. I put my arms on the table and rest my head on them, closing my eyes.

After a few minutes, I still don't feel good. I'm really dizzy and I think I might pass out. It must be complications from the concussion.

"Jade?" A man is speaking. He sounds older and I assume he's one of my professors asking me if I need help. And I think I do. The dizzy feeling is getting worse.

I slowly lift my head, squinting in the bright sun. I sit up and see two tall, very large men next to me. My heart lurches against the wall of my chest in complete panic as I realize that I can't escape whatever this is. Even if I didn't have the crutches to deal with, I still couldn't get away.

An older man, probably in his seventies, is sitting across from me. He's wearing a suit and a long black overcoat.

"Jade, I need to talk to you," he says.

His face is very familiar. The way he looks at me is familiar, too. I feel like I know him.

"Who are you?" As soon as the words leave my mouth, I realize where I saw him. New York. Rockefeller Center. He's the old man who bumped into me. The man I saw on TV with Royce Sinclair. But who is he and why is he here? My mind barely gets the question formed before he answers.

"I'm Arlin Sinclair. Royce's father. Your grandfather."

I glance at the large men blocking me on each side, then across to the man who is claiming to be my grandfather.

I have no words because I can't breathe. I think I'm holding my breath, but I'm not sure. It doesn't matter because soon I'll have no breath at all. The old man is obviously here to kill me. Here to finish the job his son didn't complete. Get rid of the evidence. Get rid of me.

I don't know why he's doing this. It shouldn't matter now. His son is dead. Nobody cares what he did.

But his father must. Because here is, sitting across from me, prepared to bury this deep, dark family secret once and for all.

54129248R00184

Made in the USA
San Bernardino, CA
08 October 2017